Bella

Annadora Perillo

D1713845

A Novel

Copyright © 2024 by Annadora Perillo

Cover design by:
Anthony Pedro

Editors:
Sally Lipton Derringer
Joseph Pedro

FOR MY FAMILY

Sweet Dreams!

Anxadora

Sweet Dreams!

Theodora

Table of Contents

Whenever you give a christening party you must always remember to ask all the most disagreeable people you know. It is very dangerous to neglect this simple precaution. Nearly all the misfortunes which happen to princesses come from their relations having forgotten to invite some nasty old fairy or other to their christenings. This is what happened in the case of the Sleeping Beauty.

—E. Nesbit, *The Sleeping Beauty in the Wood*

PROLOGUE

The Poison Apple Heart

This magic moment
While your lips are close to mine
Will last forever
Forever till the end of time
      —Jay and the Americans, "This Magic Moment"

It was just before the stroke of midnight on Bella's sixteenth birthday, December 31, 1972: thirteen long years since she'd slipped and fallen down an entire flight of subway steps and into a deep sleep.

Alex turned the television dial to the New Year's Eve celebration in Times Square. In the next ten seconds, New York would be shaken up like a blizzard in a snow globe. The city, all decked out in its glitzy bow tie of 42nd Street and lights of Broadway, displayed lofty billboards and show posters above the glossy sidewalks. From the Imperial Theatre, next to the Music Box, the iconic face of the waif Cosette looks down like an angel as the balloons and blast of boat whistles, blow-outs, tin horns, clackers, Klaxons, enough fireworks, confetti (two tons of official Times Square), and bottled up bubbly good will unleashed the virtual storm of the century.

Suspensively hovering over the plastic top hats of revelers, their paper crowns, giveaways, and glittering cardboard tiaras, from the flagpole on the tippy top of the Times Building seventy-seven feet above the city, the crystal disco ball loomed like a shiny poison apple heart.

Waiting in the wings, bands of cleanup crews dressed in white coveralls clung tightly to their broomsticks, while all the people in all the kingdoms in *all the mornings of the world* held their collective breath.

CHAPTER ONE

Nel Tempo Quando Berta Spilava . . .
In the Days When Berta Spun . . .
(Once Upon a Time . . .)

A malevolent wind blew over the ancient walls of Sabbioneta and swept through the tiny Italian town hidden within massive star-shaped ramparts—once the dream of Duke Vespasiano Gonzaga, a Renaissance warrior-prince, some called a madman.

The wind heightened the silent ghostly beauty of the city as it whispered through the mandala of its streets, stirring up the dust of antiquity about the pitted feet of the Pallas Athene, high on a Corinthian column against the ravaged façade of the Galleria delle Antichità. It breathed its air of melancholy and decay, sighing before the deserted theater and empty palaces, then swept out the gate and across the wide flat plain into the countryside where it rushed breathlessly through the doors of a church thrown open.

"We've looked everywhere," said a young boy, stopping short in the entry to catch his breath (like a larger-than-life angel with some really big news). "Antonio's gone—he's vanished."

"Ahh," said the guests collectively as they turned toward the disturbance at the back of the church—it was Gabriele, the bride's brother, it seemed, who had let in the wind. It blew in their

1

faces and through their hair, tugging at their veils of black lace and white that threatened to fly along with their best hats, their finest ribbons, and babies' bonnets. They made hopeless attempts to settle down ties, and all manner of blousy stuff billowed with wind. The priest's white vestment swelled like a sail as he strode towards Gabriele and his friends who, with passionate whispers and wild gesticulations, told how they had failed to discover the delinquent bridegroom.

"*Maledetto*—it's the curse," the old ones said, as they kissed their beads, and the broken rhythm of the rosary was set again to the movement of their lips: petitioning Our Lady with prayers that blew in the light of torches and the watery shadows of colored glass, flames of candles invoking divine intercession, and the votive offerings at the feet of saints.

The Madonna looked serenely upon a pool of white netting and hand-beaded silk that stirred at her bare toes where the serpent wound about the pedestal of cloud. Her image gleamed in the darkness of the girl's eyes. "Dear Mother of God have mercy on me and let me die I beg you because if Antonio's only deserted me," Lea said, lowering her voice already choked with tears to a conspiratorial whisper, "Papà will kill us both when he finds out what we've done." She brushed away a few loose curls that stuck to her damp cheek and wiped her face on the delicately trimmed sleeve of her wedding dress.

"You mustn't cry anymore, my child," said the Virgin, without the slightest outward manifestation, but in a voice of pure sympathy intrinsic to the wind that entered the antechamber; the scent of chrism, dripping wax, and holy water washed over them with an amber light, the rustle of pure silk, the air trembling with bells, a flutter of wings, passing. Outside, the old gods thundered.

"He's just a man," she said, "after all."

"My Lady, forgive me," Lea said, crossing herself quickly. *"Perdonna mi,"* she breathed above the beating of her heart as she hurried out the door and surrendered to the wind; butterflies and honeybees blew thick as snow in the sticky-sweet air; a warm summer breath lifted her dress, whispered *"Bellissima."* I should have known better, she told herself—wishing for someone to save me, dreaming of flight, believing in magic—that morning in the tower—playing pretend. Rescue, as it turned out, was only make-believe. Escape, just an illusion. Spells were cast, slippers were lost, golden carriages reduced to pumpkins, coachmen turned into rats and princes into frogs—in the time it took Antonio to get from *simply late* to *never—Happily ever after* . . . became the stuff of fairy tales.

Lea listened to the sound of a *filastrocca*: the lilting nursery rhyme rang through the churchyard when the flock of flower girls followed by her mother, the bridesmaids, and her sister Lavinia flitted out spinning round and round and round in a Ring a Rosie. *"Giro, Giro tondo, Cavalle, cavallando, Cento, cinquanta, La gallina canta—"*

The color of their dresses flushed the field with shades of blue so beautiful that to look at them directly stung her eyes, made Lea's heart ache. She was beginning to get drowsy, more and more lethargic: seduced by sleepy death whose voice in her ear was the whisper of pure silk and satin, crêpe de Chine, the rustle of taffeta, stiff crinolines tossed up against a shimmering silvery sky, fast-moving clouds. It tempted her with the flutter of tainted ribbons streaming in the windy sunlight, carrying the scent of flyblown fruit, flouncing perfumed petticoats, and the sound of her sister's laugh—with a pinch of something like poison in it.

Pollen, seeds, stems, and bits of freshly mowed field collected in the girls' lace-trimmed Bobbie socks; dewy wisps of straw and flax splinters clung to the insteps of fresh white patent leather shoes. *"Canta sola, sola, Non vuole andare a scuola, La gallina bianca e nera, Ti dà la buona sera, Buona sera, buona notte, Il lupo dietro la porta, La porta casca giù—"* Then, just as the door was about to fall down on top of the proverbial wolf, Lavinia's dress was caught in the spinning rhyme.

"I'a!" Maria cried out, covering her eyes as the dress tore, and, dashing to gather the train up into her hands, she smoothed the ice-blue silk (special stuff from Mantua! Her infinitesimal stitches!), examining the edge where a piece had been torn away. "Don't worry," she said when she saw the look on her daughter's face, or, otherwise, she might have broken down and cried real tears. "Go and get me my sewing basket—*e fa presta*! Your sister can't be married without her maid of honor!" she called to Lavinia, who was already running towards home—the tattered strand of blue silk trailing in the air like a remnant of sky.

The silver linings of clouds split open at the seams, spilling huge molten raindrops that fell on their heads, and just as suddenly stopped, followed by some seriously pent-up thunder, and lightning that tore Heaven into jagged-edged halves. Worried, Maria glanced over at the woods for sight of Lavinia, then turning her attention to the girls and their dresses, compelling them to go inside before the weather reduced them all to a heap of rags in front of her very eyes. Especially her very own *Cindergirl*, she thought, at the sight of doe-legged Lea dreaming alone in the corner by the chimney stones. More specifically, at the alarming state of her veil that seemed to have wings and a mind of its own, whipping about her in the wind like a wild thing—possessed, or placed under some witch's spell?

"In a minute, Mammina," Lea said when her mother tried to shuttle her back into the sanctuary of the church.

"Be careful *Bella Mia*—" Maria warned. Wishing she'd been blessed with her own mother's gift for divination, she looked into her daughter's eyes, trying to predict what was to come.

"All this wind will be bad for you."

* * *

"Blessed Mother, I'm begging you, please. Not for my sake. And not for my husband. Certainly not for that Casanova, Antonio. Fixing a torn dress—that's simple. As for the rest, if there's anything you can do, for Lea's sake and for her baby, I would be grateful," Maria whispered in staccato, inspired by the voto-covered walls surrounding her: for *vows made and grace received*; the texture of miracles incarnate. "*Ave Maria . . .*" she prayed softly, and rising to her feet with a sign of the cross, she kissed her fingertips to the statue's heart before stepping outside.

"I'm going to look for your sister," she told Lea. "Who knows where she's gone and finished with that basket." But the words were lost on the bride whose thoughts were swept up in the wind and caught; her dreams flimsy things snagged on fences.

That's the moment she took flight. At the very same moment that Antonio and Lavinia were about to take off for the New World, their sails full with lusty wind, something of the same *tempesta* possessed the bride's dress and wedding veil and lifted her high off the ground. "Oh!" she cooed, hovering above the startled witnesses assembling in the churchyard for a wedding that morning in Sabbioneta. "Oh! Oh! I can fly!"

* * *

5

L'amore ha sempre svolto romanzi, ossia l'arte di amare è sempre stata romantica.
Love has always inspired novels, or rather the art of loving has always been romantic.
L'amour a toujours vécu de romans; de fait, l'art d'aimer a toujours été romantique.
El amor siempre ha dado lugar a romances, es decir, el arte de amar siempre ha sido romántico.

—Baci, Perugina, *Novalis*

Lea woke to the convent bells that spilled pealing over the cloister walls, even before the thin pale sunlight, the silent footsteps of the nuns called to matins—on the morning after her wedding and every morning after. An air of melancholy filled the room, seeped through the solid tufa walls and fed the flower beds outside her window, so that meticulously maintained 16th century cloister gardens bloomed now with a profusion of fruit and flowers: lush lemon and tangerine, medlar and palm, hawthorn, columbine, musk mallow, and scarlet geraniums. And the air was so fragrant with the scent of orange blossoms and jasmine that the weak-hearted were driven nearly mad.

Monsignore Valentino, in his black cassock and wide-brimmed hat, leaned back, breathless, against the garden wall, basking in the lemony-gold island sunlight filled with yellow birdsong, a fountain's splashing resplendence, butterflies' and honeybees' dazzle, the distant impulse of the sea. He contemplated the moss-covered path, the worn patina of his boots, a snail's silvery thread—the pale crescents of his nails absorbed him fully for a moment. He found the cracks in the stone; his eyes traced the tangled vines up the wall to the black iron grille she looked out behind. He no longer prayed. His meditations shattered into a million fragments of songbirds singing, splintered sunlight: his soul, it seemed, soared to a higher place, seeking the sky, her face at the window, below which the nuns worked futilely to keep back the briars, thick tangles of vines, and the jasmine that grew like weeds.

"Forgive me, Father," he will say one day when he begins his last confession, telling his trespasses to his old friend who will strain to listen to the story told only with great effort.

"It was summer," he'll say, remembering clearly that slant of sunlight on potted lemon trees, long shadows from the arcade splayed onto Mother Arcangela's habit, onto her folded hands as she walked alongside him. They passed from light into shadow and into light alternately, speaking softly. Birds were restless, singing a new song. A basilisk slipped between the reeds—rushing. Convent bells sounded, summoning the sisters to the choir for prayer, their veils fluttering in the perfumed air, when he noticed, as if in a dream (both breezy and fragrant), a novice who looked more likely on her way to be meeting with some friends, or her lover, than with God. How the sight of her startled him: a young woman, both beautiful and surprising (since no one had taken vows at the convent in nearly thirty years), and although she was pregnant, her billowing robes concealed it.

Mother Arcangela followed his gaze. He asked about the girl. Of course. She'd been expecting it. "Her novice," he called her.

"A prostitute," the Madre Superiore of the convent of Santa Maggiore lied, tilting her head slightly as she watched the girl brush past a series of rose hedges, then disappear behind a wall of bougainvillea.

"Ah!" the Monsignore sighed, finding it difficult to breathe in the sultry air: the atmosphere heavy with longing and terrible ache of roses.

Arcangela took a slow, leisurely breath, and was even more expansive than usual when she shared her invented scenario, having considered the truth carefully and judged it unnecessary—to trouble a man of Monsignore's sensibilities with what was essentially none of his business. So, she told him her story, hoping he would be long gone before he heard any other. But, lately, in the silence, if one was attentive, if one's ear was pressed judiciously to the wall, so to speak, one might hear murmurs—rumors whispered in the dark, of raptures and exceptionally expressive statues—the stuff of extravagant mysticism—dare she say, *fanaticism*, and as God only knew, the world was not always safe for its living saints. Keeping Lea secret (or from flying off, as the case may be) was proving to be a bit trickier than anticipated when she first agreed to help.

"May I offer you a little something? *Una tassa di caffè*? Perhaps some cookies, Monsignore?"

Inside the dining hall, the close air made her sleepy. Arcangela concealed a yawn as she watched her distinguished guest dunk yet another *biscotto* into a cup of espresso and counted the minutes until *mezzogiorno*. She was badly in need of a nap, not yet recovered from having been wrenched out of bed in the middle of the night by the sisters' urgent, mysterious tapping at her door when her head was still filled with crazy dreams. In a panic, she had pulled a robe down over her white slip, covered her dark crop of hair with the frame of veil that squeezed her face into a perfectly formed oval. She checked herself briefly in the glass (her skin was pale with the distinctive softness of one whose life was spent in cloister, her lips long pressed to silence, her spirit surfaced in the light of her eyes), and for the first time after so many years, she was startled by her own reflection.

The sound of her heavy beads smacked against the stillness like the jagged rhythm of a prayer. She clutched the keys to mysteries, this sanctuary of palace walls and churches, cool candlelit Madonnas, cloistered secrets; locked gates. Listening to the sound of her rosary's sway, her own muffled footfall, she swept down the hall in her habit toward voices breaking on the silence of nights that followed one another like spilled beads.

Arcangela stopped at the gate, which was the last barrier between herself, and (trapped beyond it) all the world—that she did not want anymore—or need. Her breath caught as she fitted the right key into the lock and turned it with the sudden realization that she was not ready for the gate to open, or for the flood of feelings that surged toward her at the sight of her sister-in-law and her niece.

"Has something happened?" she asked when they slackened their embrace. Looking from Lea to Maria and back to Lea again, she was painfully aware of having become ridiculous, asking stupid questions at a time like this. As if their having come hundreds of miles to see her on an this island, in a convent in the heart of Palma without warning in the middle of what was supposed to be her niece's wedding night—honeymoon, at least (didn't Sister Lucia bake the cakes and sweets that she made absolutely certain were delivered—and didn't she have Father Rosario's assurances, *his solemn word,* that they had reached as far as Mantua by Friday?), was the most natural thing in the world. And, if Maria's face alone did not reveal some awful tragedy—there was her *figlioccia,* her poor goddaughter in a ghastly state of unraveling. Lea, in a sorry white heap of wedding-stuff with her black hair flying about her face like a halo, and wild eyes, looking like something spinning itself into a cocoon, or something struggling out, in one of the stages of metamorphosis, or molting, maybe, she thought, narrowing her eyes; she just couldn't help herself.

So, while Lea sat on the sofa in the parlor, quite intent on picking at the fancy beadwork of her dress, her mother attempted to explain, and Arcangela (as best she could) to pick up the threads of the tale. By dawn, it was plain that Lea *was badly left*, insomuch as Antonio left her, not only carrying his child, but had also run away with her sister Lavinia.

"I brought her here before Joseph could figure it out for himself. You know your brother," Maria said, finally.

Arcangela took another good long look at her niece, carefully considering the alternatives—a molting bird. Or a chicken—most definitely a chicken. A big, fluffy-white molting chicken. In any case, she thought, tilting her head slightly, leaving off at last— certainly, a bird. She shook her head and clucked sympathetically, agreeing to let Lea stay at the convent until the baby was born— and then? *Dio vedo e proveddo*. "God will provide the answer," she offered Maria in way of reconciliation.

The miracle of how the Virgin spoke to her and what she said and how a girl could fly remained veiled in mystery, since Lea never gave a truly lucid account of what happened that day. For someone who barely uttered a word, except in a fragmented whisper, Lea was the source of a great deal of turbulent noise. The beads of her dress, which she had been at all night long, intermittently popped off and fell loudly pinging across the floor. Sometimes, whole strands were loosed, and the resulting effect was so terrible that Archangela thought everyone in the convent would be startled from their sleep. She needn't have worried however, because the sound, apparently, had the opposite effect. Some of the sisters later confessed that not since the days of their childhood had they known such tranquil sleep: long, deep, and sweet. Dreaming to the sound of rain—big and soft and slow and warm—the sound of summer raindrops (like silkworms munching on mulberry leaves in the darkness) falling *pianissimo*.

The Madre Superiore held fast to her resolve to help her family despite the fact that they never allowed anyone from the outside to enter the convent or its *parlatorio*, much less to sit upon the sofa wildly spilling beads about in the middle of the night, without permission from the Bishop himself. Arcangela knew this, but, as she saw it, she had no choice. She worried her beads, and the wedding band on her finger, and the keys she clutched while they talked all through the long night; the conversation, inevitably, left its mark on her hands.

With any luck at all, her niece would have her baby and be back home before Valentino could blink his languid blink, she thought, folding her arms into the sleeves of her habit and adding her customary ascription—*Dio benedica*, for insurance.

In the meantime, Lea worked in the kitchen to help fill the orders for the cookies, cakes, and confections baked by the sisters of the convent who were particularly busy at Passiontide, most especially at Easter, under the tutelage of Sister Lucia, an expert pastry cook with sixty-five years experience, more or less. In Sister's hands, *pasta reale*, Paschal lambs, and hearts of Jesus materialized like magic from marzipan, which Lea then wrapped and turned out to the customers waiting by the revolving gate. The very same turntable, Sister Lucia noted as she considered her new apprentice, in which people sometimes left their infants.

Sister Lucia, guardian of the secrets of sweet-making, was cautious to be sure, perhaps, even cynical. There were only a few nuns, alive or dead, who were keepers of these age-old recipes.

Theoretically, it was possible for just about anyone to discover a list of ingredients, she thought (flour, sugar, and almonds confect marzipan, with lemon zest added, or orange; flavored sometimes with cinnamon, and the essences, other times, of flowers). But now, at nearly ninety-three, when she remembered all the novices she'd taught to bake, not even one, she realized, even if she learned what hands should do, could measure with her heart; knew, by instinct, the proportion of sugar to bitter almonds. That's what she was thinking when she set Lea to work cleaning the kitchen, dusting trays of cookies with white confectioner's sugar, or sprinkling them with nuts. Maybe this time it will stick, she dared to hope, as Lea breathed the sweetened air thick with sugar and boiled wine, candied fruit and jam, honey and citron, cinnamon, sesame, anise, pistachio, and all the flavors she invoked each day when she opened her eyes, tied on her apron, baked cakes.

Lea existed in the textures of squash *zuccata* boiled with sugar and dried in the hot Sicilian sun, of sponge cake filled with ricotta and candied fruit and covered in marzipan and fondant icing, in the sprinkling of confetti that fell perpetually before her eyes, powdery sugar and flour, in the shapes of marzipan, delicately colored and bitterly almond, in the silence so thick you could slice it like cheesecake.

The girl was a good novice, the nuns nodded in agreement: her gentle manner—*beneducato*, her dedication to work and prayer—*ora et labora*, the credo of their *patrono,* Saint Benedict—so very *benedettina*. Her silence—profound, mysterious, impenetrable.

And, *anche se*—even if her personal life was suspect (as some of the sisters implied with their glances at her stomach and then at one another when they thought no one else was watching), she was fast becoming a magician with marzipan—the molds turned out so much more—no one could say what exactly: so painfully sweet and beautifully sad that the entire convent was reduced to tears, and the Monsignore was brought to his knees. Suddenly he couldn't get enough *bocconcini*, lambs and marzipan hearts, *mostaccioli*, *amaretti, cassate, cassatine, buccellati*, honey sticks, Savoyards, *taralei, umberto* cookies, and almond pastries. Monsignore (all of the nuns couldn't help but notice), seemed to have developed an insatiable appetite for sweets, and new interest in sweet-making.

Before bed, Sister Lucia secured the pantry and the storeroom and locked the kitchen doors—and bolted them—out of necessity, to keep her stores safe from foraging pests, and to safeguard her rapidly diminishing supplies from Heaven-knew-what exactly? Until she caught the big M with his hand in the cookie jar, looking like a chipmunk with his cheeks stuffed with sweetmeats. And, she wouldn't have been a bit surprised if, when they searched his person, they didn't find his pockets full of comfits, which, she suspected, he'd been systematically hoarding in his room like some perverse and overly plump sugar plum fairy.

In fact, if he didn't leave, the sisters imagined, it was more than likely that soon he wouldn't fit through the gate—he was that huge; and his voice, which had always been papery and light, was all aspiration. He no longer slept—all that sugar coursing through his veins and fueling his heart, and so his feelings, rendered noneloquent by necessity, poured out over the tacky, sugar-dusted pages of his journal in Italian and Latin and French and Spanish and sometimes even in Arabic, his love and tenderness and longing translated to paper, his fantasies to sticky-sweet marzipan dreams.

In his dreams, Lea wore a big white dress and a veil. Not a nun's habit or veil, but a true bridal gown with all of its skirts and slips and stiff crinolines dancing up into the air like a cancan, whipped into a frenzy by the blowing wind. "My love," he said to her in his sleep, wrapped in a larval-like tangle of bedclothes, groping blindly and desperate for something to hold on to as Lea, with arms outstretched like angels' wings was straining to fly. He clutched at loosed ribbons and tattered pieces; strands of silk slipped through his fingers as the dress, in a state of furious unraveling as if silkworms were spinning insanely in reverse, was shed. And as Lea cleared the cloister walls, Monsignore Valentino blinked at the sunlight that filtered in through his dream-damp bedclothes amassed like cloud cover, while, down the hall, the sisters struggled to suppress their screams at Lea's abandoned, bloodstained sheets.

CHAPTER TWO

Winding Sheets

Maria had forgotten to take in the sheets. Her palms were sweating, and she got that sinking feeling in the pit of her stomach that comes with the sudden realization that something's lost. She squirmed beneath the baby bundled on her lap, her fingers twisting and wringing the fringes of the pink pram blanket as the train prepared to pull away from the Stazione Termini.

"*Imbecili! cretinni!*" her husband hollered at the people on the platform who pounded on the windows and doors of the train, screaming for them to open, their hysteria reaching a crescendo with the last possible chance to hoist themselves on into the cars after one another and all of their stuff. The *casino* of *valigie*, of luggage and people, *pacchetti*, and bags handed up into the gaping windows of the train was astonishing. Joseph Battista shook his head and swore at the bedlam he immediately attributed to a class of Italian, to which, thankfully, he did not belong, as he paced the car, keeping an eye out for his son who was still on the platform buying some sandwiches.

"*Managia l'America—*" he said, his stream of swearing interrupted by the sight of Gabriele with an armful of *pannini,* who (with a little help from his friends) was booted up through the window by the seat of his pants, narrowly making it aboard as the train left the station with something like a groan and a great expression of steam.

"Damnit, Gabriele! *Managia*! Are you crazy! *Ma sei pazzo?*"

"Stay calm, Papà!" Gabriele shouted back, scrambling to his feet and picking up the scattered sandwiches.

"*Zitto*! The two of you!" Maria shushed them.

The baby fussed. The sound of the train became the rhythm of Maria's distraught rocking. The Sheets! The Sheets! The Sheets! She had forgotten to take in the sheets. They flapped mournfully in the wind—her wedding sheets, washed and hung out on the line how many times? She calculated in her head. Her eyes stung at the thought of the creamy linen lifting toward sunlight—their clean bed. The line stretched backward into her past pinned with the white chrisom cloth of christening clothes, her daughter's flouncy feast-day dresses, nightgowns and petticoats, panties and slips. The laundry on the clothesline haunted her with the phantasmagorical likenesses of her lost girls, like spirits that fluttered, whispered, and lifted; straining in their winding sheets.

* * *

Maria clutched the hem of Lavinia's dress over and over again (kneeling in the windy sunlight) and wouldn't let go. She tried to find her in the still closeness of the house where she had sent her to get the sewing basket. She searched the corners and the cupboards. Her eyes swept the white-washed walls, the width and breadth of beams. Her dress trailed the tile floors. She opened the pantry and the laundry hamper. "Lavinia!" she exclaimed into her daughter's emptied chest of drawers.

Maybe she went by the old house, she had thought, hopefully squinting at the door of the beekeeper's cottage obscured by rosemary shrubs and dark flames of cypress. She half expected to find her there, Lavinia hiding under her grandmother's skirts, *sottogonna*, like a little girl.

"Shhh!" Nonna used to whisper with a finger pressed to her lips, pretending to keep her secret as Lavinia peeked out from beneath her shadow, hugging her stockinged legs, skinny as a chicken's; picking at specs of straw that stuck to the bottom of her dress, which as long ago as anyone could remember had always been widow's weeds, black bombazine. Nonna smelled like apples, cool and dark like an apple safe, like a root cellar. Hers were the old ways.

"Lav-i-nia!" Maria had called, with a voice that echoed in the chambers of her heart and was swallowed up by the soulless wind. Her hands grasped empty air.

* * *

In bocca al lupo!
Into the mouth of the wolf!

—Good Luck Saying, Italy

By the time she'd reached the edge of the woods on the way to get the sewing basket, Lavinia was breathless. She flew with the hem held high above her head nearly the whole way home, and when she finally slowed down, dropping her arm, it fluttered to her side. I'll take the shortcut, she thought, forgetting about her dressy shoes, her fancy bridesmaid's dress, but she knew the path— as children they had carved it out themselves with their wildish children's games. She wound through, pretty much unnoticed, with that sort of sashay-way she had of walking, kicking up a little dirt from the forest floor, setting some birds twittering and small things scuttling off as the dappled pattern of leaves deepened evenly to shade. Branches quivered at the edge of consciousness; the coolness of trees wrapped around her as her eyes adjusted to the dark woods. She was thinking about her sister and Antonio's wedding—inventing new endings for the daydreams she was so good at conjuring when the sound of thunder made her jump, and in the blinding flash of lightning that followed, she tripped and virtually landed on a body sprawled out at her feet. Lavinia stood rooted to the spot: mouth gaping, eyes open wide at the sight of the man scratched up and muddy, his brow caked with blood.

Her hair swept over his face, and her dress, dragged in the leaves, covered him like wings, as she searched for a pulse, poised expectantly for the warm escape of breath from his lips, the steady rise and fall of his chest, the rhythm of his beating heart. Still holding the slip of blue securely in her fist, she scrambled over to the spring nearby, and soaking the cloth with *aquasanta*, she prayed her *Aves* over and over like a spell, her words lifting off the water with the churning clouds of mineral gas, which gave up a fiery scent of burnt offerings. And because she never missed a chance to wish, she took out a hairpin, from what was by now a tangle of curls and waves, twisting it in her teeth before letting it fall into the well. She wiped his face, washing the wound on the side of his head, wringing out the torn silk hem in her hands, tying it into knots. "I love you," she said. Her tears fell like the rain in silvery slivers. Pieces of broken mirror. Bits and glass shards; the debris of a broken heart. Then hot and fast and hard as hailstones, tear-shaped diamonds dropped on his skin, melting into glistening pools. "*Ti amo,* Antonio," she whispered, her lips lightly brushing his closed eyelids, and the words, when picked up by the wind seemed to provoke the passionate storm.

Hey little sister what have you done
Hey little sister who's the only one
Hey little sister who's your Superman
Hey little sister who's the one you want
Hey little sister shotgun!

—Billy Idol, "White Wedding"

* * *

Lavinia's emotions had always been tumultuous: owing, it was said, to the weather on the day she was born. That morning, her mother had been busy with the wash: with that last burst of energy, the final effort of will (akin to madness) that "old wives" say is a sign. Reaching in for the wet things in a laundry basket at her feet, she took clothespins from her apron pocket, and from her mouth, in turn, she pinned up a blouse, the corners of a sheet, keeping an eye on Lea who was helping to wash some clothes in the soapy water of a washtub.

"Mamma," Lea called, lifting out a drippy baby bib like a cleansed soul for her inspection.

"*Brava*," Maria praised her, walking over with her basket. She bent down to plant a kiss on top of the little girl's head, taking in the sun-warmed scent. Tired suddenly, and breathless, she set down the laundry basket, brushing away a few loosed strands of hair that blew in her face. Her hand smoothed over the baby, round and full as a melon curving beneath her flower-print dress that filled with wind, fluttered papery and light like one of the scarlet poppies in the distance sprinkled among the high corn. She shielded her eyes from the sunlight that dazzled, warmed the top of her head. It caught the curve of a sickle as it sliced the bright heat, rushed through the golden shafts of corn, slanted on the bare skin and dark curls of her husband Joseph, his body arched with the rhythmic motion of the blade. Bound bundles of stalks, in triplicate, lay evenly spaced on the fields like small pyramids, flax chapels tilting toward Heaven in the windy sunlight.

* * *

There was an old woman tossed up in a basket,
Seventeen times as high as the moon;
Where she was going I couldn't but ask it,
For in her hand she carried a broom.

Old woman, old woman, old woman, quoth I,
Where are you going to up so high?
To brush the cobwebs off the sky!
May I go with you?
Aye, by-and-by.

—Mother Goose Rhyme

The old broom whispered over stone swept smooth—secrets in sunbaked tiles of terra-cotta—a lifetime of footsteps, like rain on red clay rooftops that quickens and mounts toward thunder, hushed now, as when a baby sleeps.

The house sighs; stirs with its breathing; resonant with laughter; first steps dampened: a moist spot. Children dart between raindrops; barefoot rhythms of childhood linger: elusive rhymes. A man's bootsteps tread (traces of soil, sun caked bits of earth, antediluvian dust, a wisp of field), and stop in a soft pool of sunlight where a woman sits plaiting her hair. He strokes her head; his fingers tangle in twists of flax. At the door latch he hesitates, watching as she pins up the braid, and with a handful of straw from the sheaf beside her, takes up the golden rhythm of daylight: ties rush to broom.

The old broom responded, sensing the familiar feel of the woman's fingers—distracted; fitting itself to the floor, its brush broken now, and bent, slanted to corners, carried her weightless. "Switch, switch, switch," it whispered like a spell. A slip of down evaded it, lifted into the air, settled in the sunlight with a sprinkling of dust as they swept out over the terrace of wide flat stones softened with moss, and trailing vines tangled up lichen-stained walls of the cottage where she leaned the broomstick against a ledge. In her eyes, clouds tumbled, wisps of white curled, swept over the sky's grey-blue reflection. She pulled hairpins from her apron pocket, and holding them in her teeth, took them quickly in turn to secure the thick coil of her hair.

"Something's coming," she said, distracted by a bird's distant pitch.

"Witch!" whispered the broom.

The old woman cackled, scattering seed for the birds. The stone crackled beneath the falling seed, the step and pecking of hens. The last handful spattered like rain.

"N-o-o-o-on-a!"

She heard Lea's small voice call into the wind as it brushed through fields of winter wheat—beat against the wings of honeybees, following the path to their wooden hives behind the house.

"Come on Nonna!" Lea said, tugging and pulling her grandmother along by her apron strings. "Mamma says hurry!"

Over the sky backlit with brilliant sunlight, storm clouds scuttled as Nonna's black skirts swished across the fields of maize and sugar beets, grapevines and mulberries. "Look!" Lea said pointing.

Rosa followed her finger. Off to the west, a solitary thunderhead, immeasurably dark and ominous, threatened. And the wind, which had been sweeping over the wide flat plain—stopped: suddenly replaced by an awesome stillness.

* * *

Maria was soaked with sweat; it was so impossibly hot she thought she'd suffocate. Holding a fresh towel between her thighs (the water still trickling down her legs after the surprising, first warm gush when she'd bent elbow deep in the sloshy water of the washtub), she climbed into her clean bed and shut her eyes. She must have slept, because she didn't hear her little girl calling, the sound of her running feet, or the door slamming shut behind Lea and her mother—their dresses lifted violently up into their faces by the resurgent wind as they flew in together with so many bits of straw.

The house filled with the telltale scent of lighted matchsticks, and then of the tinctures, herbal teas, and smoke Rosa wasted no time preparing. She slid open drawers and propped up the lid of the linen chest: a method that midwives used to inspire the womb. She scraped an old sheet, and laying cool lavender-scented strips on her daughter's hot forehead, alternated them with the palm of her hand, as the short, sharp pains deepened, lengthening like the jagged edge of the storm—spinning clouds collided and Maria wailed like a Banshee into the wind. Still dripping, the baby held up before the eyes of her family, howled as she cleared the water from her lungs; raining down. Lavinia Battista was born in the quick of one of the most severe storms in the region's collective memory.

"The worst of the storm is over now," Joseph said, as he kissed his wife's wind-blown hair, her forehead, eyelids, cheek, lips. He could still detect the memory of it on her skin. It mingled with her familiar scent; but, from that day on, her kiss, which had always been slightly dangerous, held traces of something bewitchingly sweet. She threaded her fingers through his, and listening for the sound of the baby's breath, sighed before falling asleep.

Except to nurse Lavinia, Maria slept for nearly six days. "I'm fine," she tried to tell them, unable to alter the worried look on their faces. Her mother's expression was fixed; her mouth set in a line as she straightened out the room, opened or closed shutters, fed Maria warm *pastina* with a demitasse spoon, crooning to her at times or to Lavinia as she rocked her to sleep. Lea came in and brushed her hair, sang her sweet lullabies, her little fingers fluttering like butterflies, like the doves outside her window and the bumblebees in the hazy heat she looked through. "*Farfallina, bella bianca, Vola, vola, mai si stanca, Vola di qua, vola di la, Poi se ne va a reposà.*" The droning made her sleepy—heavy. Her eyelids drooped. Her tongue was thick. Her milk was sweet like honey.

Joseph was busy. He'd repaired the rabbit hutches and the aviary, replenished the number of speckled hens. She would have seemed attentive and nod appreciatively, if she could, when he talked about the *fattoria*—the barns and orchards, vineyards and fields, when he came home in the evening, or in the afternoon to eat and sleep, to take shelter from the midday sun. He pulled off his soaked through shirt, swearing against the scorching heat as he lay down beside her. "The sirocco has come," he told her. "With the winds out of Africa."

Wanting to be sympathetic, Maria willed herself awake, but it was no use.

She fell asleep languishing under the spell of her dreams. Some of what she dreamed she learned long ago as a schoolgirl.

Most had become part of the region's mythology: the story of Sabbioneta, of its brooding, melancholy Lord, Vespasiano Gonzaga, Prince of Bozzólo, and Diana di Cordona, an Aragon of Spain. The story of their tragic love took hold of her romantic imagination, an obsession, which had incubated in the collective consciousness of the people like the worms who for centuries had gone at the descendants of the same ancient mulberry trees. Maria heard them eating in her sleep, saw them spin the silk for the sails that blew Diana in the wind from Spain towards Sabbioneta into the realm of her expectant prince, and the silk for the brocade gown worn by the Princess-Bride, the silk for wedding sheets, the stuff of lovers' bedclothes, and winding sheets—the silk for her shroud.

* * *

> Oh passing angel,
> Speed me with a song.
> A melody of heaven to reach my heart.
> And rose me to the race
> And make me strong.
>
> —Christina Georgina Rossetti

All that day they saw her sail spreading white along the riverbed, tilting through vineyards, cutting across fields of grain. The girl then passed kingdom after kingdom, lord after lord like most exotic treasures (spices and cloth and dyestuff) capriciously tossed along the canals, from her father's boat into her husband's bucanteur with her traveling trunks and ladies-in-waiting toward her destiny. Her dark eyes darted behind the gold-gilded edge of her fan: its fluttering concealed her quivering lips, its pulsing rhythm quieted her own trembling, and its agitated breath cooled her hot face, helping to dry the tracks of tears where her mantilla's lacy veil cast its shadow on her cheek. Her thoughts followed the flight of a gull —"Oh, Holy Spirit!" she prayed to its high-lifting wings which seemed to share the lofty secrets of her soul; her captive heart beat hard against her breast's stays as she blinked into the hot Italian sun.

"This Italy! It might as well be the end of the world!" she thought, her gaze sweeping out over the vast plain toward the distant mountains' ascent. Everywhere was gold cast from the sun sunken in the fields of maze, and barley, and wheat, and into watery fields of rice stretching as far as the eye could see: the view broken only by strands of poplar and acacia, the shimmering of windbreaks weeping. The great northern plains of Lombardy made Italy look, for all the world, like Holland or Denmark—a landscape to inspire the imaginations of morbid princes, Quixotic quests, and lachrymose ladies to sigh and tilt their fans into the wind.

Diana di Cordona held her breath as they floated past the river walls; her gilded gondola gliding and pitching until they were cast upon a new shore, where now in full view, the medieval ramparts of the Gonzaga castle, towers and turrets and spires rose up to meet them. She was afraid, as they crossed the bridge, that they'd fall into the stagnant water of the moat, and clung to the arm of her old nurse, who gave hers a pinch, in turn, as a great roar was heard in the distance. Hooves thundered to match her pounding heart, and a clamor arose as knights rode forward on fierce Gonzaga stallions: the horses tossed their magnificent heads, nostrils flared, weapons clashed against flanks, shields and swords and scabbards and flags were held high, colors unfurled in the wind, *bandieras* streamed from lances' metal glinting in sunlight, white armor gleamed. The war-courses turned into formation, bared their teeth, reared and stepped restless as the exigent blast of horns heralded the advent of their lord, powerful enough to be called prince—her prince, Diana reminded herself, casting her eyes on the knight's breastplate, the bright colors of the tabard over his heart. Slowly, he removed a gauntlet, lifted the visor from his eyes and caught her in his rapt gaze. Gathering her petticoats and courage into a courtesy, she extended a scented silky-gloved hand, and tumbled in a swoon onto the stone bridge. Her black gown, sewn with gold and jewels and metallic threads, sparkled at his feet like a spilled treasure box.

* * *

Had we but world enough, and time,
This coyness, Lady, were no crime.
We would sit down and think which way
To walk and pass our long love's day.
Thou by the Indian Ganges' side
Shouldst rubies find: I by the tide
Of Humber would complain. I would
Love you ten years before the Flood,
And you should, if you please, refuse
Till the conversion of the Jews.
My vegetable love should grow
Vaster than empires, and more slow;
An hundred years should go to praise
Thine eyes and on thy forehead gaze;
Two hundred to adore each breast,
But thirty thousand to the rest;
An age at least to every part,
And the last age should show your heart.
For, Lady, you deserve this state,
Nor would I love at lower rate.

But at my back I always hear
Time's wingèd chariot hurrying near;
And yonder all before us lie
Deserts of vast eternity.
Thy beauty shall no more be found,
Nor, in the marble vault, shall sound
My echoing song; then worms shall try
That long preserved virginity,
And your quaint honor turn to dust,
And into ashes all my lust:
The grave's a fine and private place,
But none, I think, do there embrace.
 Now therefore, while the youthful hue
Sits on thy skin like morning dew
And while thy willing soul transpires
At every pore with instant fires,
Now let us sport us while we may,
And now, like amorous birds of prey,
Rather at once our time devour
Than languish in his slow-chapt power.
Let us roll all our strength and all
Our sweetness up into one ball,
And tear our pleasures with rough strife
Thorough the iron gates of life:
Thus, though we cannot make our sun
Stand still, yet we can make him run.
                —Andrew Marvel, "To His Coy Mistress"

First light slipped through the slits of thick, drawn, damask draperies; in the distance, a cock crowed, spiriting in the dawn.

On velvet mornings like these as the Duchess curled beneath the sheets in her gossamer gown, he watched her sleep: the nearly imperceptible rise and fall of her breast, the quivering of heavy-lidded eyes, dark lashes' flutter. Her breath disturbed the long strands of her hair flowing over the pillow lace where her head rested, still full of dreams. Diana stirred from the kisses pressed to her cheek, her slightly parted lips, and to the soft undersides of her arms, clinging to sleep.

Vespasiano smudged her pink mouth with his thumb, and slid out, reluctantly, from underneath the bedclothes, first one leg, and then the other, with slightly more resolve, set onto the cold stone floor with a loud thud. He sat at the edge of the bed, and addressing the bedchamber—empty air— ran his hand through his rough beard and dark curling hair. "I don't know when I'll return," he said.

She watched him clamor around in various phases, degrees and displays of protective covering, and of leave-taking, so, it seemed to her, he was in a continuously changing, constant state of flux, until, at last, the transformation into a great Renaissance soldier-prince (a *capitano* in his *corazza di indifferenza*) from sweet knight was complete.

> What if the Prince on the horse in your fairytale
> Is right here in disguise
> And what if the stars you've been reaching so high for
> Are shining in his eyes
> —Carly Simon, "The Stuff that Dreams are Made Of"

"You will be sorely missed, my Lord," Diana whispered to the width and breadth of his back; she could already sense his straining, his muscles tensing indomitably beneath the soft butterfly kisses that lighted between his shoulders, but off-centered slightly where the spot would sting forever, his flesh bared, or burning beneath the padding of arming coat and armor.

According to her husband's impassioned plans, he was about to remake their world into his fantasy of an ideal city; a "little Athens on the Po," as Vespasiano's capital would come to be called. It was an Olympian dream of classically proportioned *palazzi* for winter and for summer use, of treasures spilling through halls of the long Galleria delle Antichità: an extensive and priceless collection of Greek and Roman antiquities displayed in magnolia-colored sunlight cast through the red brick arcade from the garden, with gilding, fool-the-eye effects, and fresco to cover the ceilings. And in these painted expanses of sky—the allegorical sun Icarus' fabled wings fly toward and are consumed by, fiery Phaeton falling from the sun god's runaway horses, scenes from Latium and horses from Troy, Daphne in her diaphanous dress, leaf like, her arms upstretched: gods and goddesses, branching and spilling from their celestial space. Looking-glass walls to reflect the dazzling distinction of its guests: intellectuals, scholars, philosophers, writers, artists, and courtesans attracted to a cultured court and its exquisite patron. In the Teatro Olimpico, audiences file into the tiers of seats (curving below twelve gods and goddesses mounted on a semicircular entablature of columns before niches of Roman emperors and frescoed Jacobean and Elizabethan courtesans that fill the backdrop) with a sweep of ermine-trimmed mantles, cloaks and Spanish hoops, starched and spidery ruffs, milky pearls, cream-colored and beige damask brocades with spun-gold lamé looped in fields of thistle flower, lotus, pine cone, palm, and scarlet-silk pomegranates—a triumph of velvet.

Sabbioneta, including a mint, a museum, a press, a synagogue, a library, and its new Church of the Incoronata, was planned about piazzas, gardens, and surprising vistas laid out on broad streets in straight rows of tangents all girded round with hexagonal fortress walls. So that in a day still to come, when the fortification was at last completed, and *Vespasiano Dux* and the date 1579 clearly inscribed on its gate, a farmer working in his field would look up to see, veiled in the mist, the bastions radiating five points into the surrounding countryside, and realize that he lived in the crotch of a star: and in the family chapel in his Chiesa della Incoronata, the Duke, knees pressed to the holystone, would pray fiercely for the kingdom that he dreamed, for the things knights guest—men care for—forgiveness for his sins and the love that he poisoned.

De ore leonis
libera me, Domine,
De ore . . .
et a cornibus unicornium
humilitatem meam.
Libera me, Domine.
Gloria Patri, et Filio,
et Spiritui Sancto
Libera me, Domine.

From the mouth of the lion,
save me, O Lord,
From the mouth . . .
and from the horns of unicorns
save my humility.
Save me, O Lord.

Glory to the Father and to the Son
and to the Holy Sprit.
Save me, O Lord.

–The Benedictine Monks of Santo Domingo De Silos
–"De Ore Leonis" Psalm 21(22)

In a day still to come . . . but for the moment, the Prince (as commander) left his dreams for Sabbioneta on paper, and went away to fight wars for the Spain his wife pined for, leaving her a lonely captive of a grim medieval fortress-castle, a prisoner of grizzly stone, of lofty flying buttresses and bastions, of haughty tower chambers—dark and desolate. Diana wandered through its shadowed courtyards and gaunt halls, trying the keys, searching the empty spaces in her deadly quest for perilous spindles to prick her pretty pink fingers on: a sleeping beauty, noctambulist, waltzing wistfully, dreamily whispering along the watchtowers, barefoot hovering by the roosting birds that swooped out reeling from beneath the shadows of castle ledges, its craggy pits, with bits of straw and loosed feathers, wind wafted wings, pieces of poems, and the love songs she sang.

Lavender's blue, diddle, diddle,
Lavender's green;
When I am king, diddle, diddle,
You shall be queen.

Who told you so, diddle diddle,
Who told you so?
Twas my own heart, diddle, diddle,
That told me so.

Call up your maids, diddle, diddle,
Set them to work.
Some with a rake, diddle, diddle,
Some with a fork.

Some to make hay, diddle, diddle,
Some to thresh corn,
Whilst you and I, diddle, diddle,
Keep the bed warm.

—Anonymous

Out from its hidden, secret places bats quivered; their sudden flight—startling—stole her breath away. Their wings, beating just above her head, shuddered against the thin, pale shadows of moonlight on milky skin, and tangled in the long-loosed ropes of her hair she let down like Rapunzel as she waited for someone to break the spell.

On nights like those when castle walls were awash in moonlight, hidden with wild vines and roses, à la *Bella Adormentata nel Bosco*, in the lofty tower chambers of Sleeping Beauty's palace, a darkling princess slept, and the wind whispering through stone drowned out the sound of her weeping. Sometimes, in her restlessness, she returned to leaning out from windows, longing through arrow loops, craning over parapets and the tippy tops of towers into the darkness: her eyes seeking out the farthest reaches of the kingdom. Her feet found footholds among the thicknesses and tangles of climbing vines. Needles pricked her fingers. Nettles scraped and scratched. The flesh of her feet and hands bled onto salient thorns. Her blood dripped onto the petals of roses, and onto her clothes, snagged and torn on barbs and briars, until she was a ragged, bloodstained bloom. And the curtain wall and the keep, the rough stone, the windows' gaping holes, great rooms and anterooms, lady chapel, chamber upon chamber, floor upon floor collapsed upon one another and dissolved into the dungeon and the dry moat's abyss as she let herself down from the latticework ladder, falling, a little way, from her cloud of roses.

The drawbridge dissolved behind her; the bailey walls disappeared. Disclosure was difficult at first, discovering the night, making things out in the pitch from the moon wizened shadows and marsh fog. Diana stared at shapes (hunched and humped suspiciously), and twisted, black transmutable forms which stood off adamantly, or revealed themselves in a sudden rush as soft hayricks, thatch, and straw. She was fleet. Throaty frog calls filled the air as a million frog legs leapt dripping from the silvery black liquid surface of rice fields, their songs filling her head with stories of enchantment, and fireflies sparkled in the fields that unfolded and wrapped around her like a mantel, like a cloak of velvet *alluciolato* looped with spun gold.

* * *

Orlando sighed under the weight of the stars; he was bone-tired and buoyant, having spent the better part of the night up a laboring donkey's ass, a perspective he always found enlightening. He bid goodnight to his friend (and fellow midwife) Nero, with a gesture so full of bonhomie, so warm and generously administered, that the poor creature nearly toppled. But Nero's smile, slightly skewed, was filled with infinite patience, a mixture of gratitude, tolerance and love for Orlando who saved him from "a fate worse than death," as he was once far worse off than this donkey coaxed with curses, sticks and endearments, with treats and caresses.

"*Buona notte, Bella*—Good night, Beautiful," he said and stroked her head, singing her lullabies in a language only a donkey could understand.

Nero's hearing was not so good, which was something of a blessing, because the barn was a lively place at night: rocked with snores and sneezes, wheezes and shuffles, squawks, squeals, bleats, peeping, pawing—restless arrangements. There were heaves of beastly sighs, nit picking, the settling of feathers and the shaking out of great dusty coats, scattered stomping and intermittent scuttering, the whir of iridescent wings as insects fed on dung piles, and in heaps of straw small things gnawed and burrowed. Fluttering sounds filled the rafters where birds roosted, and bats, dangling high above him, pealed out to hunt. All told, the noises, smells, drafts, and draughts together with the pinchy straw were bad enough to drive Caliban crazy, but that didn't keep Nero from his dreams. He knew what it meant to sleep in a warm bed, having been a former favorite courtesan pet; run away from the dwarf apartments of the Duchess of Milan and the miniature trappings of the past: ruffs, ruffles, and little pointy doll shoes, which was precisely why he loved the flea-infested drap-cloth: preferring to snuggle up to a soft donkey *culo* for comfort over linens of delicate lace cutwork, downy coverlets, and the binding of ribbons he stilled railed against in his sleep, as legions of silk threads flew and whipped about him, stinging. To Nero, the threshing floor was *terra incognita,* dross turned to wonder.

Something gleamed in the corner of his eye, caught in a shaft of early light. He blinked it away, rubbing at his sockets as if they were bothered by glittering gold dust and not just sticky with sleep. But it stubbornly persisted, glinting just at the periphery of sight. Something shimmered. A leftover fragment of a dream, no doubt, he thought: a nightmare-shard, a gaudy memory chipped sway at, a hellish trinket come to haunt him from his past, a fandangle, bauble, a bead. Something quivered at the fringe of awareness, caught in a specific beam of sunlight broadening to reveal the colors of baked earth and shadow—terracotta and *terra di ombra* (umbers burnt and raw), terra di Sienna, yellow ochre and brown, sepia, Tuscan red, chestnut, dark, warm, dappled donkey-grey, and all of the ferruginous colors of his new life burnished in the half-light, in the still somber tones of his awakening, and set in it—a fleshed-out foot, a little toe encircled with a ring exposed from beneath the edges of her gown made of yellow lancé velvet with cloth-of-gold sleeves. The woman was wound in warp or chain and weft of silk winding vine-shoots and inflorescence, pearl ropes and dangling silver, belts and bracelets, and clasped at her breast, caught up at the center of buttery filigree chemise was the *rosa dei venti*, the sixteen-pointed swirling windrose star of the Gonzaga.

Nero crouched, his face close to nearly touching the girl (her hair the color of raven's wings, her pale cheek spattered and streaked with blood) asleep on the straw in a blanket of spun gold brocade. Before she could wake up, however, startle and scream at his fantastic face, his capricious grin, troll-like demeanor, and wide, toady-eyed stares, he hobbled out in a hurry to find Orlando.

Diana stared unblinkingly, with cool fascination at a spider spinning a perfect web between the angles of wide flat boards above her head; gossamer threads of spider silk shimmered, flickering in space as the dark creature spun intently, flinging itself high and single-mindedly across the ceiling beams. She brushed away the hay that scratched her face, and her brow furrowed as she winced at the pain it caused her to stir, at the effort of emerging. She stretched her long creamy neck, extending each cramped leg, each slender arm, uncurling fingers and toes from the crumpled stuff of her dress. A little tattered and torn, the lustrous fabric crackled like glass; a Spanish farthingale hoop sprang up and bounced back again, stiffening, it swirled about her as she straightened and picked off scraps of straw, wooly bits, and feathers that were stuck in the crinkly folds and the wrinkled dampness of sleeves, unfurling.

As Orlando pulled the door open, sunlight poured through, gathered in her hair; her eyes sparkled like winking jewels. The air filled with the heady sweetness of roses, petals clung, caught up in the glittering caul of golden net, in the sheer luminousness of veil, in the long curling tendrils and lush tangle of her hair. Orlando saw this through the dazzling, mote-filled sunlight, streaming—an opalescent flurry of something scintillating, dispersing straw, bits of fleecy wool and down, particles of dust, and his heart startled too, as at the sudden flight of a winged thing flushed from a covert.

His hulking figure loomed darkly in the doorway against the gleaming backlight of the sun; amused, more than a little, at the seemingly hopeless dilemma of this curious creature, he tried not to laugh, as she, imagining herself so obviously cornered, so horribly and irrevocably trapped, desperately tried to find a way out. Darting first one way, and then the other, helplessly blocked, with no alternative, Diana, dazed and dizzy, dashed finally, headlong and flailing, into Orlando's outstretched arms, and fainted.

He laid her down in a tufted bed of cool, green grasses, and sprays of wildflowers just outside the opening of the thatch and stone crèche, counting on the healthful benefits of fresh air and warm Italian sun to revive her. He found her pulse and felt her flesh warm beneath his touch; translucent eyelids fluttered and blinked, springing open with an ever-widening look of panic as she ran off, draggle-tailed, in every direction. All around her, the morning mist was lifting from the fields, burning off with the sun that made her damp dress steam and shimmer. Some haze, caught low among the trees still hung in the mulberry field. A blue light colored the air around her, white clouds raced; her dress tossed across a cobalt sky.

"*Dai! Aspetta*! Wait! *Non temere!*"

She didn't stop, necessarily, but only tripped off a little way and faltered: the sound of his words was reassuring; but moreover, the little strength she had was failing.

"Don't be afraid!" he called out. "No one is going to hurt you."

She made a fresh start but was too weak to run; her head was reeling, and before she got very far, she sank down onto the ground with a shudder, as if given up to prayer or preparing to be sacrificed. "It's no use," she said, her voice trembling as she fought back tears. "Despite what you may or may not intend it seems I haven't any defenses left."

"You've been defending yourself, then?" he said, appraising her wounds—resting his eyes on bare extremities.

She spread the dress out over her feet with their telltale cuts and splinters of thorns, diffusing the fabric around her, twisting and twirling her hair, which fell like a mantle over her shoulders, past her waist and onto the floor. "I merely encountered some nasty briars," she offered in way of some explanation. "Some especially warlike roses." Fidgeting nervously, she wriggled, wet, wrinkled, and bedraggled, on the soft tussock where she leaned up against a mulberry tree, in the quivering shade of leaves. Her honey dress drew the bees, its milky sap stained; birds gorged themselves on pale pinkish berries that made a sticky mess as they fell around her. Butterfly wings dusted her cheek, wing beats whispered in her ear, spiders and lacewings and moths spun their wild silk tussah, while buried beneath the ground in their sticky yellow eggs, thousands of silkworms were waiting to be born.

"My Lady," he began slowly. "Since you are here, stranded, more or less, with only myself, a poor silk farmer, and my friend Nero, poor as well—and a gentleman—you are not likely to have any further cause to defend—anything. I am called Orlando," she heard him say, as if listening in a dream.

Diana reached for the hands he held out, an extension that sent a sharp, stabbing pain across her shoulders where he noted both the blood that seeped through the cloth of her dress in the very center of her back over the scapular and the conspicuous absence of wings. The pain left her breathless, and she was conscious, suddenly, of a terrible thirst.

"My name is Melissa," she lied, although this memory grew fuzzy, like so many details of the days that followed: a time seen through a haze of effulgent sunshine as if filtered through a powdery palette, a swirling kaleidoscope of brilliant color and pattern on skin as transparent and thinner than cellophane stretched over the delicate veins of whirring butterfly wings in a frenzied dance towards a first embrace, a first sticky-sweet kiss—suspended in air.

* * *

Beating the air madly with the wings of the flying machine strapped to his massive arms, Orlando positioned himself precariously on the roof of the barn and threw himself off the top. Whirling, hurtling through the high air, he hovered for a moment, frantically flapping like an enormous bird, then crashed spectacularly into the waiting bed of hay below, where Melissa ran on cue to brush off straw, and to help mend the broken wings, the shattered hopes, and dashed dreams that tumbled into the trusses of hay where they attempted to unravel the mysteries of flight, and those mysteries, deeper still, and more elusive.

Melissa freed Orlando from the trappings of his flying machine and the fastenings of his course hair shirt. Once his doublet was discarded and the obstacle of breeches pushed aside, there was an allowable access for a small hand—reaching—and as her mouth brushed his chest, she lost herself in anoetic delight, in the dark downy immeasurably warm vastness of flesh.

Orlando fumbled with minutia. "A million buttons! *Dio buono!*" he cried, with enough of them undone, finally, to expose a pale expanse of breast: skin the color of unbleached wax, a barely visible tracery of veins and nipples tinted the pale creamy-pink of pressed and faded rosebuds, which with just a brush of his fingertips released an intoxicating scent—a mixture of tallow candles and beeswax, balm and burnt honey. In his head and in his heart and in his soul beat a million pairs of wings: madly dancing, whirring wildly, the swarms suspended in the sweet warm air surrounded them like a cloud.

They lie in the shadowy twilight, listening to the sound of their hearts beating, the sheer breathlessness of words like whispering silk. All of a sudden, the world was bewitching— because of the waxing, luminous moon, the impossible closeness of one another, and the glittering profusion of stars—astonishing: their light scarcely diminished after a dwindling eternity of burning toward extinction. And because they were ignorant of the fact that stars were only holes left, sooner or later, deeper and darker than a lover's tomb—than the tomb of Juliet, and emptier still—they wrapped themselves in their lovers sheet like shiny spun silk against the inconceivable, the incessant murmuring of the stars—slipping, and the sound of the feeding silkworms, which fell on the night like rain. Their lips pressed in a kiss, their limbs entwined—locked in an eternal embrace, bare bottoms tilting toward the sky.

* * *

On his lips the taste lingered, his eyelids drooped, his flesh felt thick, heavy and warm, remembering. Already the sun beat down on the fields and on Nero at the lead of a string of women and children. From a distance, the pickers, with their mulberry baskets strapped to their backs, looked like a small army of ants, and then upright bunnies with their great straw baskets stuffed with colored eggs. The sun glinted on the small, scissor-like knife blades strapped to their fingers as they stripped the trees of shiny green leaves for the insatiable appetites of silkworms. Orlando was not hungry. He ate only a peach from his lunch sack, hummed to himself like a honey-covered Pooh, sun spilling on his flesh streaked with sweat and milky tree sap, peach juice, and burst mulberry; his thoughts returned to sweet Melissa.

* * *

Menocchio—"I have said that, in my opinion, all was chaos . . . and out of that bulk a mass formed—just as cheese is made out of milk—and worms appeared in it, and these were the angels."

—Carlo Ginzburg, *The Cheese and the Worms*

Orlando fanned the fires; in his head, he already reeled out the silk, winding the lengths of thread into his dreams; weaving. He picked up a fat egg-shaped bundle and held it in the palm of his hand. "Each cocoon the worm spins," he explained. "Every one is almost exactly like every other cocoon the *baco da seta* has spun for thousands of years. *Sempre identico, e l'unico. A*lways the same, and only one cocoon in all of its life. One perfect one only." He rubbed at the course fuzz that covered the outside of the tightly wound case, to reveal the fine soft silk underneath. "*Meraviglioso!*" he said, holding it out to her.

She touched it tentatively. The pale yolk-colored cocoon bounced back from the soft pressure of her fingertip pulled away with a sharp intake of breath, which, catching in her throat, sounded something like "H-ah!" Barely discernible. She had learned that whispering was requisite in the silk-rearing shed, that it was necessary to tiptoe about the spinning worms. If startled by any loud or sudden noise, they stopped, and the silken threads snapped. Or else they might spin a snag, a rough, bumpy spot in the otherwise flawless 1.6 kilometers of continuous, unbroken thread, and spoil the silk. Everyone walked on eggshells when the worms began blindly winding—loop the loop—around their tiny curled hooked shapes. They covered themselves with quickly and ever-thickening cozy coverlets; their spinnerets spinning out bunting twenty-four hours a day for three and four days until, at last, every blessed drop of liquid silk was squeezed out and spun into one long and glistening gossamer ribbon wound into elliptical cobweb-like cradles. Clinging to the small bunches of twigs and straw supports, all snuggled up, the pupa slept *come bambolette,* like little baby dolls.

Orlando pulled the largest, heaviest specimen from its winding place, and held it up between his forefinger and thick thumb before the backlight of the fire, which illuminated the tangle of course golden silk sticking out about the cocoon like the soft strands of hair on his forearms and naked chest. When it got hot enough, the pupa would die in their dark secret sleep: kept from their evolution, their silken sheathes turned to winding sheets, into tiny shrouds for those meant to die for loveliness' sake, their destinies fulfilled. But a select few, male and female, were spared. Orlando chose those carefully, weighing their lives in the balance. He threaded them to a line suspended from the ceiling; there, dangling like strings of pearls, they could complete their magical metamorphosis.

"The Romans ate them, you know," he said as they stepped outside into the twilight.

"Yacht!" Melissa covered her mouth. "I can't imagine anything more disgusting. You?"

Orlando laughed. "Honestly, no. But sometimes, when I think about the worms—their savage hunger, that awful yearning," he said, looking up into the sky, "I wonder could you grow a new skin? Cast off the old one? Change as well?—If you ate them, swallowed their secret, took it inside—Could solid flesh become q*ualcose' altro*—something else? Some winged thing—*qualcose' alato*? And I watch them—*farfalle, farfalle nottura, falene*—butterflies, night butterflies—moths. I study the flight of birds. I make sketches, fill up notebooks, and over and over again I throw myself at the ground. So far, I've discovered that I need wider wings—bigger, stronger arms," he said, opening them to full breadth.

"Not for me, *amore*," Melissa declared, folding herself softly inside them as dusk settled and they held one another like the shuddering shadowy forms of moths resting (on the depthless velvet of night-blooming flowers) with outstretched wings.

* * *

Busy old foll, unruly sun,
Why dost thou thus,
Through windows and through curtains, call on us?
Must to thy motions lovers' seasons run?
Saucy pedantic wretch, go chide

Late schoolboys, and sour prentices,
　Go tell court-huntsmen that the King will ride,
　　Call country ants to harvest offices;
　Love, all alike, no season knows, nor clime,
Nor hours, days, months, which are the rags of time.

　　Thy beams so reverend and strong
　　　Why shouldst thou think?
　I could eclipse and cloud them with a wink,
　But that I would not lose her sight so long:
　　If her eyes have not blinded thine,
　　　Look, and tomorrow late, tell me
　Whether both the Indias of spice and mine
Be where thou leftst them, or lie here with me.
Ask for those kings whom thou saw'st yesterday,
And thou shalt hear, All here in one bed lay:

　　She is all states, and all princes I,
　　　Nothing else is
　Princes do but play us; compared to this,
　All honor's mimic, all wealth alchemy.
　　Thou, sun, art half as happy as we
　　　In that the world's contracted thus;
　Thine age asks ease, and since thy duties be
To warm the world, that's done in warming us.
　Shine here to us, and thou art everywhere;
This bed thy center is, these walls they sphere.
　　　　　　　　—John Donne, "The Sun Rising"

Melissa measured time now in new ways: by the lengths of long-lingering kisses and airy thread. She had learned to unwind the cocoons, reeling silk like a throwster, a regular Chinese empress. Orlando gave her a few to work on while he took the rest to market: leaving while she was asleep, his wagon filled with the golden cocoons, she imagined, like a brilliant cloud. She thought of this while she soaked them in a basin of water, dissolving the gummy substance that bound them together, and as they bobbed and swelled, her deft fingers quickly lifted out the floating end of loosened thread and wound it once and again about the hand reel.

"It's impossible to reel as fast as the worms have spun, even working from dawn to dark it will take several days," he had explained, smoothing the way for his departure with his fingers tracing over her face, committing it to memory, analyzing it like a cartographer—the depths of its valleys, the reach between her eyes etched on his heart like a map for the long journey home.

Orlando will be back by the time the cocoons are all unwound, she reminded herself, turning the reel, spinning his promise round and round in her fingers like a prayer. Sometimes, when he was gone, she set her work aside, and ventured out for long walks instead. She skirted the perimeters of the farm, marking out the borders that bound the edges of her existence, and which, in contrast to the confines of castle walls—this swatch of land, a tapestry of verdant weave and crimson lake caught up with the glittering threads of sunlight, golden grain fields, French (pink mulberry) knots, tangled threads of tomato vines and grape garlands, riotous poppies, patches of melon, and sugar beets— seemed endless. Women wearing wide straw hats, like the habits of destitute nuns, tilted them at the sun as they waded barelegged in the paddy-fields, weeding rice—the long slender reeds lifted dripping into their baskets from the silvery sheet of lagoon. She wound along its marshy banks, past the women with their mulberry baskets and the hatching trays they rinsed.

Rushing wide and fast and dark and deep, the river ran more swiftly now, dividing the plains of maize, barley, wheat and rice fields, guiding the icy Alpine rains towards the gates of distant cities before spilling into the wide Adriatic Sea. Stopping on a spit of sandy shore to rest, its rhythmic lapping and its rushing, hypnotic surge made her sleepy as she leaned dreamily over the edge, trailing her hand in the tantalizing pool. "No one would know if I were to bathe here," she said to her own watery reflection, already wriggling out of her clothes, casting them about, carelessly littering the beach with thrown off vestiges of her wardrobe.

The water felt wonderful; she was enjoying it so much that she never noticed a pair of eyes looking on blinkingly from between the reeds, fixing her in their gaze until she emerged quivering like Aphrodite from the foam to dry in the warm sun. Her wet slip clung. She trembled in the breeze that made the windbreaks shimmer and swept a silk scarf up from the sand. It sailed—this bright ribbon, a streamer unfurling, fluttering in the breeze like a *bandiera*, waving like a flag, her own colors flying off and landing on the head of a peeping frog. The sight of this grotesque creature, absurdly posturing in its hat, struck her as so preposterous that she might have laughed aloud, had it not been leering at her from behind that veil with an all too disconcertingly human expression of lasciviousness tinged with regret. She shuddered, as the frog turned, rasping deeply, as if words were stuck in its throat, before it lopped off wearing her scarf on its head like some fantastic caul.

Melissa wasn't certain if the bells she heard were real. Hawk bells. Most certainly. She'd seen the men with their falconers and the hooded birds. She heard them again, and this time there was no mistaking it: the sound of silvery double bells—the kind her husband ordered specially from Milan, the very best and most expensive. From somewhere, not too far away, came the call of the falconer raising his black-gloved hand. Long pointed wings flashing past were gone in an instant like the glint of an expert needlewoman, stitching, and Melissa slipped back into the enchanted storybook world she'd entered through a minute opening she believed to be as infinitesimally small as the eye of that needle, and settled there again with a sprinkling of something like butterfly dust.

* * *

Meanwhile, the traces of a lost princess laid at his feet, so incited the lovelorn prince that his speech, which was characteristically Spartan, became the raving of a madman, and he executed the messenger at once, slitting its throat with his razor-sharp sword—no amount of pleading on its behalf would have spared its life—poor misguided frog. Vespasiano thundered like a legendary giant, his voice boomed, echoed through the empty halls, and rocked the towers; his bootsteps made the earth tremble everywhere for miles around. Reaching out, he and his men scoured the land: their inquiries judicious, often bloody—and there was no use in hiding in haying fields, in the lofty limbs of trees, or under rocks—not a stone was left unturned.

The trail of his wife's sweet-adulterant blood like the scent of witches (heretics, magicians) excited the hounds to the chase. The sound of their howling infected her sleep, tainted her dreams. She woke soaked with sweat to the silence, a monstrous quiet bunched beneath the bed; it coiled in the dark, and breathed down her neck with its sulfury dragon-breath. She followed its billowing form out the door where it gathered, its outline blurred, in the smoky, *sfumato*-smudged dawn, leveling its wings. She stared into its yellow eyes.

The fields were burning along with the rearing shed, and the barn where Nero, in his customary night-battles with finery, grappled with the *silk pointes*/noose slipped around his neck, and his legs, though short, kicked fiercely, until he hung, puppetlike, from the rafters above the bonfire—the way they dangled witches and burnt effigies.

Smoke rolled over the waveless plain as Orlando driving his wagon (empty now except for the mechanical wings he had brought along for repair) towards home, whipped his tired horse, and they fairly flew on the fringe of his fields on fire with the Prince's frenzied pack, *canaglia* at their heels. "Melissa!" he wailed into the inferno, racing to find an opening through the maze of burning wheat. "Go to the Devil!" he swore, lashing at the dogs closing in, nearly blinded by the smoke that overcame him. What can it mean? he thought at last as his horse startled and bolted, throwing him and his wings high and clear of the wagon at the same time that Melissa (once again called Diana) was dragged from the fire and rendered to the duke, chafing against the metal trappings of armored guard and horse that spirited her away from the torched farm and burning fields. Within the belly of the earth something shuddered, and Heaven quaked when doom dragged its monstrous tail writhing, lashing, and seething. It rented the plane just as they leapt to the other side of the chasm where Orlando, his hair in flames, his wings on fire, too, was falling to earth like a star.

Once I rose above the noise and confusion
Just to get a glimpse beyond this illusion.
I was soaring ever higher
But I flew too high

—Kansas, "Carry on Wayward Son"

They returned Diana to the duke's stronghold and laid her down on her old bed where she wavered in the borderland between waking and dreams, fascinated by the silk panel that decorated her wall. The concept of metamorphosis absorbed her fully for a moment as the Putti, strolling along acacia branches on the slip of embroidered linen, were changed into dragons; and the pigs too had been strangely stitched—under the same leaves that fed the hungry caterpillars—she thought, keeping her head turned sharply from her lover's shattered lips, his splintered eyes, wasted limbs, and the burnt shards of his wings, which they had laid out beside her.

All through the long night, Diana mourned for Orlando and his ancient dream of Dedalus. Railing against her restraints, she cried out for mercy in the name of the Lord, calling for her mother and her father and for her old nurse buried here so far from Spain without so much as a friend to lay a sprig of rosemary on her grave. But despite her ardent, tearful prayers, it was no merciful redeemer, but only her husband who appeared daily with poison, she thought, clearly on his mind, and a goblet of wine which he put to her lips and bid her to drink. She refused until, on the third day, he came and untied the cloth binding from her wrists. "*Bevi!*" he said, once again handing her the cup from which, at last, she drained every drop.

For the next several hours she thrashed about in agony as hundreds of tiny worms gnawed at her bed sheets and her sleeping gown. Because she insisted on pulling the gloves off her hands, tearing at her skin and her head where caterpillars nested and moths lay their eggs in her hair, they bound her up again with ribbons and strips of rags. She tried to speak, but her mouth felt stuffed with cotton: moths flew out when she opened it, and thumping blindly, they streamed from her lips and fluttered upward—even from her fingertips. With a fever of wings beating in her brain, she gathered her angels—whispering saints, and rose above the bed where the Holy Spirit hovered, his wings on fire.

Brooding in the self-imposed exile of his garden, Vespasiano Gonzaga, Prince of Bózzolo, future knight of the Golden Fleece, reached into the emptiness. "God called my wife suddenly to himself before she could utter a word," was all that he offered in way of explanation when he finally emerged in bitter mortification, a dark figure in long, black mourning cloak.

Hundreds of torches lit the night as he led the procession of mourners following the hearse to the church. There, where the priests dressed in black waited on the high altar among the purple draperies and the flickering tapers of unbleached beeswax, the echo of armor, whispering silk, chanting, and dirges for the dead, Diana was delivered to her requiem; her body (which gave off the telltale scent of bitter almonds masked by the overwhelming perfume of roses) anointed with the chrism of salvation. Dressed in her finest gown: a silk brocade winding sheet, her hair wound with gold as well, she was a glittering feast for worms: her flesh the host for larvae who fed on lost dreams, born again to fly away on powdery, white wings.

> The force that through the green fuse drives the flower
> Drives my green age; that blast the roots of trees
> Is my destroyer.

And I am dumb to tell the crooked rose
My youth is bent by the same wintry fever.

The force that drives the water through the rocks
Drives my red blood; that dries the mouthing streams
Turns mine to wax.
And I am dumb to mouth unto my veins
How at the mountain spring the same mouth sucks.

The hand that whirs the water in the pool
Stirs the quicksand; that ropes the blowing wind
Hauls my shroud sail.
And I am dumb to tell the hanging man
How of my clay is made the hangman's lime.

The lips of time leech to the fountain head;
Love drips and gathers, but the fallen blood
Shall calm her sores.
And I am dumb to tell a weather's wind
How time has ticked a heaven round the stars.

And I am dumb to tell a lover's tomb
How at my sheet goes the same crooked worm.

—Dylan Thomas, "The Force That Through the Green Fuse Drives the Flower"

CHAPTER THREE

The Law of Storms

. . . upwards I may go or round.
—Dante, *Purgatory*. Canto VII, *The Divine Comedy*

Poi piovve dentro all'alta fantasia . . .
Next, showered into my fantasy . . .
—Dante, *Purgatory*. Canto XVII, *The Divine Comedy*

Now loosed, Lea's soul was trying to find its bearings. Somewhere over the Atlantic, she hovered like—as nearly as she could figure—a burst balloon. That's how it felt when she began to rise up in the first place, like a balloon when a child lets go of the string and "OOOhwwaahh" there's that awful sinking sensation that you feel in the split second when you've let go of something—your dog's leash, your baby's hand, a balloon. She found herself falling like an upside down Alice, sinking up, up, and up into the sun: a lovely white balloon lifted higher, higher and higher until, quite unexpectedly and much to her surprise, she burst, and what was left was just energy like gas, helium, and bits of balloon that were still stuck like eggshell and continued to drop off of her along the way.

It was exceedingly dismal where she drifted out over the sea, brooding—over her past life: love, betrayal, birth, death. Her head was spinning. Positively ionlike regrets pulled toward her, drawn to sadness like dew to salty grains of sea spray, particles from fires, burning meteors, and volcanic eruptions—clinging to dust. She was dark clouds gathering, at the mercy of her thoughts, which were blowing out to her at sea as land breezes. Cold gushes of air assailed her all around, changed the blood in her veins to ice water, and with the tropical heat from the equator blasted up inside—her thoughts distilled where the scent of bananas and pineapple and rum drifted upwards over Guadalupe; snow fell like tears, the accumulation of a lifetime.

She scuttled. Although, it was not as if she could go anywhere she liked, but was pulled along, compelled really, a crazy wind-tormented thing, a madwoman, *una pazza* driven to distraction with a mindless, wild storm-driven obsession; she was huge and moving with the force of a continent like Africa drifting away and breaking off. A hurricane wind with the power of the atomic bomb, she was hot-pink and headed dead-on for the coast of Brazil where Lavinia (in a small boat) feverishly slept alongside Antonio, turning in her wind-tossed dreams as weather stations and meteorologists everywhere tracked the storm.

Their weathervanes whirled; satellites probed, inserted like thermometers up her rectum: monitoring changes in blood-red lines of mercury, recording dew points. Balloons measured the dimensions of upper air; the base height of clouds. They made predictions, basing them on maps of spliced-together expanses of sky, pieced-together pictures of cirrus, stratus and cumulus (alto and nimbus) that merged and collided (cirrus, cirrocumulus and cirrostratus, altocumulus, altostratus and nimbostratus, stratocumulus, and cumulonimbus), classifying clouds whose names filled the air like incantations. They cast their microwaves out into the blue, penetrating the darkness, piercing the impenetrable, and with the homing instincts of pigeons, their radar reached out to find her and bounced off, echoing her low wail, her soft sobs, her mournful sound in bursts and pips and pulses. Her reflection beamed in waves. It fluttered back, a whirring beat of wings displayed on their scanners, as if originating from monitors strapped to her heart.

Her pulse beat in blips, quickening closer. "Blip . . .," she said as she radiated outwards from the center of the display—converted to light. "Blip . . . blip . . . blip. . . .." The air heated up. The barometer dropped. They projected, forecasting disaster.

Lea roared in as anticipated, only she came much sooner than expected, and she forced herself higher and faster and was more powerful than anyone ever might have imagined.

> I've stepped in the middle of seven sad forests,
> I've been out in front of a dozen dead oceans,
> I've been ten thousand miles in the mouth of a graveyard,
>
> And it's a hard, and it's a hard, it's a hard, and it's a hard,
> and it's a hard rain's a-gonna fall.
> —Bob Dylan, "A Hard Rain's A-Gonna Fall"

* * *

In their small boat off the coast of Brazil, the lovers sailed, oblivious to storm warnings. Lavinia swelled. Having ignored the early warning signs, she was now in distress. It began, innocently enough, as a tickle: a feather that floated in on a breeze from a faraway place and stuck in her throat. She washed the cough down with wine, stifling it with kisses, stopping it up with accommodating parts of Antonio. But it got worse, and one day after their swim she shivered uncontrollably as the sailcloth slapped against white wind-filled clouds. She dismissed this, attributing it to having taken too much sun, to overexposure and a bad burn in places that had never before seen the light of day. It wasn't just sunstroke making her head spin or the motion of the sea making her sick— it was the dizzying dazzle of love. Love made her knees weak and rocked her off her guard, leaving no one to stand watch. And while making love required a hypervigilance to details like teeth and toes and fingertips, the breadth and depth of kisses, hollows, degrees, ascendance—it necessarily precluded paying attention to the ordinary, the extraneous. While the sunset was bursting, she was on fire, and while she should be gazing wide-eyed while a halo was spinning itself around the moon, she was feverishly kissing Antonio with her eyes closed. And he—he could barely see through the haze of her hair obscuring the pillow like a cloud or gathered in the velvety darkness between the sheets. With bedclothes for a sail and whispers driving the wind, a whole ocean washed up between their thighs.

* * *

Floundering in Lea's wake, in the churning aftermath of the storm, Lavinia dragged herself onto the shore. Exhausted, nearly drowned, and coughing up gallons of salt water, she was fascinated by a flare from the beach. It seemed to wink at her as it tossed out light shards, sparkler-like, more brilliant that the sun-bounced spangles off the sea, spray, glittering particles of sand, pieces of pretty pale-colored sea glass, shells, polished pebbles, smoothed and tumbled stones, or the foam with which she'd washed up. On the beach, just beyond the breakers, she could see that someone was lying spread-eagle on the sand, and stuck between his legs, tangled in seaweed, was the most awesome sight she had ever seen—there, pulsing in the sunlight, flaring with the brightness of a binary star, was a giant hailstone, or diamond as big as a coconut (with the burning blue clarity, with an absolute magnitude of God-only-knew, how much), and right away she knew that that someone was Antonio, brightening as she came up closer on the scene like a supernova exploding.

> After the cloud embankments,
> The lamentation of wind,
> And the starry descent into time,
> We came to the flashing waters and shaded our eyes
> From the glare.
>
> Alone with the shore and harbor,
> The stems of the cocoanut trees,
> The fronds of silence and hushed music,
> We cried for the new revelation
> And waited for miracles to rise.
>
> Where elements touch and merge,
> Where shadows swoon like outcasts on the sand
> And the tired moment waits, its courage gone—
> There were we in latitudes where storms were born.
> —Arna Bontemps, "Reconnaissance"

* * *

Maria sorted booties, in all the possibilities of pink. Sparks flew from the heat of her hands as she matched and smoothed countless pairs, folding. She stacked them neatly in piles, added a small sock to her basket of mending, regarding it disdainfully as the latest addition to the growing heap of her failings, guilt, sins, incompleteness. A lifetime of things left undone, snags, pulls, tears, of seams unraveled, missing buttons, fallen hems, holes—a monument to regret. Sighing as she turned away, she shouldered their reproaches, petty little taunts, nasty accusations, afraid they might decide to fling themselves magically about the kitchen and fly into her face—the harpies—animated like the pictures in the "*Walter Sidney*" show that her son and her husband were so crazy about. Maybe, if they sprang to life, she thought, getting ready to wash the floor now, her mop handle swiping at the air, maybe then she could simply reduce them to the rags that they really were.

As Joseph turned on the television set in the den, she heard the strains of stars spilling from Tinkerbelle's magic wand across the blue-black picture screen on the *Magical World of Disney* they watched every Sunday night along with the *Ed Sullivan Show* and *Bonanza*.

He whistled to her: his high, sweet birdcall, but she wouldn't come now; he could sense it in the momentum of her mopping, imagining her lip's resolve, her back's arch—resistance. The hartshorn fumes drifted up from the wet floor, wafted off the woman working with a fury. "Mrs. Clean," he thought, imagining the bottle with the genie winking on it, and wondered what wishes she was squandering. They swished and sloshed by the sloppy bucketful: wishes stopping up the sink; clogging the drain. A soapy, atmospheric film settled over the surface of the wash water like the frothy scum of tiny pools continually effervescing and swirling with the motion of miniature eddies, small whirlpools, continental drift, of glaciers—melting, melt water, outwash, of frozen lakes and islands of ice, the friction of ice sheets passing, snow drifting, clouds, colloidal particles under a microscope. Bacteria. Tempests. All pulled swirling down the cleared drain like a genie sucked back into his magic lamp. Alakazam!

Winding through the labyrinth of sewer and water systems, eventually this backwash of wishes emptied into the sea where its microscopic bits of grit and particles of dust entered the shells of mollusks, who in defense of their soft flesh against these invasions, covered the irritants with secretions. And so, attached to shell walls and growing in the silvery darkness of oyster bellies, the intolerable intrusions of wasted wish-sediment, of dream-till and sludge, were very slowly over time turned into pearls.

Only partly paying attention to the television tube, Joseph watched Pinocchio dance on his puppet stick legs and flap his skinny little wooden arms about on stage like vestigial wings as he sang his *canto libero,* the emancipation proclamation of a puppet who'd lost his strings and was on the point of becoming a real boy—owning it. Joseph, aware of the magical and painful transformation yet to come, sighed for poor old Gipetto: for in the end, he knew what it would take to save him—the son who had been begging rides from pigeons, and nothing could prevent his fated sojourn into the belly of the whale. *Coraggio!* If a boy got lost, he thought, half-conscious of his wife winding down in the kitchen, a man knew how to get hold of a boat. But what about his daughters? There was his Lea, already spewed from the mouth of the dogfish, so to speak, and he could not fathom what monster had swallowed Lavinia.

Maria came in balancing a knife and two ripe pears on a white plate. Joseph pared the fruit as she sat with her sewing, the sound of her needle flicking against silver thimble tip, protecting her finger from pricks, as the chain of stitches came quickly and spaced tightly between. Sometimes it was the flash of knitting needles or the jagged rhythm of crotchet hook and pearly pastel threads, the curve of her neck and the entranced look in her eyes that made it seem like a powerful spell was being cast as the net grew with each stitch and he was caught. Gradually, she slowed down, cooling like an iron after being shut off, and he listened to the sound of her softly ticking over rock and roll on the *Ed Sullivan Show* and Gabriele singing wild in a language, it seemed, he was born understanding.

> Baby, do you understand me now?
> Sometimes I feel a little mad
> But don't you know that no one alive can always be an angel
>
> Animals, "Don't Let Me Be Misunderstood"

Even before the start of "Bonanza," his friends came to get him. "*Attenta, Gabriele. Mi racomando!*" his father warned.

"*Si, Papà,*" Gabriele called on his way out the door—his nose already growing longer.

* * *

Under the big Bronx sky, Joseph's spirit soared, his heart pounding to the theme of the Ponderosa as he adjusted the sprinkler head and turned it on the green lawn of his yard. He heard the water course through the hose, and stepped back as it spurted out sputtering, pulsing as the wide high arc shifted first to the right, straight up, and then left, invisibly falling except for intermittent sparkling in the darkness amid October's tangle of moonlight and vines climbing the garden wall.

Maria came out in her slippers to look at the stars before bed, and sighed, fixing her eyes on the one that she wished on. The mysterious power of its beauty exerted on the imagination, restored in reality from the diminished twinkling of its nursery song. She had, by now, committed "Twinkle, Twinkle" to memory, gotten it by heart from the *Mother Goose Rhymes* she read to her baby granddaughter Bella before bed. She divined meaning from the drawings and imagined what she sensed the sounds might mean, but put together with what little English she knew, what she pictured was bizarre in the extreme: a company of mice, babies bunting, and ABCs jumbled together like a burlesque of the *Commedia dell'Arte* featuring Harlequin and Pierrot and all of the characters from fairy tales.

When she was feeling tired, which was often the case, of this cacophony tripping phonetically or stuck, mostly, on her tongue, she sang Italian songs instead, finding solace in the familiar sounds, words, reassured by the repetition, worn old refrains, the effortlessness of her voice conjuring up the wolf, revealing him behind the door and letting the ax (or, in this case, the door) fall cleanly, once again as her hand smoothed circles over the baby's freshly powdered and diapered backside, Bella's breathing nearly imperceptible as she drifted off to sleep, snug in her bunting like a warm bundle of rising bread dough.

From the open window next door, Maria and Joseph heard the sound of a record playing. Rosemary Clooney's voice drifted out into the night. "Hey there, you with the stars in your eyes . . ." Holding each other close they danced like conspirators—where a lizard slept, mice dug, burrowing by the soaking roots of nightshade plants along with a rather large rat, among pumpkins as big as coaches—and made love to "Mambo Italiano."

* * *

When I was just a little girl,
I asked my mother, "What will I be?

Will I be pretty?
Will I be rich?"
Here's what she said to me:

"Que sera, sera,
Whatever will be, will be;
The future's not ours to see.
Que sera, sera,
What will be, will be."

—Doris Day, "Que Sera, Sera"

Bella gazed into the long looking glass, hardly recognizing herself dressed up for Halloween: they had added wings to a First Holy Communion dress, ballet slippers, a magic wand, and diamond tiara from the Five and Ten Cents store. While Teresa, their downstairs tenant and dearest friend, made up her face reminiscent of movie stars and dolls she had known, her son Alex shook one of the boxes of Good & Plenty candy that she bought him for the party at school, singing as he straddled a chintz armchair. "Good & Plenty, Good & Plenty, Good & Plenty, Good & Plenty."

He climbed down when he was done, put the candy in his lunchbox with the picture of Napoleon Solo and Ilya Kuryakin on it and strapped on his six-shooters. At first, he had wanted to be a knight like one of the round table in King Arthur's court, or Robin Hood, or one of his merry band of men, but all of the fuss over the costumes changed his mind. He decided just to wear his belt instead, his old cowboy hat and a bandana, but couldn't resist the package with the silver plastic bullets when he saw it at Woolworth's, and the badge that said Sheriff of Dodge City. He fired alternately at Bella. "Bang! Bang! Bang! Bang!" and blew imaginary smoke from both barrels. "What's she suppose to be?" he asked, replacing the guns in the holster riding a little too low on his hips.

His mother, lost in concentration, loaded a tiny brush with black cake to darken the delicate arches of the little girl's brows. Frowning, Bella screwed up her face, but Teresa, not that easily discouraged, swooshed pearly blue over each crinkled-up, nearly translucent lid, rimming her big, dreamy eyes with black cake liner, and while her long lashes fought to flutter and close, she swiped on some mascara. Maria took the rags out from her grandaughter's hair, releasing the banana curls that fell about her in dark ropes. Rouge was rubbed onto the pale porcelain of her cheeks and lipstick applied. "Go like this," Teresa said, demonstrating the proper way to purse her lips, which were set in the exaggerated, petrified pout of the uninitiated, and gave her a hug before she could run away. "In case you need to put some more on later," she said, tucking a little Avon lipstick sample in the pocket of Bella's sweater. "Come back. Close your eyes." A pink powder puff tickled her face, the soft scent lingering, suspended in the air like a sprinkling of fairy dust.

"What's she supposed to be?" Alex asked again, trying the question on Nonna this time.

"A princess," Maria answered, straightening her granddaughter's already crooked tiara. "Isn't that right, *Bella di Nonna?*" she said, giving her a big hug. "A *beautiful* princess."

"A *bea-u-ti-ful* princess," Bella echoed, as if bewitched, her words caught in some witch's spell.

"How come she's got wings then?"

"She's like . . ." Teresa said, realizing that she was stuck. "She's like a *fairy* princess," she explained, untangling the fairytales: poisoned apples, thorns, and glass caskets, Sleeping Beauty, Snow White and all the enchanted princesses, as Bella tried to catch the glitter on her dress.

"A *fairy* princess," Bella repeated. Laughing, she stuck her tongue out at her friend.

Alex remained still for a moment as a story came to him, characters and incidents converged: an old frog, a good field mouse, a blind-rich mole. Flowers and colors unfolded in his head—a bird's wing beat, its quickening heart, the shape of a swallow remembered in his soul. "Ohhh, like Thumbelina?" he asked.

"Like Thumbling," said Bella, lighting on a leaf somewhere, as delicate as a snowflake. Someplace a pretty princeling as fragile as glass brandishes his bright wings; sets the tiniest golden crown upon her lovely little head. Spinning, Bella flapped her arms.

Maria stopped her.

Alex shrugged. "You look good," he said.

"*Andiamo, bambini?*" Joseph called as the little troop made their way down the stairs. "Ah!" he exclaimed, playing at his breath taken away. "*Guarda*, Miss America! Look how beautiful she is," he said beaming at his granddaughter. "And let me see—who is this bandito? Or could it be Mr. John Wayne?"

"Reach for the sky," Alex said, determined to shoot it out with poor Nonno, who was killed in the end, with bravura.

"*Ciao, Valentino mio,*" Maria called, blowing her husband an exaggerated kiss like famous lovers of the silent screen as she waved, "Bye-bye kids."

"Mom!" Teresa called out to her mother-in-law, who was sweeping leaves in the yard. "Hurry up. You're gonna miss them!"

Alex's grandmother, Anastasia, rushed to the porch, signaling good-bye with her upheld broomstick.

"Bye Babushka, Nonni, Mommy!" Alex and Bella waved.

Anastasia, Maria, and Teresa waved back from the porch until Joseph and the children had practically disappeared out of sight, headed down the street toward the El, and then all three went back into the house together.

* * *

Anastasia and Teresa had prepared for Halloween—the Feast of All Souls, *Festa dei Morti,* by leaving out some lentils, lima beans, and Jujubes before they went to bed. They cracked open all of the windows so that the dead could come in. Anastasia's entire family: mother Alexandria, father Nicholas, her big sisters Olga, Tatiana, and Marie, and her baby brother Aleksei had all been killed during the Revolution; her husband Arturo died in the summer of 1942 before their son Aleksei II's first birthday. That's all anyone ever got to know about Anastasia. She didn't like to talk about herself or her family; her life was a riddle. "It's like some big secret or somethin'," Teresa would say when her friends asked—some of the biggest questions in the history of the Bronx were raised about Anastasia's past, but she would take the answers with her to the grave.

In 1958, being Russian was not exactly a coup, an ostrich feather in your cap. The more people speculated about who and what she was and where she came from the more reclusive Anastasia became the more they speculated until they made her out to be some sort of spy—just like that Natasha on the *Rocky and Bullwinkle Show.* The fact that her only son (U.S. Army—Airborne) was missing, had been captured and tortured or killed, was lost fighting their losing battle, apparently made little or no difference whatsoever to anyone, especially the neighborhood kids; to them, everything was a big joke. Any time now, those little hoodlums would be tossing toilet paper rolls into the fruit trees, stealing the pumpkin from the front stoop and smashing it in the street. They would egg the house and soap the car just as they did every Halloween. Come morning, Teresa would be sponging the words "Commie! Pinko! Spy! Witch!" from the windshield of her red Mustang convertible, wishing she could wash their mouths out with soap instead. All through the day they would continue taunting— ringing the bell and running away. Ever since Teresa started selling Avon, the prank had become simply irresistible. "Ding dong! Avon lady!" they called as they scattered and hid, doubled over, thinking it was hilarious—how life could be a scream.

But Teresa wasn't laughing: though still so very young, in her life, she too, had suffered some heavy losses. Her great-grandfather, both of her grandparents, her mother's brothers and sisters, cousins, and their caretaker's entire family were killed after the armistice and before Italy's final liberation in 1945 while the SS units were wasting the countryside. Much of this story had been fleshed out with photographs from *Life* Magazines and her father's books, which she secreted away at night. Under the tent of her sheets she poured over black and white images of war with a flashlight, highlighting, in particular, those dog-eared pages with underscored words, sentences, or entire underlined passages.

> The possibilities for destruction in no way exhausted, rather seemed endless, as partisans fought a war of popular insurrection and hatred, and the Germans retaliated, executing ten Italians for every German who

was killed. Thirty-five thousand partisans and civilian martyrs to Nazi-Fascist terrorism died after the armistice when the whole country was turned into a battleground, a cluster of villages called Marzabotta disappeared from the face of the earth after two SS companies herded their one thousand eight hundred and thirty inhabitants into a church and massacred them, stringing the corpses from lampposts, trees, and the balconies of buildings like rotting fruit. In the village of Rionero Sannitico, sixteen civilians were shot as a reprisal because an old man tried to kill a German soldier he caught stealing his chickens.

—Henry Adams, *Italy at War*

Every person in the house was murdered, except for Teresa's mother, because Marisola was in the habit of sneaking off to meet Nicola, the caretaker's son, in the barn or the wood or the haying field where they humped like rabbits and was not in her bed like the others *al primo canto del gallo*—at cockcrow.

Day after day, without exception, their rooster would climb to the top of the woodpile to wake the sun. Charlemagne stretched his long neck, lifted his handsome face, and focused on something only he, with his golden crown and mystic rooster's eyes, could see. His wings when swept open, beating, eclipsed an entire village. "*Chicchirchí!*" he sang out, boasting the voice of an angel. Every morning's wake up call said, "Remember, so far you've survived," or "You've survived so far," and was remindful of the rhythm of normal life: now, when most everything they had was gone—husbands, fathers, sons—men and precious, meltable metals—iron bedsteads and wedding bands of gold, silver, and platinum sacrificed much earlier in the war when Mussolini's men marched through taking scrap, herding cows and ducks and geese and pigs and horses and rabbits away like sheep to the slaughter two by two as if they were filling up the ark.

The family succeeded in saving at least a couple of necks from the Fascists wielding axes. Before the soldiers could find them, they dressed three little pigs up in christening gowns and stuck hats on their heads. They tied huge bows in the bonnets around the hair of their chinny chin chins and painted Miss Piggy pouts on their lips. For at least three quarters of an hour Teresa's grandmother, Camilla, had played nursemaid to those Moppets while the soldiers prodded and poked and overturned family treasures with their guns. The whole while she pushed them all in a baby carriage—stinky little pigs in blankets—rocking and singing them *nina nana*.

"*Giro, Giro tondo, Cavalle, cavallando, Cento cinquanta, La gallina canta, Canta sola, sola, Non vuole andare a scuola, La gallina bianca e nera, Ti dà la buona sera—*"

"Little pig, little pig, let me in!" hollered the big bad wolf, pounding on the door. "Or I'll blow your house in!"

"Huff and puff till you're blue. See if I care!" thought Camilla, racing to build a big fire in the chimney. "*Buona sera, buona notte, Il lupo dietro la porta, La porta casca giù, e lupo non c'è più.*"

The children hid bunnies under their hats and a chick or two up their sleeves, so with some sleight of hand, a few simple illusions, they managed to save what poor innocent creatures they could. They were almost convinced they had wintered the storm when the war ended and the Germans came to take what the bombs missed, stealing from the meager menagerie Mussolini's men had left behind, which didn't amount to a hill of beans. There were a few raspy chickens in the kitchen, and Charlemagne, their fabled black rooster sometimes called Charlie and sometimes Charles the Great or the King of Lombardy, because it was a widely held belief that he had been around since the first Crusade. A legend in his own time for more reasons than one, Charlemagne was thought by some to have graced the seal of Chianti Classico, that he was the original *Gallo Nero*.

Nobody ever raised a doubt that he was the one responsible for the unusual peace that reigned among Domenico DePasquale's small, happy, healthy flock of birds and the strange, delicate, fragile beauty of their eggs whose shells came in pastel shades—of pink, pretty flamingo, pale blue, olive green, turquoise, and peach, which the children sorted by different sizes and colors into boxes by hand. Some people liked to eat the large ones themselves and saved the little ones for their children. Each morning Domenico's wife Camilla fed the chickens on good, plump golden grains of corn and let them have free range. They roamed the fields or wandered into the woods at will, sheltering from the wind and rain under the trees in the copse wood. They got plenty of fresh air and full run of the farm, easy accessibility to lush grass: going out to eat worms, fuzzy caterpillars, pill bugs and other crunchy crawly creatures. Although they laid fewer eggs than plain old ordinary chickens (four per week instead of seven), what they lacked in quantity they made up for in sunny yolks, and whites that were never runny.

Anyone who'd ever eaten those eggs (hard boiled with a sprinkling of salt and pepper the way Camilla liked them, beaten up with some sugar and vanilla bean for their babies, egg yolk, sugar and *marsala zabaglione,* whipped into a *frappé di caffè*, soft cooked and served in little egg cups with thin strips of buttered toast for children, sunny-side up, down, or over-easy, scrambled with fried peppers, in a *frittata* of baby artichokes, asparagus or leeks, baked into Easter cakes, mixed into semolina dough for *tagliatelle*, dropped into a clear broth of bow ties and grated cheese *straccatella*, made into white or green leaves of lasagna, fried with bacon, poached in a pot of zucchini, deviled, or "in Purgatory": the favorite of Domenico himself, who cooked them in olive oil, tomato sauce, and melted, smoked mozzarella and ate them with salt and pepper and slices of crusty bread) said they were better by far than any other eggs from anything on the planet with wings.

The eggs were especially popular at Eastertime as the centerpieces of bread wreaths, crosses, and lambs. They filled bowls, baskets, and crocks, were hidden in the grass for children, and spilled over the tops of milk pails left in clean quiet houses while families went to church. The DePasquale table was laid with a fresh white tablecloth, set with a big bowl for s*paghetti carbonara* (*pancetta, parmigiano,* parsley, and plenty of milled black pepper into which Camilla would whisk some raw eggs and spoon in the boiled pasta, carefully, so as not to set the eggs), their best dishes, plates of tender fava beans, and vases of blue cornflowers. Braided palm crosses and fronds fanned out above the faces of peasant Madonna's with almond eyes who looked down from the walls above their freshly made beds. Beds, baskets of bread and eggs alike awaited the priest's visit and annual blessing.

Though he did crow three times to commemorate Peter's denial, and though there were many towns in Italy where the crucifixion was enacted annually, where, on Good Friday black-hooded penitents wound through the streets at dusk, or cloaked in white, carried candles and the instruments of Christ's Passion (crosses and chains of heavy beads) symbolically to Cavalry, the Place of the Skull, it was the joy of the empty tomb that Charlemagne celebrated with his beautiful voice on Easter morning:

for the people of his village, cock crow was a time of nativity and of resurrection. They were Easter people. Theirs was a procession of baby angels, and of bearers racing through the streets with the Madonna on their shoulders. In Florence, cheers rose up from huge crowds gathered in front of the Duomo. After the priest recited the Gloria, a mechanical dove on a wire flew down to a cart, setting off the fireworks just like Tinkerbelle in Disney World. Simultaneously, Domenico DePasquale released his doves. They fluttered up like hearts and leaves of poetry into the luminous blue and sailcloth clouds of the sky on Easter morning.

It was exactly on such a morning that, despite the fact the sun rose as big and round as a host, Charlemagne never made a peep. For the very first time in his life, Domenico woke without Charlemagne's call, and also to find his wife Camilla (who had passed away in the space of time between the start of the war and the armistice) sitting on the bed (her short legs dangling over the edge of the mattress so that even the crepe paper soles of her feet were visible), though the sun was already up. Ordinarily banished at cockcrow, eidetic images and spirits that had been out and about remained afoot, afloat, aloft, alight from night into the dawn of that dark and terrible day. Obviously upset, perhaps by present circumstances, past problems, and/or premonitions, Camilla fretted; wringing her hands, she babbled on and compulsively obsessed.

"*Lo fatto cadere le uova,*" she repeated over and over, dredging up the past, stuff out of ordinary time like the night a fox raided the henhouse, the day she dropped some eggs: recalling a time when the world was still so lovely and filled with magic that it made her want to cry, when the aviary had been alive with the bubbling, effervescent life of birds—lifting and falling—air, and sunlight. When spinning straw into gold seemed entirely possible;

fields of plain pumpkins were near to bursting with soon-to-be-turned-into-carriage-like potential, princelings cloaked in purple velvet with ermine trim and silver linings searched the countryside for peasant girls who, at the stroke of midnight, might have fled from masked balls as fast as their legs could carry them, having lost, on the travertine steps of Renaissance palaces, or in the torchlight piazzas of Medieval towns, as they flew through the gates, their slippers made of glass. That morning Camilla pulled one out of her apron pocket along with a few sticks of straw and handful of corn spilling like jewels onto the ground where sunlight cast tessellated patterns as it poured through the rusted chicken wire fence she shut behind her; smiling back, she crossed the yard, holding up the sail of her white apron (almost flat against the sky) full of pale pink and blue and brown-speckled eggs like fresh miracles.

* * *

Still sitting on the bed, Camilla's spirit wept, sobbing softly like the coo of a dove, lamenting unlatched gates, dropped eggs, useless wings. Her small, freckled hands fluttered—opening and closing. An invisible wind ruffled her white nightdress and the down of the thick braid that wound to the floor onto which tears dropped, spilled over like seeds from her empty palms. Feathers fell around her.

Domenico, finally exasperated, gave up trying to make any sense of his dead wife's cryptic messages, and went out to the barnyard to find an explanation for Charlie's unprecedented silence. He searched high and low for the rooster, who was nowhere to be found—at least not in any of his usual places—not atop the barn, fence, or the henhouse. But then, from near the woodpile, he heard a straggled breath and found Charlemagne lying under the derelict tractor; his neck had obviously been broken, but he was still alive. Domenico lifted him out gently, stroking his mangled feathers. "*Biltà di donna e di saccente core, e cavalieri armati che sien genti; cantar d'augelli e ragionar d'amore,*" he recited as he carried Charlemagne over and laid his head on the chopping block.

> Beauty of woman and of wise hearts, and gentle knights in armor; the song of birds and the discourse of love; bright ships moving swiftly on the sea; clear air when the dawn appears, and white snow falling without wind; stream of water and meadow with every flower; gold, silver, azure in ornaments.
>
> —Boccaccio, *Decameron*

"Who could have done such a thing?"

"Stop!" someone shouted just as the ax came down. Not more than a few steps away stood four German soldiers; one pointed a pistol straight at Domenico DePasquale's heart.

"*Assassini! Assassini!* You murderers!" screamed the old man. His clothes and face and hands covered in Charlemagne's spilled blood, he lunged, ax upheld, at the soldier with the gun. The soldier fired. And while Domenico lay dying, all the rest of the family (Nicola's included) were herded out of the house and executed one by one.

Waking up in the field of wildflowers, where she had made love and fallen asleep, Marisola was last to hear the world explode. Nicola heard the first shot, and as she opened her eyes and smiled, he clasped his palm over her mouth in case she might scream. "*Zitta!*" he whispered, releasing his grip, but never really letting go. They watched, stock still, their limbs taking root, coiled deep into the ground of that blood-drenched place. Fingertips digging into the field, they clung together like vines, their sun-warmed skin sending out shoots and tender young leaves that wound around their waists, threaded through their hair; blousy petals brushed their cheeks, blew about them, sighed in the charred air of that fragile morning exploding into *disjecta membra poetae*, leaves of poems, wildflower seeds, feathers, and fragments of delicately colored eggshells. Leaving a trail from the fallout that covered their clothes and their hair, filled their mouths, stuck in their eyes, and continued to drop off them, they escaped their shattered village and made their way to the newly liberated city of Sienna.

A few short weeks after they arrived, Marisola discovered that she was pregnant. She and Nicola were married in a war-torn church that had been flooded by snow and rain. They recited their vows and kissed as water fell through a hole in the ceiling and pooled about their ankles.

They did not vow to be poor, but were, nonetheless, still grateful to be alive in the aftermath of such tragedy. They prayed to Saints Margaret for food, shelter, and the safety of their unborn child, and to the city's beloved patron Saint Catherine for the strength to survive the terrible lack thereof. But things were starting to look better, nearer the birth, Nicola found some work with the restoration, and they were able to find a tiny room amidst the burnt rooftops of Sienna. One morning after Nicola left for work, Marisola, big as a sail, scrubbed down the entire room from floor to ceiling till it sparkled like the inside of a jewel box, washed up in the chipped basin, changed her dress, combed her hair, and lay down on her clean bed where in just a few short hours she would give birth to a baby girl. She lived long enough to hold her one time only in her arms and to name her Anna-Teresa. After the funeral,

Nicola took his baby daughter, packed an American Girl doll-sized trunk, and left for New York in the United States of America. Teresa's earliest memories were of seeing the sights of the city from the vantage point of her father's horse-drawn carriage: of silvery harness bells and pink plastic flowers threaded through the horse's hair as they pulled away from the Plaza, and she, riding up on the seat beside her father in his dress-up clothes, happily pretended to be a princess in a storybook: fairy bells, skaters flying on the frozen rink below glittering skyscrapers, Alice in the wonderland of snow falling in Central Park. Later on, he bought a junk wagon, which eventually evolved into the "Cinderella Salvage Company."

* * *

Because it was the Day of the Dead, Anastasia was distracted during coffee, saying very little. Her eyes darted around Maria's second-floor dining room from family photos placed on lace doilies to the waxy leaves of philodendron and fixed on the reliquary of the china cabinet where she lost herself in contemplation among creamy Capodimonte baskets, Fontanini angels, colored Moreno glass, and an assortment of confetti-filled *bonbonieri* tied with ribbons and tulle.

So many spirits stuffed into such a small room, Teresa shuddered, looking at her mother-in-law, aware that like herself, she must have been trying hard to suppress the fear that her son (Teresa's husband) might be not merely missing but among the dead. The thought hung heavily in the air between them, a palpable presence.

"I dreamed about a curse—" Anastasia whispered, looking at Maria over the top of her china cup. She carefully placed it in the saucer, her hand's slight tremble made it rattle, the air filling with the sound that accompanies all such psychic and supernatural phenomenon.

Teresa tried changing the subject to the white sale at Alexanders, not wanting to hear Anastasia's dream, least of all today. By now, even Maria had heard how she dreamt of the death of her parents, her brother, and three sisters before they were executed, and offered her a Stella D'oro Anisette Toast instead. Anastasia dunked it into the cup of Medaglia d'Oro espresso mixed with warm milk and was just about to pipe up again when the alarming ring of the telephone cut her short.

Maria replaced the receiver, untied her apron, exchanging it with a shawl hung from a hook on the wall and spurted out something about Bella, "*le scale*," which meant *steps* and some kind of "*emergenza!*"

"It's the curse! I told you so—" Anastasia called to Maria, who went flying downstairs: crepe paper witches and dangling seven-legged spiders fluttering behind her; the screen door slammed shut in her wake.

Teresa gave her mother-in-law a dirty look.

"I was only just trying to warn her."

* * *

What good were I told you so's? Maria wondered as she raced down Fordham Road, her stomach tied in knots tight as a witch's ladder, the wind whipping at her face and the fringes of her shawl entangling evil. The time for premonitions was past. The Piper was back once again and what's more? —it was payday. A lifetime ago, she had been warned—she was sick to death of warnings. Keep your eyes open. Be leery of gifts. Beware of strangers. Having always to be on the lookout until she was scared of shadows and still her daughter was dead—in the end all the precaution and wariness in the world couldn't save Lea. Now her beautiful granddaughter was lying on the street, having tripped on the hem of her fairy-princess dress and fallen headfirst down the full flight of metal stairs.

At the train station, Maria stood on shaky ground. Her unsteady legs threatened to come out from under her at any moment. The incoming cars caused earth tremors: a giant monster on the loose with terrible teeth and claws, pointy scales, terrible roars, and metal screaming. The sci-fi sound track swallowed sentences alive—words whole, which ultimately made no difference whatsoever to Maria as she seemed to have entirely lost the ability to speak or understand any English. Her husband, the police, and the paramedics opened and closed their puppet-mouths, made incomprehensible motions, gesturing and waving their arms around like the Japanese actors in *Godzilla*, and then they turned on the sirens.

Teresa, having heard only some sketchy details, imagined the unthinkable. Until she'd tracked down Alex (sitting with a policeman in the emergency waiting room at the hospital where they'd rushed Bella) and saw for herself that her son was all in one piece, she didn't know how she'd survive. She prayed for Bella as she held on to her boy, and made a sort of vow, promising herself that in the future she would pay more attention to the crazy things her mother-in-law tried to tell her, and then she went outside and lit a whole pack of Marlboros almost at once, vowed to quit, and not to miss mass on saint's days. For the rest of her life, she kept one out of those three resolutions.

At home, Anastasia answered the door to three little ghost-girls, dropping boxes of Sugar Babies into the plastic pumpkin lanterns they held out as they stood in the orange glow of the porch light. Their mouths were smears of red lipstick; black mascara ran down their rouged cheeks. The wind whipped up the leaves around the stoop, swirled around the hems of their white dresses, and lifted their veils. She shut the door and bolted it, belted her robe more tightly, and poured a glass of cognac from the crystal decanter before going to bed. In the distance wolves howled.

Maria heard them too, as she fell asleep beside Bella's hospital bed, reliving the past, and blaming herself once again for the *curse*, which she believed she had brought down on them all.

* * *

> *Quando è il tempo delle cieliegie,*
> *Le ciliegie si vanno a cogliere,*
> *Si vanno a cogliere col panierino,*
> *Questo è il frutto del mio giardino.*
> *Il vestito lungo, lungo,*
> *Le scarpette apunta, apunta,*
> *La cintura stretta, stretta,*
> *Balleró con me, balleró con me.*

—Italian Nursery Song

"Maria, *basta*! Get that boy out of your head—" her mother had warned her when she was still just a young girl. "I'm saying this for your own good. You know when you wish someone evil it comes back to you. Not just once, not twice, but three times," she said counting curses out on her fingers and holding them up ominously like a charm. "Don't even dream it."

"But Mamma, I'm not wishing anyone any evil," Maria tried to explain, sincerely, convincingly. "I don't want to harm a hair on Sabrina's stupid little head. I just wish she would disappear. I want to make her go away so that Joseph will be free and we can be together."

"*Em be?*" her mother said, arching her brows. "You believe there's a difference?"

Maria thought about this, passing long afternoons dangling upside down in the clouds of pink and white fruit trees blooming in the *frutteto* at the edge of Joseph's fields. Her pale pink blouse, her skirt and petticoat tumbled inside out about her face, concealing her, a cherry blossom hanging in the branches, stealing glances at Joseph from among the boughs and tear-shaped leaves as the clouds and sky, an inverted wedge of blue, spun slowly between her thighs; in the open-air, scrapes and scratches were raised up on her arms and legs as she swung, clinging, arborescent.

She dozed in the sweet shade of the cherry trees, in the cool depths of the shadow cast by Joseph on his way to the fields, or curled up in the hollows of his footprints, playing giant steps in his trail to rabbits, to spots where deer had just been sleeping, deer licks, chasing elusive tails: after the fox that Sabrina had been aching ever so long for—to throw over her shoulder; she'd requisitioned it with a minxish smile, slipping her arm through his. And though he'd discouraged countless intruding foxes by firing shots, setting snares, by throwing his sickle when nothing else was handy to keep them from terrorizing his hen houses and rabbit hutches, he never in a million years imagined the impression one would make pressed up against the dress of his fiancé, the sly grin on its little fox face now clipped to her collar. He flinched from the beady look it gave him with the black glass set in the sockets of its once flashing eyes, and at Sabrina shaking her tail as the fox's swung sadly between her shoulder blades.

"That mangy cat—that *gato spelacchiato!*" Maria humphed at the thought of her archrival, her cousin Sabrina dressed to the nines, decked out in *pelliccia*—a Sabrina in fur. "Yacht!" she said, spitting out a storm of cherry pits that riddled the air. "He loves me he loves me not, he loves me he loves me not," she repeated, slowly plucking the petals off daisies by the ones, tens, hundreds, thousands so it always came out right. Until the air all around her was a storm of dismembered daisies, of feathered seeds blown from the puffballs of dandelions—love thoughts carried on thistle wings to her sweetheart, windblown hopefully in the right direction, and the spewed pits of the cherries she ate until her stomach hurt. Sometimes she sang, other times danced, with cherries dangling from her ears like jewels that brushed against the fresh scratch marks on her cheeks, while carving a heart with berry-stained fingers in the bark of a tree: the full-blown fruit quivering with the iridescent wings of beetles. She practiced kisses with the cherry-stained lips that kept insisting over and over again, passionately, sometimes pleading, sometimes sulking, sometimes as she was stomping her feet—for her mother to pretty please make her a spell. But Rosa wouldn't budge, be swayed, enticed, bribed, coaxed, persuaded, convinced, won over, baited, or fooled. Tricked? "That's it!" she said, thinking she just might have found something up her sleeve that he hadn't yet tried as she scrambled down the crooked split trunk ladder propped up against the tree.

"*Senti*, Mamma. Listen," said Maria, placing the picking basket onto the table. Rosa's eyes lit up at the sight of the *panierino* spilling over with cherries and she set to work on it immediately, picking over the fruit, lifting her eyes, inconspicuously, now and then to the girl's face. "Suppose," Maria continued, trying to sound as matter-of-fact as possible as one could with cherries swinging from her ears. "Just suppose that a lady comes to you—"

"What lady?" her mother wanted to know. Rinsing the cherries off in the sink, she dried them thoughtfully one by one.

"A lady like, like Sonia Louisa and say Sonia Louisa needs help, *poverina*, the poor thing is desperate because she's in love *capisci?* And he's about to marry someone else and if she can't find a way to make him fall in love with her . . . well then she says she might as well die."

Rosa looked up from trimming the tops of the cherries with a sharp knife. "I see," she said. "It's obvious that what poor Signorina Louisa needs is a love spell. Tell her to come and see me," she said, sorting the cherries into a collection of clean, bell-shaped jars.

"It isn't her exactly," said Maria, taking heart as the cherries looked on like conspirators. "Remember, we're just pretending. But could you make a potion for someone in her place if you wanted to? What magic would you use?"

"*Stai attenta, bella mia*, be careful what you wish for," Rosa warned, wagging a finger in her face with an "*eh*" for emphasis. You know I'm right, so don't look at me that way. "*E vero eh*? It's true. And that's that," she said, bathing the cherries in brandy and screwing the lids on tight.

"But *Mamma, Mammina, cara, tessoro, dai!*" she pleaded, calling her Mommy, dearest one, treasure: fussing round and round and round. Pressing her hands, kissing her cheek. "Only this once a little spell just a very small charm *piccolo piccolo piccolo piccolo, per scaramanzia*—for luck it will be nothing for you, I've seen you do it a hundred times, *un cuore de picicone*, a wish, a prayer, a pigeon's heart and I'll never ask for anything ever again I give you my word I promise *Dai! Dai! Ti giuro!* I swear! I beg you! *Ti prego!* A love spell! A potion! Just a drop! Just a drop! Just a drop! Just a drop!"

Her mother sighed and shook her head, shutting the jars of cherries away in a dark cupboard to steep. "Sit here with me," she said, pulling her onto her lap like a little girl. "*Siedeti qui.* You're going to make yourself sick," she warned as she rocked, laying a cool hand on her hot forehead. "Now stay quiet and we'll see. *Vedremo,*" she said, shushing her still.

While for the moment Rosa believed she had staved off the Devil, her daughter was busy brewing something up. She gathered what she'd learned of magical love spells and collecting all of the charms in her possession, she tied them together in the red velvet sack, the talisman with the salt inside it, and when her mother's back was turned, she concealed a candle and some honey beneath her cape, and slipped out at midnight with her bag full of tricks—so armed with the power of her desire—Maria was a numinous witch, indeed, and cast a potent spell.

* * *

Sabrina screamed as spiders, spilling unexpectedly from the drain spout under which her face was poised, dropped into her open mouth. She had been impatiently priming the pump, desperately driven by the desire to drink, or die of thirst. It was like a terrible, unscratchable, unstoppable itch motivated no doubt by the days and weeks of drought, a sun that conspired to burn everything and everyone to a crisp, and a wind to whip up the dust. It was the kind of heat that manifested itself in the deeply evolving shadows of sweat: moon shapes materialized in armpits; soggy crescents defined the undersides of breasts. The kind of heat that made men cast off soaked-through t-shirts and cover their heads with kerchiefs like old women fanning themselves in doorways. While the *contadini* sought sanctuary under grape arbors and the overhanging shade of chestnut trees, in the city the heat wave forced shop gates to a clamoring close, and old men and babies to siesta forever. It was the kind of heat mirages were made of, the kind that dried up a fountain and choked it with nesting spiders that spilled onto Sabrina's face, tumbling on her head; they dangled in her hair, fell into her eyes and filled her gaping mouth, stifling her screams. So many spiders that they scattered in every direction, dripping down the opening in front of her blouse, crawling up her skirt: an especially big, black hairy one jumped on her ankle—the last thing she saw before losing consciousness. The memory of its sting left a lasting impression.

Although, when she was sent for, Rosa knew that it was more-than-likely a nursery spider that frightened Sabrina away, after a short time she emerged from the girl's room and, commanding the attention befitting a wise woman in a place where she was held in the highest regard, she said, "Sabrina's been bitten by a tarantula! Send for the musicians! She has to dance!"

Everyone gasped. There was no precedent for this ritual in the collective memory of the region; like the spider for whose bite and particular pathology it was an antidote, it originated in other, sunnier, antediluvian places in the Mediterranean: Lecce, Puglia, Brindisi—the place still called Magna Grecia where the Dionysian-inspired dance had begun, because it was there that the tarantula stung from the dawn of time until the present with great tenacity and effect like an ardent lover. Rosa knew that the bite itself was technically not harmful to humans (a *tarantata*, in fact, never had to be bitten at all), but it was believed to be poisonous. The belief was what inspired the disease (actually caused by the kinds of things that attacked a woman's spirit and made it sick) and the cure, which was a rite of liberation. An exorcism.

Rosa sent to Puglia for the musicians. Dum da dum da dum da dum, dum da dum da dum dum da dum. Arriving in the middle of the night they visited the somnolent *Tarantata* in order to evaluate the strength of her demons and plan the ritual accordingly. The tambourine was hung above her head like a pale paper moon as they tuned the guitar and the strings of the pear-shaped mandolin respectively, attempting to find the right key out of four possibilities: A major, A minor, G major and D major. Sabrina groaned. Exactly the reaction they desired.

"*Brava,*" they said, and went off to get some much needed rest, because these old men who had sent countless women whirling, knew that beginning the following morning when they played the Tarantella, Sabrina (with her family, friends, and the whole town in attendance) was going to dance herself into a frenzy, and it would more than likely be necessary to play for several hours, or even days at a stretch; they would have to play for as long as it took in order for the girl to cleanse her heart of toxins, to rid itself of whatever evil was poisoning her soul.

Sabrina danced for a week straight wearing all of the many kerchiefs that had been placed about the room like boas draped around her neck, tossed over her shoulders, tied in her hair, and clenched in her teeth. She stuffed each one in her mouth, in turn, took in a whole spectrum of colors—red, orange, yellow, green, blue, indigo, and violet and all over again in reverse—violet, indigo, blue, green, yellow, orange, red, and even a few colored bows like juicy lifesavers. Swirling, her arms thrown open wide, her head tossed back, back arched, she flew way up, as high as the Witch of the East ("behind the moon, beyond the rain"); somewhere between the sun and the cataract she swallowed a rainbow.

Crashing to the floor, at last, Sabrina fell into a trance, and the musicians got a break. *"Finalmente!"* Their ears perked up at the mention of food, pleasure plainly registered on their faces. *"Vengo! Vengo!"* The old tambourine-man trilled, passing his fingers through his thin, straw-colored hair, stretching his long, skinny legs, the parchment-like skin of his face crinkling with a capricious smile as he sprung up quick as a cricket with his walking stick.

Clicking his assent, the guitar player sawed his jaw. "I'm coming too," he echoed, rubbing his hands together and smoothing them over his legs, bones cracking as stiff joints began to move.

Only the doleful mandolinist shook his head, feeling his eyes slightly heavy. *"Fra poco*—in a little while," he said, more tired suddenly than hungry. And with a great yawn, fell fast asleep in his chair—alongside the reclining Sabrina who floated on a white sheet and pillow spread out for her on the floor like a cloud—his arms resting at his sides like folded wings.

The guests swarmed the buffet, brushing against one another to fill their plates and settling down anywhere there was space available at the table, on folding chairs, propped up against walls, or underneath mimosa trees, they chewed their lunch and furiously fanned themselves with napkins, a whirring plague of hungry locusts.

Everyone sweated like pigs. Everyone in that whole town turned out for that *brutta*, flea-bitten Sabrina. Imagine that! Maria fumed, her heart leaping at the sight of Joseph; she tormented herself over what she believed to be the fault of her badly mismanaged magic, which only succeeded in making Sabrina the center of attention, and Joseph more in love with her than ever.

What a weak spell! What a sad sorry little witch! We all may as well be cooking in a pot over a slow fire, she thought—stewing in her own juice. It was so hot and muggy it seemed they'd been stuck up inside a rain cloud.

> Here I come, *Menne vengo,*
> *Piano, Piano,* Slowly, slowly,
> Quietly, quietly, *Zitto, zitto,*
> *Come un gato,* like a cat.

A telltale stroke of lightning tore the sky to ribbons with its jagged fingernails. Thunder grumbled. In the west, a storm was brewing, clearing its throat. "*Menne vengo, piano, piano*—" Maria sang to the children, sneaking her fingers "*Zitto, zittto*—" up a toddler's arm "*Come un gato*," and tickling underneath. Singing rhymes to pass the time and to distract the children from the approaching storm, which was making some seriously menacing noises, but mostly, to distract herself from thoughts of her own abject destiny, to keep from wallowing in revelations that smacked of her own wickedness. For as she was singing little ditties, she memorized Joseph's mouth for the ten millionth time, divining a promise from those pillow lips. What she wouldn't give for a kiss. To what lengths, she wondered, would she go—mad? Anything but murder maybe? Her thoughts turned dangerous, wandering lustfully in the dark like gypsies sweeping across deserts, their caravans rumbling over the plains.

Balls of lightning rolled from the storm's white-hot fingertips like witch-fires, the horrible roar escalating into a thundering of hooves. "*Menne vengo*—" she sang. Two black, raggedy clouds like bundles of unsacked fleece, one moving north and one straggling south at the same time, met, stopped and perversely reversed themselves, whirling like dervishes in a circle.

"*Zitto, zitto—*" (*Gli zingari arrivano*, the pilgrims and fortunetellers park their *caravanserai*, barefoot gypsies dance, their bonfires blaze like funeral pyres where widows once burned with the painted wagons of the dead).

"*Come un gato—*"she teased with a tickle and a cackling to the sound of the thunderclap. The children pressed closer or flew off in every direction like so many baby chickens as Maria smoothed their ruffled feathers. (Inside her painted wagon as pretty as a horse-drawn pumpkin, the bride sits like a princess upon her mattress: the bed piled high with wedding gifts, gaudier than any pirate's treasure. The sparkle in her eyes rivals the jewels glinting from her crown, heavenly bodies—hosts, her *corsetto* made of stars—a constellation. Clinging to her elephant-toy like a party favor, the most darkly beautiful queen of all the gypsies stares into her lover's eyes. The bridesmaids *ballano*, the colors of their marvelous skirts swirl halos around the moon, bracelets jangling like gold lavished for the bride price. Dancing to the invisible beat of wings: bright scarves slash the night, flames of tango-colored firelight *saltino—* spit, vanishing into thin air, into smoke—*fuoco*. And the bride and groom jump over the broom).

"A twister, a twister!" the guests outside screamed at the sight of the demonic black cloud insanely spinning round in a heartbeat and single-mindedly moving forward at three miles a minute, madly gyrating, shamelessly as any bawdy barroom mama. The monster paused as parasitic whirls writhed, and, coiling like the tendrils of an enormous octopus, reached out relentlessly demolishing everything in its path with an astonishing roar like the sea. Farms were picked up and dashed down, scattered to the wind like toothpicks, while Sabrina, just outside her front door, resumed the dance, whirling to the whipped-up froth, to the spellbinding howl of the vortex.

"We're up inside the cyclone!" Maria shouted, gazing out the open window at the sepia-colored storm showering debris. It snowed bits and pieces of unsacked fleece, the livestock tossed up into the sky: horses, cows, sheep, and pigs flew through the air as the farm lifted higher and higher, swirled above the ground like a possessed spinning toy, and dropped.

Baby Sophia flew in on her broomstick—faggot end down—sweeping her tracks from the sky, and landed just in time to see what had become of her little sister.

She is capable of bringing down the sky, suspending the earth, making springs dry up, sweeping away mountains, conjuring up the spirits of the dead. She can weaken the gods, put out the stars, light up Hell itself.

—Apuleius, *Metamorphoses*

CHAPTER FOUR

Our Lady's Bedstraw

At this day it is indifferent to say in the English tongue,
"she is a witch" or "she is a wise woman."
—Reginald Scot, *Discoverie of Witchcraft*

Baby Sophia was a witch. Her mother was a witch, as was
her mother before her. The women in Sophia's family were witches,
had always been witches, they said, but two of her ancestors were
infamous: Felicitá Caprice, a shepherdess known as *La Capricciosa*,
after her temperament and the goats that she tended, and Felicitá's
grandmother, Perpetua (The Witch) who lived together in the
Camonica Valley during the sixteenth century.

The Camonica Valley, or the Val Camonica, as it was called in
Italian, was steeped in the *mezza luna* of mountains separating the
vast Italian plain from the rest of Europe. It was north and west of the
cities, courts and castles, distant from the priests and principalities—
the princes and *principese* of the Po Valley: far from the Ferrara and
Modena of the Farnese, from Sabbioneta and Montua, fief of the
Gonzaga (where Romeo got his poison), the Milan of the Sforza
and Visconti, the Scaligeri's Verona—its balconies. The valley was
further north, still, above Lake Iseo and the cone of Mont'Isola and
wedged up high between the Alpine peaks.

Relatively isolated, free and clear of those feudal lords—to the mountain people at that heightened perspective, the stuff of Renaissance legend was to be of even less consequence than the traces of the legacies they'd one day leave behind (Lucrezia's love letters, a lock of her golden hair, the lofty stars on the ceiling of Isabella's Paradiso, a princess' silky winding sheet, a pair of bracelets fashioned from pieces of Juliet's pink marble tomb, chipped away at), as imperceptible as their poisons gone undetected.

And if the palazzi of the glitterati were to be imposing, great even, they would never be impermeable, but imperfect: the rough walls of fortresses, masked by veils of majesty for centuries, scarred, pitted, and pockmarked; inherent flaws weakened further still by time and attacks by their enemies. The keepers of the gates would be assailed by arrows and ghosts of kings, and of damsels and great ladies who walked headless along the watchtowers for birthing baby girls and falling short of princes, or for sinning with lovers bound in basements wringing their manacled hands and rattling their chains in the dungeons with dead men. Eventually, the very fabric of the courts was corrupt, the materials of palaces—marble, stone, and mortar disintegrated. Their castles crumbled, tumbledown towers returned to dust. Ashes to ashes.

The primitive places inhabited by the peasants and shepherds, ironically, were the magnificent mountains cast from the same indigenous stone as the playgrounds of the rich and famous: metamorphic marble, rock from older mountains dissipated, and wasted beaches once laid down in a now extinct sea. Some of the Earth's crust, it seemed, crept northward slowly toward the ancient mountains, crunching up against them eventually, exerting enough force to fold the bottom of the sea and uplifting them sky-high so to speak; magma—molten rock bubbling up through the cracks until they reached astonishing heights of something above fifteen thousand feet.

Postorogenically, they were acted upon by subtler forces: transforming them over the course of millennia, nature's agents such as frost infiltrated the cracks and chiseled the jagged faces of peaks and ridges, snow incessantly melted and froze, forcing rocks apart in tenths until they shattered like glass and the sharp splinters fell away serrating summits in high relief, snowmelt and showers imbued streams that welled to rivers that scraped and swept away as river-wash the routed scrap of landscape from grit to boulder stones. Those cataracts cleft mountainsides like mighty wet saws wielding enough power to pulverize bedrock: they ripped potholes, tore valleys wide, made terrible gashes at faults where wild rapids rushed and waterfalls plummeted over steep ravines and depthless gorges. The snowfields turned to *fogli di ghiaccio*—sheets of ice slowly advancing and receding over time, and where those cirque glaciers worked their magical transformations—where they scoured out and filled bow-shaped basins around peaks, frosty horns were formed and ridges were sharpened into pointy arêtes like stiff meringues.

When the *ghiacciaio* melted, in the way of finishing touches, sometimes they left tarn lakes—paternoster lakes strung over the mountains like liquid beryl rosary beads and gardens of glaciated stone just begging to be inscribed with the stories and spirit-thoughts of primitive artists. Specifically, in the part of the Val Camonica known as Naquane, with their pointed instruments and their chisels, the Camuni people (the tribe the valley was named for) struck in and scratched out thousands upon thousands of images from the polished bedrock. The carvings begun when the sun set on the last ice age proliferated for eight millennia. By the end of the first century B.C., in the day of Octavian, when the Alpine people were completely overwhelmed by the Roman legions and their lands rendered back unto Caesar, they had covered the smooth outcroppings like empty gallery walls; the world's fresh canvases, once blank pages were filled with wagons, wheels and sacred deer, warriors with their swords uplifted and shields spread beneath the wing-petals of *Camuni Roses*—like pinned butterflies.

There would have been silences too profound to imagine, or the sound of bone, then, scraped against stone—percussion, an echolalia of voices, maybe, birds beating their wings hard above the snowline, reeling clouds, ice melting, flowers forced up through the snow, the iridescence of enormous dragon-fly wings suspended in air. Living things had just emerged from the primordial stew, still trembling from the big bang, catching their breath, shaking the fallout from their coats, wiping the cosmic dust from their eyes and squinting at the world through the swirling mist. Wild creatures crawled out from their caves, chased their fury tails and left fresh footprints in the lily-white snow—roving and hunting.

An old woman squeezed herself out from between the cracks, sniffing the wind. She raked her filthy fingernails, black as obsidian, sharp as flint, through the silvery-metallic roves of her hair, scurrying off to forage for food, to dig up rootstock for her medicine bundles. She roved over the snowfields, this *strega altissima*— an old crone, a relict searching the frozen landscape for scattered branches, for the bones of dead things she collected over time, carting them off home: her back bent, the snow breaking with the weight of her stick-bundle. She rested, stock-still, snaggle-toothed, bristly, in the shadow of tall firs shaggy with winter. Wild hares hid in their snow-white bunny-fur, kenning hawks who hunted on the wing. The wild goats climbed, shaking ice from their beards. Their horns clashed in the musk-charged air. She stomped the snow from her boots, shook out her coarse-hair coat, the terrible tangle of her hair. Her breath billowed white with the bucks' roar and the low-slung bellies of the nanny goats swinging, pealed like a carillon of bells in the high cold air.

The old woman cackled, crouched in her cave space cluttered with cook pot—fire: a bone yard filled with her cache of clavicles and cavernous skulls, of enormous dinosaur toes, bat fingers and little tiny bird feet, ancient reptile wings, fossils, and gas-filled ammonite whirls, cuttlefish bones and antlers and still-velvety horns, Jurassic rocks and cockle shells and curled up trilobites all in a row. She dug up the loam with her fingers, treasure-troves of tails, carious bones, and dragons' teeth she'd sewn into the earth, sifting through piles of tinkling bones, of quiet dust, for the missing pieces to the jigsaw she puzzled over: setting an airy, sutureless skull to the rickety framework of a skeleton which seemed human, otherwise, but had a short, deep rib cage, hollow air-filled bones and a carina—a keeled breastbone, ridged like a bird's—batlike, flanged. "Ahh," she exclaimed when, at last, she'd found the key she'd been searching for in the shape of a couple extra coracoid bones and fitted them in to brace the sternum, the big breastbone against the spine, the shoulder blades—powerful scapula. She hummed all the while as she forged them into place, wondering at the outrageous proportion of these wings and the nature of this flying-thing with three times the wingspan of an albatross.

Her buzz filled the cave as the skeleton gathered itself up by its jock/bootstrap(s) with a windchimelike tinkling of brittle bones, brash. It stood shakily, at first, balancing precariously, teetering as it warmed its long leg bones by the fire, the low humming of her voice singing it to life. Her pungent breath filled the cave-air with a smell like hot tarmacadam, fertilizer, burnt matchsticks, brimstone—sulphurous, stormy—stirring it up. The wind swooshed around the chattering bones, whistling through the empty sockets of its eyes, lost ears, hissing through its teeth, appearing to provide just the impetus it needed to lift its birdlike arms like a raptor.

The old woman grimaced as outside the mouth of the cave a blizzard was blowing and the white surface of the snow cracked—from the vibrations of her breath, the force of those terrible wings pulling on the downbeat, or maybe it was the stress of just one more snowflake trembling as it touched down that triggered the avalanche. With a sound like thunder underground, the snow was loosed and began to slide, crumbling into a river of white powder and icy blocks, tumbling down, dragging trees along in its path: with such momentum, mindfully, it seemed, as if the course of its destruction was hell-bent. She heard a demonic roar and the last thing she saw as this *rara avis*, this skeleton-bird alighted, was the sight of its naked tailbone, which left her in awe of life's little mysteries, petrified, pondering during the rapture, anabiosis, how it was possible to fly without benefit of tail feathers, before the world was buried beneath the snow.

* * *

Felicitá's beauty was legend. In fact, it was a widely held belief that no woman who had ever lived on those high mountains' snowy peaks, pristine hills, in the depths of their impossible shadows, deep recesses, dappled valleys, those blank ravines, intraversable passes, treacherously steep cliffs, amidst the alpine lakes and icy springs, mists and wildflowers, magical herbs and damselflies, secret places, in the grottos *e nelle caverne*, in the hidden caves of the mountains older than time itself, had ever been lovelier than

Felicitá. The desire for her was unanimous. To poor boys, like the peasants and shepherds (whose world was flat, but still very high), a fleeting glimpse of her was like blinking before the flash of a star. They would follow her anywhere, their longing bringing them perilously close to the ends of the earth, to the tops of the world where they were in danger of tumbling from the dizzying heights they clambered to—just for a peak. And if they were surefooted and fleet enough to find her, they would inevitably fix her in their Gaze and all that staring, like looking directly at the sun for too long and too hard, even eclipsed, would damage their retinas, so that her image burned there, stuck, pasted behind their eyelids like gold paper stars as they dropped off to sleep in fields where they lay snuggled up to their fires. On those mornings they woke slightly scorched—the hair on their chins and forearms singed as if they had fallen like angels cast from dreams, having just grazed the sun.

And because *the bigger they are, the harder they fall,* as the old saying goes, and since few, if any, were immune to her charms, the rich and powerful were equally smitten: obsession which ended for many in torch-(goat-)song, *tragedia*. Even the Podesta, who should, by rights, have focused on official matters regarding his flock— quite literally, as often it was the sheep and goats brought before him whose fate he held in his hands, had his fantasies whipped up by the earthy smell of livestock, conjuring up images of Dionysian orgies like a true bacchant, imagining sex with the goat-girl.

As to the magical effect of her charms, and the extent to which certain young men and old magistrates were said to have become entranced, the extent to which she may have bewitched an entire village, held them spellbound—Felicitá never had a clue. Her life, rather, revolved around the daily routine requirements of goats. Rising each new day as the sun rose, during the *rapsodia*, the high drama of dawn breaking on the snowfields, she fastened her bodice in the crackling dark. Bunches of dried herbs dangled from the cradling, illuminated by a halo of sun, which flooded the medallion window opening in the wall above her. Felicità fluffed up her bed, sent bits of her makeshift mattress-stuff flying about in the tiny hut, lifting up into the broadening light like snow flurries, but this *fiocco di neve* was made up of the buttercups and Our Lady's Bedstraw she used to fill her sleeping bag. It was soft and fragrant, because it was the same stuff (they say) that had been laid down for Mary's bed in the manger, and its flowers (as the story goes), once merely white, were graciously thereafter, miraculously changed to gold.

"*Mannaggia al Diavolo!*" her grandmother stormed, as she was awakened by bits of Felicitá's bed flying in her face. "You would think," she said, swiping and blowing at the settling specs as if they were swarms of angry locusts. "You would think that an old woman could get some sleep around here and not be continually plagued by storms in the middle of the night. "It should interest you to know that at the moment I was wrenched from my dreams, it so happens I was very far away, further than I've ever been before," she said, gone off on one of her tangents. "It's a good thing I was able to get back, or I might have died in my sleep." Still lost somewhere in a dream where her thoughts had flown off—taken flight like a bird. *Trapped behind its eyes, her spirit searches, rakes the earth, scours the seas, drags the oceans for her stolen daughter—lost girl. She's been rent alive, her soul laid bare. Her heart pulses only as long as it's held aloft, caught in a raven's claws, beating beneath the shadow of its black wings. Entrails drip from its fierce beak like a valentine message in the mouth of a dove. At the cave's mouth, she stops; her ruffled feathers exchanged for a mother's mourning weeds. Draped in the dirty dreadlocks of her hair, bowed beneath* moonbeams, *she drags herself, drawn to the glow of the witch's fire within, tripping inside, over the bric-a-brac of coughed-up stones, sticks and bones, bound bundles, Neolithic tools, unidentified objects, rubbish, a trash heap of useless old junk that, surely, women who had never lived in a cave would have no use for. Her eyes sift through the scene, sorting out stuff. Deciphering petroglyphs. She spots something hunkered up, slumped against a wall. Something else swishes out from the shadows, and converging in the watery light of flames they become a woman of substance. The witch holds out her hands, with their long bony fingers and black nails curled like chicken's feet, over the warm fire. The images crackle and burn, the colors heat up: melting warps the sound, make it quavery; drowns it out. Everything becomes distorted, fluid, as if under the sea where it's difficult to speak and breathe and move against the resistance of water.* The limbs of the dreamer felt impossibly heavy then, her body pinned to the bed like a dead weight.

"*There was a deafening roar as the earth opened up—and I heard her cry out,*" says the witch. "*Like someone torn away,*" *and then pausing for what seems like an eternity to attend to her cook pot, she stirs its contents ever-so-s-l-w-l-y while salamanderlike flames leap up under it. Tormentingly slow, the sound of snow melt magnified ten thousand times as drops drip—drip drop, drip drop, drip drop, forming puddles at their feet.* "*There was a terrible thundering of hooves, the roar of a unicorn,*" *she says, choosing her words oh-so-very-carefully when she finally continues.* "*I heard a gasp—an enormous gulp (sparing no gory details) as if something was being swallowed alive,*" *she says, intent on stirring the fire with a forked stick that sends live sparks dancing all around them*—but before she got any further, the embers, confused with flecks of bedstraw from Felicitá's mattress, woke Perpetua, who was cranky from her dream, dripping from night sweats, and feeling heavy as a drowning victim. Sparks flew where cinders continued to fall, ashes settling over everything like a warm blanket.

Felicitá, was not always, but could be, oblivious to her grandmother's tirades. She turned absently away, her attention caught by the tail of a diminutive creature, a little grey mouse who, she was certain (on account of her own hunger) had failed in its efforts to find even a crumb, a morsel of cheese, scrap of bread, or the remotest possibility of greasy spatterings of any kind. The planks of the floor that her grandmother swept religiously, anyway, were bare; the small cupboard bereft. Felicitá took up her staff from its place in the chimney corner, watching as the *topolino* scurried off and disappeared beneath the boards. "Mice are nesting in there again," she said.

"And so they will," her grandmother answered as she gave up an apricot cheek to the girl's goodbye kiss along with that solemn assurance.

As Felicitá opened the gate to the pale, her goat greeted her with customary enthusiasm, raised a raucous bleating and butting in its characteristically nanny-goat way. The creature owed its life to her, since Felicitá had come to its rescue some time ago. Having fallen off a cliff, apparently, into a deep snow bank—snowbound, the stranded kid struggled to free itself and would certainly have died in vain, frozen to death and/or been devoured by hungry wolves which Felicitá staved off, bravely. She christened the goat Tiramisú, after the dessert, because of its coloring, which especially reminded her of that wedding-cake-like confection made from mascarpone, and was the stuff fed to bridegrooms, but mostly because "Pull me up!" is what the word meant, and "*Tira mi su! Tira mi su!*" was exactly what the little thing pleaded as it looked up at her, helplessly trapped.

Tiramisú, in turn, was prized and cherished for the snow-white milk that the grandmother also made into cheese, stirring it in the big kettle, for soft wool, which was cleaned, combed, spun and knitted into sweaters and warm socks, for wool wax, for love unbridled, fidelity, and fantastic leaps of faith. It was the same blind faith that enabled Felicitá and Tiramisú to navigate the treacherous mountain terrain: for the way down the mountain was winding and wicked, especially in winter when the snow was deep, the slopes treacherous—steep, and snow was unstable. Often, as hard rains turned stretches of water into mud, the roads became impassable, and since it was several miles, she might be prevented from accessing the village for as many as six months. The holy bells rang on the Sabbath day, and rang clearly, clamoring to call in the high cold air stray members of the flock to worship, but for Felicitá, and other inhabitants of the Val Camonica, those church bells were as esoteric, as remote as the Heaven they glorified—the lofty paradise they aspired to, and just as ethereal.

From high on her perch on the mountain, the stars were so close they caught like cheap tinsel, dime store garland, and glitter in her hair: so close that she could touch them with the tip of her shepherd's staff, which ignited like a sparkler, a Cinderella/Fairy Godmother's wand.

Snowy frosting transformed the Alps into some kind of frozen confection—baked Alaska, glacé icing, mountains of meringue, the tiers of a great cake. Glaciers spilled over, trailing white endlessly like a lavishly, hand-beaded wedding train, spangled and sequined and all-dazzling with pearls; they cast icy glass slippers precisely fitted to her feet. From behind her snow-lace veil, Felicitá listened to the bells, lifted up her face and reached out her hands greedily to grab them, only to find that they'd dissolved like the snowflakes she caught on the tip of her tongue. In her life, she had swallowed snowflakes ad infinitum, given birth to a million snow babies, and a blizzard of flyaway dreams.

Hunger was tangible; hard work was real—death from starvation was commonplace among the peasants, and disease struck down the fleshpots as well as the poor. While she had (without complicity), driven men mad with desire—what she desired most was painfully simple: she aspired to eat and to rest, she wanted a respite from the ache of wanting—*riposa*. *Want* made her wistful, made her waiflike. She cinched in her skirt waist *centimetro* by *centimetro* each day as she lost flesh, became a little lighter. Every morning she found that there was less and less left of her corporal self to concern herself with. That magically beautiful quality which men were mesmerized by was, in reality, the result of continual fasting, the lack of regular nourishment, which brought her to the brink of starvation. It was the flush of fever that suffused Felicitá's cheeks with high color, and fever that sparkled in her eyes. She was taper-thin, fair, tall, and translucent as wax, incinerating, a torch song, her life-flame going up like a candle.

Her fantasies, however rich, were the lush, hunger-driven hallucinations of the poor. Her empty stomach made her mystical: most often the result of some mushroom she'd eaten, some root that she'd dug up, or other, some grass she'd gathered, some leaves and wild herbs she'd climbed especially high for, because the goats gave spicy delicious milk when they'd munched on some of those rare weeds. On those particular occasions, when it was too much to climb and then to come back down the mountain again all in one day, Felicitá fell asleep up there counting goats. She always started the same way, with Tiramisú, and enumerated the others, to whom she had given names of the saints as powerful talismans for protection. "Tiramisú," she began, listing them slowly one by one, except when she got past Joan of Arc, who came just before Saint Clare, she cringed and left off, counting stars, instead. This change of heart was brought about by the memory of what had happened with the Podesta, to whom poor Clare was earmarked. The very idea of that man filled her with a nameless dread—waiting to ambush her in the dark.

She'd been stopping to pick up one goat or another at the Podesta's house for years, and although his behavior had always been aboveboard/suspicion, and though he could never be accused (up until then) of having done a single thing you could really put your finger on—he gave her the creeps, just the same. Some days, as soon as the door swung open, she could sense his presence in the goat shed. The smell of something spoiled, a sour smell curdling in the corners like rennet. Something festered, waiting for her in the wings.

"*Buon giorno, Bella Mia,*" he belched out (his spirit always buoyant on account of his full stomach) in a manner suggesting the chance meeting of old lovers on a sunny Italian terrace instead of a shitty goat shed. Felicitá garbled her *buon giornos* and grabbed the opportunity, while he was momentarily distracted (scraping some *caca* off his shoe), to get the goat by the rope and make a beeline for the door.

"*Brava! Bravissima!*" her little audience of goats bleated brazenly. Shamelessly loud. Applauding proudly. And she would graciously have taken a bow two, after she sprinted out into the sunshine, if she had not been trapped by Signore, the Podesta's spontaneous expansion.

"Baby! O! Where are you going in such a hurry?" he wanted to know, blocking her way as he reached out to detain her with his heavy limbs, groping with inflated fingers.

Felicitá sucked in air in order to make herself smaller until she was the size of Toppogiggio, the little Italian mouse, and the tiny fleas she shook off herself pitched their three-ring circus tent down his pants. "Old flea-bag!" And now if she could only, she thought, holding her breath, just squeak by—which she did, with a "pop" like an Asti Spumante cork escaping.

"Smooch!" went the sound of a big *baccione* as his kiss hit empty air, and while the Podesta was left standing there foolishly foiled *managia!*—his arms around nothing, Felicitá, with a sparkling-like-effervescence flew with her little entourage, trippingly headoverheels overhooves down the mountain.

The Podesta's wife Nina had all-at-one-time both the advantage and misfortune to observe the higgledy-piggledy, flurry-scurrying pandemonium flying out the goat-shed from where she stood getting the breakfast of melty cheese, pink links of *cervellato*, crusty bread, and foamy white goat-milk on the table. She decorously set the salt cellar down last and when she did, she literally spilled over with pride, which far from being contained, revealed itself in a bustle of her biggish bustle, and bustiness that held aloft the fluttering ribbons of her wimple. Because salt was such a precious commodity, and its abuse made her considerably more prone that usual to swelling up, hot and cold sweats, dizziness and fainting fits (during which the guilt-ridden Podesta, afraid she would die, vowed every time he stuck the bottle of vinegar under her nose and slapped her silly into consciousness, that he would change—bargained with God, sealed pacts with Satan, and promises he had no intention of keeping while he poured kisses on her sodden, salty, skin), she used it only sparingly. Sometimes she would place a grain of salt or two or three on the tip of her tongue as she looked out over the snowfields, icy mountains' majesty and imagined that they were *grande mucchi di sale,* great salt domes instead of snow stretching as far as the eye could see, and she was the richest woman in the world—efflorescent, a salt queen. She saw her sparkling crystal palace and princely consort (the Podesta) licking salt out of her hand, which went a long way in making her able to put up with her husband's indiscretions, in making her marriage palatable.

Nina's thoughts raced ahead (while the air was still steamy with cooking smells and preparations for the morning meal) to clearing and cleaning the platter from which the greasy slicks of fried sausages would be been mopped up with fresh hunks of bread, and the dubious success of that rag-picker (chiffonier) who called herself a Laundress, in eliminating the stains from her husband's good shirt and her much cherished napery. She had been stewing about all of that for a while when the Podesta came inside wagging his tail behind him. *Bravo buffone,* she said to him with the slings and arrows of her eyes (*What kind of fool was he? What kind of idiot did he take her for? Did he think she was stupid? Did he think she was blind?*) that shot him daggers. He tried his best to dodge them.

She was most certainly not stupid, she told him, *tutto agitata,* obviously distraught at having to set him straight on this point every so often—on the contrary—she had eyes of her own and they were wide open. She could put two and two together. She was nobody's fool. "I know what you've been up to with that peasant girl," she screamed, waving a fried sausage in his face.

The Podesta squirmed, and with his back pressed up against the wall began with "But, Nina. *Amore—*" which was always a definite indication that he was about to turn his little circus antics into a full-blown creep-show as the fleas fired up their act in his drawers. "Just wait until I tell you what happened," he said, scratching his balls. "One minute she was standing there big as life," he attested to his wife, telling tales through his luteous-stained teeth. "And then— pof! She vanished into thin air. Disappeared. *Sparito!*" he said, dramatically pausing: Puncinello's puppetmaster pulling the strings in the theater of the Grand Guignol, his commanding stage presence conjuring up the scene over which he waved his magician's magic wand with a grand sweeping Houdini-like flourish of his dark cape. His cupped hands held out. Empty! So, his wife could see Felicitá escaped like a dove right before their very eyes, which now followed the bird as it flew up toward the ceiling. Their attention directed to the air high up above the center ring ("Ladies and gentlemen and children of all ages. *Signore e signori, attenzione! Il Gran Circo Italiano e lieto di presentare Felicitá! Ecco la meraviglia delle meraviglie!* Wonder of wonders!"). Felicitá wowed them with her death-defying feats as she flew through the air on the flying trapeze and balanced without a net on the high wire, then settled herself in the rafters from where she cooed and pooped irreverently on their breakfast things.

"Pof! Just like that?" his wife said, so absolutely flabbergasted by this cheap parlor trick that she had stopped in her tracks, so to speak. About to cut off a piece of sausage with her carving knife, she kept it poised, instead, hovering above them in mid-air.

The Podesta, who observed that his wife's eyes had opened wide, watched that disembodied, freewheeling knife, and considered that maybe, just maybe this time, possibly, he had gone too far: but by the time he arrived at that revelation it was already too late. He was forced to repeat his story over again and again and again. Explain. Elaborate. Embellish. He began to sweat under direct, scrupulous cross-examination like a man pinned spread-eagle to the wall by all of the knives his hot-blooded, sharp-tempered wife (fire-eater, sword-thrower extraordinaire) had wielded at him over the years. And who, now after wiping her hands on her apron, stood back, razor-sharp stiletto clenched tightly in her teeth, and turning her back on him (drumroll please!) prepared to throw it backwards between her legs and hit a mark between his ("—*Nuccioline! Noccioline! Noccioline belle, tostate e croccanti! Noccioline e mele candite! Limonata fresca!*").

"Disappeared?"

"*Sparita!*" the Podesta repeated, itching uncontrollably.

"Pof!" she said at last, wiping her bosom with the handkerchief she stuffed inside along with that juicy tidbit like a plum for safekeeping.

Perhaps, no harm would have come from the story, if it had not fallen on the big ears of that busybody of a maid with the blackbird snippet-of-a-nose, whose skill as a laundress in no way equaled her talent for telling a washwoman's tales. A talent and a gift. A reputation which earned her the title of *Chiaccierona,* town gossip equal to none—who had been fortunate enough to have stopped just outside their open window that morning where she saw and overheard plenty, peeping in as at a raree-show, piled it up high on top of her basket and brought it with her down to the river where the women did their washing so that she could air their dirty laundry in public—hanging Felicitá out to dry. Her name would soon be on the tips of all the women's tongues, and they'd flap with it like sheets in the wind. That tattletale of a laundrylady told the story almost at once, wagging away. She worked it up into quite a lather with some strong lye. Before long, every one of them was up to their elbows in the soup, eating it up: a hotchpot of nightshirts and leggings, a boiling cauldron of bloomers and chichi underthings churned, wrung, twisted, lashed, and beaten out on stones.

ALL
Double, double toil and trouble;
Fire, burn; and, cauldron, bubble.
—William Shakespeare, *MacBeth*

It filled them with a bubbly feeling that foamed up into their mouths and escaped their pouty lips with sudsy sounds and expressions of surprise like a bowlful of goldfish. Before long they were blowing bubbles ("I'm forever blowing bubbles . . . pretty bubbles in the air"), a regular soap opera. Bubbles bubbled up fluently with their words in streams of sparkling effervescence; some grew bigger than big, bursting in startled, bubbleized faces. From then on, they blew bubbles whenever they talked like it was always New Year's Eve on the *Lawrence Welk Show*. They went around with the frothy white foam of telltale bubble shadows lingering on their upper lips like milk mustaches, and giant shadows of bubble clouds were cast over the valley. A little one hovered over Felicitá like a perverse guardian angel, a bit of cloud-fluff that followed her everywhere. It snuggled up against her shoulder, and with Tiramisú lying at her feet she was soon fast asleep among her flock, under cover: a frightened wolf-princess among all those sleepy sheep.

"StarlightstarbrightfirststarIseetonightIwishImayIwishImight-havethewishIwish. . ." While—

All along the watchtower, princes kept the view
—Bob Dylan, "All Along the Watchtower"

* * *

That night there was someone else who couldn't sleep. Someone so tall that when he strode along (this lord along his watchtower), a rolled-up starmap in his hand, the top of his head nearly touched the clouds. He was weightless, walking on air as his white Dominican's robe flew up against the nightsky, streaming behind him like the fiery tail of a comet. Someone else who tossed and turned against the firmament, found comfort in forbidden planets, clung to constellations, spun dreams in the dross beneath the moon and beyond the Milky Way; someone else who wished on stars. Cosmologist, astronomer-priest, philosopher, visionary, mystic, a magician of majestic proportions. Bruno Falcone had a soul with wings: mechanisms which, despite the obvious limitations of his astonishingly dark and beautiful (if only too human) form, enabled his spirit to soar, exploring the universe at will. A man who lived like someone had lit a torch under him and it was his mission to keep it alive—a King of the Magi, a priest of the sacred fire following a bright and mysterious star. No morbid prince, the glittering universe he held within his heart, whose wonder he had assimilated, made his teeth flash when he smiled, and his eyes give off sparks. His handshake was especially warm and his kisses so impossibly hot that when he made love sometimes the bed caught fire.

He was a man on a voyage of the kind of discovery that would forever after alter the way people looked at the world, a whole brand new perspective and, unfortunately, to some his revelations gave pause; they labeled them heretical and sounded the alarm. Though a proponent of the earth-shattering, contra-Ptolemaic view of the cosmos, Falcone, pledging allegiance to Copernican theory as had other independent priests and high-minded men of his day, even expanded upon it. Some might venture to say that he absolutely defied the limits of reason and good judgment, calling his ideas preposterous, radical and ultimately dangerous. Not only was the universe sun-centered as Copernicus claimed, he said, but more than that—there were—Falcone believed—beyond it many more universes, innumerable solar systems made up of an endless array of galaxies, infinite possibilities of stars whose frothy systems covered the surfaces of vast bubble-spaces. The universe was boundless, and because God was infinite, he raved, so, it stood to reason, was the Heaven he inhabited—

> *Tutto lui e in tutto il mondo, ed in ciascuno sua parte infinitamente e totalmente.*
> The whole of him is in the whole world, and in each of its parts infinitely and totally.
>
> —Giordano Bruno

His theory, not grounded in science or math, could not be counted out on fingers or reduced to mathematical equations the way Galileo would measure the width and breadth of Dante's Hell by the size of Lucifer's arm, but developed solely by instinct, and tested by personal contact.

For the Pope, this proved to be a matter of no small consequence. Since he both challenged and threatened church doctrine by his public declarations of these beliefs, Falcone was a man to be reckoned with. And as the climate of witch-hunting changed and they turned up the heat, things got ugly. The Inquisition broadened its search and scope to include Protestants and heretics (artists, intellectuals, and scientists) as enemies of the Catholic Counter-Reformation, and accusations of heresy were rife. The most powerful of all Jesuits, the Pope's Cardinal Senzagioia, the great Witch-Hunter General himself, geared up to make a shining example of the starry-eyed astronomer, hand-picked him for his pet peeve, and Bruno Falcone had a personal prosecutor of his very own.

They prepared the Star Chamber. Summoned on several separate occasions and subjected to ruthless examination, he remained steadfast: but when his own mother was accused of witchcraft and they threatened her with the stake, he felt compelled to leave Venice in a hurry. Holed up in the mountains where he had taken sanctuary in a family stronghold; with an unobstructed view of the sky, he felt free, and the sudden appearance of a bright new light which he first gleamed there, which would prove to be his nemesis, had not yet revealed itself to be some evil star.

While the case that the gung-ho high priest was building against him in Rome incubated, something, which posed a greater and even more immediate threat closer to home, festered in the stars. Ironically, and completely by *coincidenza,* a bizarre chain of events beginning with Felicitá's encounter with the Podesta, would come home to plague them. For right about now, the Podesta, who had been molested by pesky flees and lay awake all night scratching uncontrollably (with painful swelling in his groin, burning up with fever), wished that he would die. Clueless really, he had no idea how quickly his wish would be granted—unmercifully, and not before the pestilence spread.

The vermin's traveling circus packed up their act, which included the disease with a deadly punch, and took it on the road. They appeared all over town, performing multiple engagements, hitching rides with wild rodents, mostly with rats; the sickness spread rapidly, quickly reaching epidemic proportions. The people called this plague the Pink Death. As a consequence of so much dying, all of life's beautiful colors were washed out; but while the world turned gunmetal grey, the afflicted themselves, as the disease progressed, turned from *a lighter shade of pale* to a shocking postmortem pink—luridly beautiful. The color, like a bad Cat in the Hat trick, left spots on everything it came into contact with. The washcloths used to quench the feverish foreheads and extremities of the afflicted were covered with pink polka dots. When wrung out, they turned the water in the basins pink as well, and as people emptied their washbasins out of doors, pink flowed like blood through the streets of the village. The stigmata of the disease colored everything, and snow, being especially vulnerable, soaked it in. Eventually, whole mountains (as if God had covered them with a giant baby blanket) turned fuzzy-pink, and anyone lucky enough to be still alive, looked at the world through rose-colored glasses.

Because of the possibility that the sky was falling, or, in spite of it, Bruno Falcone stood in the center of his octagonal courtyard, looking up as if through an enormous telescope at the octagonal slice of sky up inside of it. The sun's shadow shifting around him was the only reminder he had that time was passing. He was a megalith, a portal in an astronomical monolith that utilized the sky—like Stonehenge, like the great pyramids at Giza—the gnomon on the face of a giant sundial. From God's eye-view, he looked like a fleck of glass in a kaleidoscope which, when turned, created nearly limitless patterns, fantastic arrangements, impossibly beautiful accidents of shifting light and color.

However, while Bruno was out there preoccupied for the better part of the day, others could not be so easily distracted. Falcone's mother, Donatella (who in her old age was simply called Contessa), on whose seemingly frail but very capable shoulders the awesome burden of housekeeping rested, did not take her responsibilities so lightly. Far from it! She would not, could not ignore the audacious packs of furry plague-bearing rats that were ransacking the castle. Was she expected to sit idly by as they grew bigger and more rambunctious each day: sacking flour, stuffing themselves like gluttons on her foodstores, noshing on the very walls? And how could she close her eyes at night when she knew how they liked to nibble, with their razor-sharp fangs, on the earlobes of little children as they slept.

The very notion filled her with revulsion, with such ineffable horror that she waged herself a war of sorts, beginning it with a declaration of fierce purposefulness; with spanking, brutal determination she took up the cudgels. It was a lively war of flying distaffs and flailing broomsticks whose battles they fought in the sixteen trapezoidally-shaped rooms: eighteen beautifully balanced bedrooms to a floor like the iambic stanzas in Spencer's "Faerie Queene." It raged on through the amazing labyrinth of the castle. The pitter patter of little rat feet could be heard all hours of the day and night as the rat packs ran continuously up and down the devious series of spiral stairways, its convoluted halls, winding in the tangled arrangement that led up and down the eight octagonal towers. In the kitchen, they slipped undetected into stew pots, more than a few were baked in a pie.

It was a war of cleverly conceived schemes, a war of wits, strategy, and poisoned bait, a bloody war—sad to say—she was in danger of losing. When at least one ladies' maid threw herself screaming from the nearest window with her skirts pinned over her face like a slack parachute, a thick stream of rats rising up like black smoke from the tail end of a plane going down, all that the Contessa could do, all that anyone could do was to throw up their hands, powerless as the carved creatures who looked on with expressions of blank horror from the diagonal groins and rib ends of cross vaults.

Sanitary lines were drawn. Bands of traveling Flagellants lashed one another to within inches of their lives, but their scourging could not put a damper on the disease—didn't even touch it. Despite flogging, the plague spread like wildfire. Each morning death hung in the air like napalm, doomwatchers kept their eyes on the mushroom cloud, and the Contessa, who now believed that the only recourse left to her was prayer, had everyone in the household down on their knees in the ladychapel for hours, fervently praying for a plague-ridder with the magnetism of the Pied Piper, when suddenly their prayers were answered.

Perpetua, far from being surprised when sent for, only wondered what had taken them so long, and Felicitá who, plague or no, was delighted to be taking up residence in a castle, saw it as a reprieve, a temporary stay from the prying eyes and meddlesome tongues of mountainwomen and townspeople too. The bubble-cloud that the idle gossip had created, far from having lifted, had grown enormous, taken on a life of its own. It bubbled up, a monstrous brew pushing against the filmy wall of her universe, threatening to explode at any given moment and blowing her world sky-high. A cosmic storm. An apocalypse of milky stars. She had been cowering in the dark beneath it, outcasted, an exile, but now she was dancing in a rainshadow, headed for higher ground, towards a bright plague on the surface of the sun.

By the time they shut up their house, tucked a few things in a rucksack (roots, lady fern, angelica, poultices) and were ready to go, rumors were flying thick and fast as the rats running rampant. So, by the time the castle appeared in the distance, an enormous octagon girded round by eight towers that cast the imperial shadow of a ruby crown on the already pink snow surrounding it, and she led her grandmother toward it, with Tiramisú in tow like Toto, she looked like Dorothy in the crystal ball at the first gleaming of OZ. A little dwarfed and a tiny bit shaky, but secretly her heart thrilling just a weensy bit at the thought of meeting face to face with the darkly mysterious master of that dream-haunted mansion, already the subject of so much fantastical speculation.

Their arrival shook up the scene briskly like a blizzard in a snowglobe. So very Zhivago. Bruno turned from his enraptured, stakelike trance in the courtyard, dreamy drifting, simulated flight, toward the travelers who seemed to him to have an uncanny connection to the sudden snowfall and the phenomenon of downy flakes so luxurious that the six-pointed-star patterns of each one individually were made clearly visible to the naked eye, drifting down as Felicitá and Perpetua passed through the rose-marble light of the portal.

Come di neve in alpe sanza vento
As snow falls in the mountains without wind
—Dante in *Inferno* XIV.30

Almost at once, their spirits measured the space, did the necessary math, and made the adjustments. They didn't need a guide to verify that its architect consistently and obsessively applied the principle of divine proportion in its aggressively unusual plan— this was architecture of the heart, a castle of the soul. They could feel their hearts soar in the vaulted entryway, and through the door which opened onto a courtyard where their eyes were drawn upwards to the pointed arches of the octagonal walls, like looking at the sky (from the bottom of a well) out of which, pink-tinged snow was falling. The space wrapped itself around them, as it will in a temple, in any and all of the mystic places of the world: magic manifested itself in an instant. Everywhere they looked, Felicitá and Perpetua spied out the hand of God. Felicitá saw revelations in stone—the faces of angels in the countenances of wall adornments, shy shadows, dust motes' dance. Perpetua heard the tinkling of tiny harps in the trembling of frozen spiders' webs and felt the whoosh of a snow angel's blizzard of wings, the white rush of Bruno's robe as he turned to greet them. She was drawn to the magnetism of his face, and Felicitá to both the power and beauty of his eyes.

Although the snow was falling fast by then, Bruno was virtually unmoved. For as he returned the girl's gaze he had gone lost in the fiery depths of her eyes and was fighting a losing battle with the irresistible impulse to take her face in his hands. She had the flashing eyes, and at first blush, the look of fever on her cheeks so easily mistaken for good health or the effect of cold weather, "a smile that glowed Celestial rosy red" like an angel in *Paradise Lost*. According to Raphael:

> Whatever pure thou in the body enjoyest
> (And pure thou wert created) we enjoy
> In eminence, and obstacle find none
> Of membrane, joint, or limb, exclusive bars:
> Easier than Air with Air, if spirits embrace,
> Total they mix, union of pure with pure
> Desiring; nor restrained conveyance need
> As flesh to mix with flesh, or soul with soul.
> —John Milton, *Paradise Lost*, VIII

He looked up at the sky, falling into the falling snow and felt that there was nothing left to deflect his flight. He was no longer a tethered star-traveler, a hunted heretic, and this lovely wild *creatura* on the arm of the plague-ridder was no ragtag and bobtail shepherd-girl. She was a would-be-princess with her fairy godmother from once upon a dream.

Transformed on the spot, Felicitá was caught up in the light and particles of snow which swirled round like cotton candy, spinning a dress of pink taffeta, ambrosial strawberry *frappé*, a Bob Mackie dress, a waltzing gown studded with ice crystals and seeded with snow like her crown, *scintillante*. And her shepherdess' crook became a scepter. And the Ugg boots, *pantoufle de vair* on her feet, had turned to Cinderella slippers of glass. Perpetua who had been in wool was now dressed all in blue from her head to her foot, tied up with a pink satin ribbon like any respectable fairy godmother— *Bibbidi Bobbidi Boo!*

> I know you
> I walked with you once upon a dream.
> I know you
> The gleam in your eyes is so familiar a gleam
> "Once Upon a Dream"
> from Walt Disney's *Sleeping Beauty*

Bruno—who felt himself possessed, suddenly, of some awesome latent power, with the practiced patience of the Prince holding out his silky-gloved hand, apologized, as he led them inside, for being the cause of so apparently long and arduous a journey. He called up from the foot of the stairwell for someone to attend to the unlikely pair of visitors come to deliver them, as without warning, the Contessa came whooping down on her broomstick with her merry band. Perpetua felt only the warm gush of wind as the lady of the house flew by, screeching like a banshee, with household staff at her heels trailing close behind like a pack of witches on a wild hair-raising ride, kicking up a row banging pots and pans, flailing their broomsticks, sorghum stalks and battleswitches, brandishing distaffs and spindles like bright swords at the enemy—in this case the rats which they had on the run.

At the sight of the plague-ridder, the Contessa stopped in midair, so to speak, breathed a sigh of relief so big it expanded to fill the castle she raised the siege of; disbanding her troops, her grateful regiments scattered to the four winds now that the big guns had arrived. She took Perpetua and Felicitá under her wing, primed them both with food and wine as they warmed themselves by the fire where coverlets were laid over fresh hay for straw mattresses and these *pagliacci* placed in the warm chimney corner. Felicitá wondered at the fact that her little goat's new digs were more luxurious than she had ever, in her life, seen before, and at the cushiness of her own accommodations with rosy marble walls and the baby angels that abounded on account of the splendid church window through which fat cherubs tumbled like clouds, sticking to the soffits and ogives. The flocks of putti frolicked in their overhead playland as if the ceiling with its flying buttresses were just another patch of sky. They filled the room with their distinctive babies' breath, reminiscent of pabulum and gummed up rusks, zwieback toasts, sweetcakes, and biscotti till the air was moist and smelled of Downy, melting snow, vapor, like the foggy silvery-white lining of a cloud. She caught a damp white pinion feather as it floated to the floor and ran her fingers over it pensively.

Their hostess spared them nothing as she related the infestation story with a general's attention to detail and the sadistic slant of a professional exterminator. Perpetua listened with the kind of quiet reserved for the confessional, or the breathless silence before the snow; listening in a way that only priests know how to listen—priests and wolves—until the Contessa had told all.

"Leave it to me," Perpetua said on the fly as she got to work quickly and efficiently mixing up potions, batches of poison cocktails with her own specially concocted prayers to purge this mouse house of the plague. Spells were cast all around. She ushered in goats and sheep, anointing them with asses' milk to attract the fleas from bedding and human hosts: advising the latter to wash with a decoction of black alder bark. She laid down rat poison thick and fast.

However effective, this aggressive treatment was not without serious side effects—by breathing in large quantities of the dust there was always a danger that the blood could become thinned and otherwise healthy organisms compromised. But luckily, because of the literally high living in these frozen extremities, in adapting to the cold, their skins had gotten thick like their blood. White arsenic fell like snow.

And then that winter there was a fabled amount of snow. Felicitá liked to imagine, as she dreamed by the fire, how it spilled like feathers from the Snow Queen's sleeves or flew like bedstraw from her mattress as she shook it out—how the feathers of falling ticking turned to snow and then into flocks of wild geese rising into the high cold air like smoke. The cities were paralyzed by slews of blizzards the likes of which they had never seen before and the population buried, sunk into drifts of despair from which they had begun to believe they would never—dig as they might, shovel their little hearts out—get themselves from under, day after day after day no matter how hard they tried.

No sooner was there a glimmer of hope in a just-cleared pathway when a new winter storm dumped several more inches. The streets were virtually intraversable: already icy and brimful, the people added to it as they pushed the heavy snow from off the clay-tile rooftops. Everywhere it piled up sky-high in heaps and mounds and snowbanks. They attacked it with shovels and bats and brooms, went at it with chisels and little silver hammers and pickaxes like snow miners. Snowbound, snowblind. Shop gates rattled closed and stayed shut, classes at the university cancelled. Frozen stiff. Faculties, societies and academies engaged in icy, heated debate as everywhere huge lancelike icicles dripped menacingly overhead, and as the sky continually threatened more—snow removal became the order of the day.

Desperate times called for desperate measures. City authorities mandated residents to clear the snow from the streets around their homes or face serious fines.

People scooped and shoveled, scraped and spooned and pitched it into their carts overflowing with bales of white that spilled over onto the streets as they lumbered along as if they were hauling loads of clouds down to the rivers and canals to dump them. To make matters even worse, citizens who were hard-pressed to find a horse, were strapped for wagons and had no money to dispose of snow with, cleverly devised a way to get rid of it: they melted it—in huge snow fires. This seemed innocuous enough at first, but soon the air was dank with burning snow. Toxic snowclouds clotted the atmosphere with a smell like the too-toasty marshmallows of a zillion overly zealous Campfire Girls. The sticky-sweet smog proved particularly hazardous to public health. Gradually the sky darkened and rained down the sooty ashes of snow, and what they coughed up from their lungs looked like the remains of charred marshmallows. Terribly infectious. Zymotic disease of the lungs and pleurisy rapidly became widespread and the Pink Plague, which thus far had only beset those God-forsaken regions of the north they were beginning to resemble a little too closely, was breathing down their necks. The winds of communal contagion were blowing, gathering in the chock-snow-full-of-storm-clouds overhead. They began to see pink in their phlegm full of innuendo, in the sky suffused with pastel hints of fever, and interpreted them as signs spelled out as plainly as the skywriting Wicked Witch of the West's *Surrender Dorothy*—the stuff of superstition: storms, plagues, curses, and cosmic disturbances—the bad omens that witch-hunting madness is made of.

CHAPTER FIVE

Damsels and Dragons

When facing the nighttime wind and cold it helps to have
the perseverance of an arctic explorer, the heart of a poet
and the patience of Job.

—David H. Levy, *Comets, Creators and Destroyers*

We are beings born of stars.

—Carl Sagan

Much to his mother's chagrin, Bruno was not mindful, general-
ly, of the forecast; despite potentially hazardous weather conditions,
he could still be found contemplating constellations in the courtyard
all hours of the day and night. Bitter cold and gale force winds notwithstanding, he walked along the battlements braving the elements
to see the moonrise, and thereby would discover the nearly imperceptible glimmer of a never-been-seen-before light in Sagittarius.

Some consequence, yet hanging in the stars . . .

—William Shakespeare, *Romeo and Juliet*

Risking overexposure, defying all reason, he courted death
as if it were a homecoming princess as he literally hurled himself

into deep space. He discovered firsthand that viable life existed in the clouds of Venus and Jupiter, and, for a fact, that there were organisms burrowed beneath the surface of the moon and in the blazing dross of comets. He learned, beyond the shadow of a doubt, that the spirits who clouded the sky were so plentiful that they could be skimmed off the top like cream, that the angels which abounded, and who were given credit for turning the cranks that set the celestial spheres spinning—were otherwise engaged.

He personally plummeted through the outer limits, toward the double planet Pluto, although at the time it was known by some other name. He basked in the spectrum of starlight until he glowed from within, his visual purple splitting so fast he was blinded. He cut a wide swath through the old ether, ran rings around Saturn and the scientists stuck in the mire of their earth-centered universe, spinning their own wheels. He made fantastic voyages to and from space, orbiting the earth many times, and it was this particular view of things, this knowing how really high—high is (that same vision which would one day be shared by people everywhere when some six hundred years or so into the future, they would glimpse the first pictures of the planet taken from outer space, and everyone would get goose bumps as an awestruck astronaut exclaimed, "Oh what a heavenly light" at the sight of the earth rising—Colonel John Glen broadcasting his amazement across the airways of the world from the cabin of Friendship 7) that kept his spirit from sinking. It was this perspective from a falcon's pitch that held it aloft, made him shine, luminous like the clusters of stars lighting his way in the darkness. It kept him from going lost in dark matter, wallowing in warm nebula, drifting into dead stars, collapsing. It kept him from burning out like so many others, one by one, who now had black holes where their hearts should be.

Bruno Falcone navigated by the stars, set his course with his heart, the fathomless reach of his wings. White dwarfs, cool super giants, hot blue neutron stars, pulsars and quasars were his signposts, the inter-and extragalactic markings he followed in much the same way indigenous people used inasuks, stone carvings, and notches in the barks of trees. Deneb, Altair, Vega, and Polaris like a glittering string of runway lights were his trail of breadcrumbs, untouched by fairy tale birds. Sparks like fireflies flew up into the dark, alighting from scattered bonfires to guide him home: welcoming as a beacon's fire (the Lanterna of Genoa), or the warm glow of a porch light left intentionally lit. He flew like an eagle and always landed on his feet.

Perhaps there was truth to what people ultimately believed— that it was this skyrocketing around the universe that caused such a stir, disturbed the old order, made a sensation, radically changed the sky. Could so many pairs of eyes deny what they so plainly saw, mistake a triple conjunction of planets? Because there, all three in a row, were Jupiter, Saturn, and Mars. Quite possibly Falcone himself had willed them into this new alignment, created an asterism, shook something loose, dramatically altered Heaven as surely as if he had done it with his own hands. For him it would have been easy, as simple as tampering with the Styrofoam ball planets in a schoolboy's mobile model of the solar system. And as if that weren't enough—there was a new light, which he so boldly pointed out. Hadn't he been the first to bring it to everyone's attention? Then, maybe it was the pull of his own imagining, the force of his yearning, the magnetism of his dreams—flying into deep space with the gravitational force of a meteor passing that disturbed the vast Ort cloud—pulled it out of the halo in which comets were born: a dirty snowball made of black ice, gas, silicate grit and cosmic dust melting in the blast of solar wind so that it streamed a miles-long tail as it orbited the sun. And in the end, it was the eccentric path of this planetoid (beautiful extraterrestrial trash) and not really a star at all (as people wrongfully believed) which would finally bring the sky crashing down on Bruno Falcone's head.

In those few final days of grace, before the impact of his discovery hit the world like an asteroid, he shared it with Felicitá. Because they were star-crossed form the start, it was only a matter of time before they found themselves doing a death defying act on that highwire of a castle top which was a little like walking a tightrope across the falls, considering the dangerous combination of height, wind, and weak-in-the-knees sensations they experienced one especially moonlit night when they were seized by vertigo, and the rest, as they say, is history.

Felicitá had taken to climbing up into the towers and onto the ledges and rooftops: it was true she couldn't be comfier than there in the castle, but still, she sometimes felt confined in comparison to the wanton freedom of goat herding, and she missed, especially, the dizzying heights of her former life, climbing to the high places, the icy precipices, the frozen pinnae which had formed the snowy wings of her transcendence. She was threatened by civilization fast encroaching upon her in the form of refinements. Lovely slippers pinched her toes when she walked, and corsets painfully constrained her flesh as her steady new diet put a little meat on her bones and she began to fill out the gowns munificently given her.

Her hair, however, was a different matter entirely: no matter how much time and effort they put into styling it into submission, it seemed to have a mind all of its own. The Contessa, who was always up to a challenge, at times saw to it herself, satisfied when every last strand had been coifed into place, dressed with pins and pearls, bits and scraps of lace. Then moments later the whole affair would begin to unravel itself and Felicitá would turn up sheepishly wild, once again, attempting to tame the flyaway cloud with all the success of a *mufflone* trying to hide its fluffy tail.

She had resigned herself to the fact that nothing came without a price but determined that it was a relatively small one to pay—considering. Although, she may have chafed against tight shoes and breast stays in general, she had to admit that only a fool would protest against being warm and full, certainly better off than she (or her grandmother) had ever been before. Magically, her life had been transformed overnight. She felt as if she'd awakened suddenly after having been asleep for a very long time—warm, incubating, brooding in the dark. A drab larva-cum-nymphet who only hours after leaving the murky water had turned into a fluttery insect, an iridescent winged-thing, a damsel. And Bruno, with his capacity to fly, stand and fight, dream and quest, whose fiery eyes held her spellbound, was the one she took to like a bird takes to the air. He was a sorcerer with kisses so hot they scorched her lips; the touch of his hands raised welts up on her skin like a dangerous outbreak of hives as she experienced total meltdown, her will reduced to ashes. The air heated up when he was near, filled with the scent of fire and powder that prefaced his appearance—dragon-heart, slayer.

And he was like a butterfly called across the vast bubble spaces of the universe, across deserts and wastelands, irresistibly attracted to the very air she stirred; the pulse of her wings pounding in his brain with the force of helicopter blades that had begun to surge somewhere in the ether before time.

I can hear her heart beat for a thousand miles
And the heavens open every time she smiles
And when I come to her that's where I belong
Yet I'm running to her like a river's song.

—Van Morrison, "Crazy Love"

She kicked up a cosmic storm of pollen, such a raging pheromone cloud around her that he was worried about the possibility of mass migrations, about every flying thing in the universe *called* from impossible distances: swarming. She meant the world to him. She was the sun, stars, and the moon that Romeo swore by. As for the earth (as far as Bruno Falcone was concerned), it was Felecitá who made it spin. A testament to Galileo's principle of inertia, she was a body moving freely and it was obvious that it was going to take some serious interference—cosmic or otherwise— to stop her, or for true love to change its course.

* * *

Glittering with the gifts he had given her (rings for her toes and rings for all of her fingers slipped inside a sable muff lined with satin, draped in silk and unending strands of pearls), refractive, she headed down the runway. Cold light glowed all around her, the luminescent cloud of a brittle star. Her wedding dress was the stuff of dreams, made of wishes, silver and white watered silk, gossamer, invisible threads, a pattern older than time itself. The weight of its voluminous skirt, folds and hem and veil were born up by butterflies and lifted in the mouths of birds, which lit on the jeweled net, crowning her hair. Fluttering was all around; they brushed her face and tickled her legs encircled by the great hoops spinning round her like Saturn's rings. Petals soft and slow as snowflakes were scattered ahead as she took her first steps, instinctively testing the ice before skating out onto the frozen lake, a glass carpet. Through the blizzard, she could see the predicant and Bruno, waiting. White petals fell, blanketing the aisle like a galaxy of faintly luminous stars, the path of the Milky Way lighting her way in the dark. She was a streak of light, a great gush of wind as she streamed by nearly blowing out the flames of candles, backscattering.

Her hand automatically reached for the amulet, which Bruno had placed around her neck as they knelt on the velvet cushion at the foot of the altar. Prior to this, she could not even have conceived of so splendent a thing. Perhaps, a bezoar, in her estimation, was more valuable. Her own prized possession was a stone about the size of a pigeon's egg—a tried and true anecdote for poison, a cure for chronic and painful diseases: a charm with great magical powers. By the eighteenth century, a charm like that might fetch many times the price of an emerald. But then, no matter how you sliced it, a stone coughed up by a toad couldn't hold a candle to the beauty of the Byzantine cross of gold and green enamel that Bruno gave her. Her fingers fluttered over the delicate floral pattern, the facets of hogback diamonds, lighting on the fire opal, a singular *girasole*—or sunflower—shining out from an emerald jewel-field. She could feel heat emanating, imagined rays glinting, light beaming like blazes from her breast. Suddenly her breath caught as a thread from her sleeve snagged on one of the prongs and pulled, compromising the setting: the stone holding on precariously. The idea that this meant to be some kind of sinister omen settled on her like an ice fog. She tried to clear the premonition away, swore a sacred oath to have the cross fixed immediately, promised: but the terrible vision of the stone cast off and lost in the snow remained fixed in her mind's eye as, over their bowed heads, the priest pronounced his blessing.

Just then, the most remarkable gift of all was revealed, off center slightly in the huge fleuron church window. It was the baby star she hung her hopes on. His star she hitched her wagon to. The largest diamonds ever found—Star of Sierra Leone, Star of Africa, Hope diamond, Drescion, Koh-i-Nur would all pale in comparison to the exotic star, which Bruno had discovered and subsequently named Felicitá's Nova. And since by their very nature comets continually hail down, during the "Angel's Prayer to Mary" (as if it were a show at Disney World) it poured water, organic building blocks, commentary debris to the tune of nine tons a second (*Ave Maria, Mater Dei, Ora pro nobis peccatoribus* . . .), pieces of comet dust—shooting stars, a meteor shower to rival the drama of creation.

The wedding banquet surpassed all fantasy. In her wildest dreams, she could not have envisioned that feast. One would first have to be acquainted with quinces to warrant six of them baked in a pie, but there were a dozen or so quince pies together with some pheasant-filled —and rabbit. There were twenty-five different dishes in all, each one stranger than the next. The first course or *credenza* of sweet antipasti and the last course of desserts, however, made quite a hit with the new bride, Felicitá having recently unearthed a powerful sweet tooth. She'd only just begun to scratch the surface of her obsession for *dolci* until that night when she went to town on the sweet and savory treats prepared by the pastry chef like *una bambina* let loose in *Candyland*. Her eyes (and her mouth) wide open with equal measures of pleasure and surprise plainly registered on her face as she masterfully excavated *cannoli* cream from Turkish hats with her tongue, sucked the crystallized sugar coating from rosy *cotognata* chunks and crunched on *granita,* ice (which was kept in caves) flavored with *cedrata*—syrup made from sugar and citrus flowers. She even licked the features off the gold gilded marzipan figurines of miniature birds that graced the table and was prevented from very nearly obliterating a chubby angel and a marzipan god (whose heads she had been seriously considering biting off for some time) by the servants who cleared the banquet table, resetting it down to the cloth and little sugar sculptures. A fresh scene and completely new change of setting for each of the six courses.

The second *credenza* of meat and wildly imaginative soups was abysmally disappointing in comparison. She could only venture to guess what on earth those poor drowned and burnt offerings may once have been (game birds, squab, hen, wild boar, capon, veal, partridge, pork, venison, hare, suckling pig), couldn't even imagine the creatures boarding the ark, much less recognize them served up as supper (spit roasted and skewered without benefit of fur or downy feathers).

Freshwater fish (trout, sturgeon, duarade, and pike which were grilled, spiced and dressed with lemon or as fillets and patties, caught in Lake Guarda, the Mincio River and the Po, and served with a mélange of imaginative sauces) were probably as plentiful as they must have been when Peter once cast his nets. Hundreds of crabs, *grancipori* were sacrificed to the table of giants as the ritualistic bang of silver hammers came down on their little heads. Felicitá had to stuff up her mouth with her napkin to stop from screaming "Run for your lives!" as platter after platter was successively brought in and everyone merrily smashed away, indelicately sucking on the tiny little legs and pincers like straws, carelessly flinging them onto the growing bone yard of crushed orange crab shells.

Credenza numero three rated far better, as Felicitá, who had always been a vegan by necessity, loved the taste of slender asparagus spears, celery and artichoke hearts reminiscent of the wild greens she foraged for in familiar Alpine pastures, her old stomping grounds.

At the end of the meal, they showered the guests with Torrone candy.

> In Cremona, Italy in 1441 . . .
> at the wedding of Francesco Sforza
> to Bianca Marie Visconti, the
> buffet featured a sweet made of
> nutmeats, honey and egg whites in
> the shape of the famous tower
> of Cremona "*Torrione.*" Hence
> the name Torrone.
>
> —Ferrara Bakery

Hundreds of pounds of sweets were tossed out like confetti as ribaldry prevailed and tumblers brimming with wine were raised in raunchy toasts to the bride and groom as the guests drank round after round to the couple's health—*Salute*! Long life—*Cent anni!* Male children—*Figli Maschi*! To Love! To Life! And to love again!

Felicitá was still picking bits of vanilla nougat candy (particles of white wafer, honey clouds, chewy castle) from her teeth when it was time for the revels to begin.

Swept up in the dance before she could catch her breath, Bruno's warm hand clasped hers and they threw off sparks like tops spinning round to the music against the background of the dancers whirling in elliptical orbits, satellites circling round, forward and in retrograde, vertiginous.

Well, it's a marvelous night for a Moondance
With the stars up above in your eyes
A fantabulous night to make romance
'Neath the cover of October skies

—Van Morrison, "Moondance"

The trail of steamy puddles left in their wake had barely enough time to cool before piles of wedding clothes collected on the floor of the bridal chamber like cumulus, pillowy, gathered like silver clouds, mounds of coconut, stiffly beaten egg whites and sugar, meringue, whipped heavy cream, angel food cake, snow drifts from which delicate seed pearls and glass beads glistened, ice crystals glittered from folds of watered silk, pools of ice cream, melty lemon ice, like frostwork before fingertips tasting like lady fingers soaked in Amaretto di Soronno traced lips sticky sweet with vanilla, honey, almonds, banana, Gandmanier, ice-cream, candied violets and mimosa, maraschino cherries. Tenuous touches raised red welts up on milky skin like bee stings, burned like frostbite. Slow moving and molten hot kisses and caresses melted into one another until temperatures rose to the boiling point, scalding, hot enough to bring flavored sugar water to the hardball stage by the candy thermometer until it all went up in smoke, combusting— alight in flames like a flambé.

CHAPTER SIX

The Blessing Witch

But it were a thousand times better for the land, if all Witches, *but especially the blessing Witch* might suffer Death.

—William Perkins, *The Good Witch Must Also Die*

The Podesta's wife had done coddling up her husband; for months Nina had been feeding him *in bianco*, forever spooning out soft-cooked eggs, potato dumplings—*gnocchi, pastina, stracciatelle,* invalid's gruel. Wiping spittle and milk from the corners of his mouth like a wet nurse and changing his dirty diapers. Unlike the others who prayed for mercy, the pigheaded Podesta lingered far too long, hanging on past all hope, clinging past care, past . . . dying only when he had just about exhausted his only-so-vigilant wife's legacy and patience. One morning when the cock crowed feebly at a prophetical dawn which spread like a deepening bruise—bad black and blue, broken capillary blood vessels, webs of spider veins trailing off into a pale pasty sky—a pretty Parisian pink stained his cheeks with high color like two biffin, deep red cooking apples. They laid him out on the ground to speed up his death and removed the roof of the house to expedite his soul. In the case of the stubborn Podesta, even this, which for all intents and purposes should have meant curtains for him, was excruciatingly slow. Color seeped in like blood in vitellus; his pop-eyes two bloodshot yolks. An extreme pink invaded his tissues, similar to squid ink squirted into his skin, the viscous liquid in a lava lamp or gushes of grenadine in a Tequila Sunrise, Campari in soda. Her audible sigh of relief was justifiable then, when the Angel of Death flew overhead at last and his skin blushed all over the shade of strawberries soaked in Marsala and sugar. Nina was overcome by the sight of her husband's oedematous and pink body and the heady scent of sweet vermouth (wormwood, *Gorgonzola)* that filled the air.

Eventually, she was brought round, and when she came to, the bereaved widow began preparations for the corpse's cremation for which all of the deceased dead were necessarily doomed. *Kyri-e e-le-i-son.* Darkness was drawn all around: she drew the heavy drapes, hung black crepe to warn the world away from her door, secured the shutters fast against the insufferable tatty pink reflection of sunlight on snow. Beneath the veil she now always wore, her eyes had succumbed to shadow, receded into the sallow folds of her cheeks, sunk in the depths of despair. Abandoning her bone corset like an exoskeleton, her figure misshapen, mollusk-like, skulked in sackcloth, deep morning. All of her meals were taken on the floor, whereby the light of a single candle she'd plop herself in front of a plate of leftovers, whatever she could dig up from her root cellar and the unreplenished stores of her pantry. She was but a shadow of her former self, and seeing her slumped on the cold hearth that way, she might have passed for lots of things not quite human: a mysterious pile of *something* and the tears she'd been reduced to—coal, rags, seaweed? A blubbering, salt-marshy beached thing—whale, walrus, seal, a manatee maybe?

It was in this sorry shape that she was discovered by her brother Massimo, who happened to be out witch-hunting in the mountains by order of the Holy Office which meant to wipe out the magical folk (i.e. heretical) ways of the mountain people, and who, upon hearing about the death of his brother-in-law (who he had always secretly referred to as *that Scaramouch*), set out *pronto*. This prelate, hot-gospeller, the mad and infamous Max would have put his hand to fire to be at his dear sister's side in her hour of need, such was their propinquity, although it meant taking a hiatus from his mission of evangelizing lost souls when he was really on a holy roll. He had already pointed the finger at hundreds of women suspected of witchery, leveling charges of *maleficium*. Why, in just one year's time he had nailed a werewolf, had a spell-caster whipped and banished for administering love potions (among other things), prosecuted a particularly nefarious old woman who'd become so completely convinced that she *was* a witch that she named three chickens as her familiars, a cunning woman whose prophylaxis had caused the village priest to lose his penis, a necromancer, a blood-letter, bewitcher, magic-worker, conjurer, card reader, herbalist, bone-setter, bewitcher, layer-out, diviner, sorceress, wizard, magician, counter magician, curser, shape-shifter, storm-raiser, gynecologist, healer, wise woman, washwoman, a spinner, libber, prophetess, treasure finder, dowser, charmer, astrologer, exorcist, wet nurse, weaver, a possessed nun, storyteller, a *malandante* and a *benandante*, a whole gaggle of witches. He was personally responsible for contributing to the rising influx of *Anguane* women who, in order to escape certain condemnation from the Inquisition, hit the ground running, vanishing into the Val Camonica where they sought protection in the hidden caves of Naquanne.

He felt smug enough, as he journeyed out to see his sister, trudging through the backwoods of ice, a man equal to just about anything. But he was in no way prepared for the flies, for the holy hosts of wriggling parasitic insects, her skin crawling, her overall lousiness. He found her in a state of utter wretchedness, abjection, *miserabile*, a disheveled heap, the lengths of black veil draped over her shoulders like bats' wings, her hair hung in snaky gorgonlike dregs, her flesh cankered, scaly with boils and carbuncles clinging on like barnacles. "*Che puzzo!*" he couldn't help but exclaim to Donato, his beautiful young assistant who had already stuffed up his nose and mouth with the sleeve of his cassock upon entering the house, which swelled and stank from so much crying, like poop decks, cheap seaside resorts. "*Porco a miseria!*"

She recoiled in horror at the sight of her brother, shrunk away from the alarmingly alien, black-robed Dominican inquisitor, demonologist, who stood prefectorially alongside his protégé and fixed her in his gaze. But such manifestations were well within the parameters of Max's personal experience, the realm of his expertise. Without a moment's hesitation, he concluded that what he was dealing with here was a clear-cut case of *perfect possession*. His sister was possessed by a demon, by demons or *perhaps,* he thought, (considering the slightest revision) *by Satan himself.* (Matt. VIII, 16: They brought unto him many that were possessed with devils and he cast out the spirits.)

She met all of the criteria and then some. Her countenance was terrible to behold; she swore monstrously, fiendishly spewing curses, flashing him nasty snaggle-toothed grins, assailed him with invectives. Because (unbeknownst to him) of the profusion of polyps and of foreign objects lodged in her throat, her words were warbled and bumbled, making it next to impossible to make out what she said, a croaker whose ravings were mostly about animals as near as he could tell. A huge hare figured predominantly in one hallucination, and she raved out of control as it came for her, apparently, clawing and scratching with its giant bunny paws, knocking at the door. Typical. Ultimately, it became necessary to have her gagged and tied to the bedpost with rags to restrain her from a satyr-like compulsion for dancing obscenely about like a goat and acting out other perversions of the demons. But when the stigmata "A*iuto*! —Help me!" appeared scratched in her distended abdomen like Braille from the inside out, there could be no doubt— as far as he knew she had never learned to read or write—it was plain as the nose on her face.

"*Adjure te, spiritus nequissime, per Deum omnipotentem,*" he began. "I adjure thee, most evil spirit, by almighty God."

He fed her the host and had her drink the wine of the Eucharist; had the Laundress, Father Donato, and the newly employed housemaid, tie her up, tie her down, hold her nose while he poured Holy Water down her throat. Then he plied her with questions as to the identity and nature of her demon(s), scrawled the names of them all on slips of paper (Satan or Dis, Molech, Chemosh, Baalim, Astoroth, Ashtoreth of the Crescent Horns— known also as Astarte Queen of Heaven, Azazel, Mammon, Tammuz, Dagon, Rimmon, Asmodeus and Lilith, Lucifer, Baal, Belial or Beliar, Beelzebub, Lord of Dung, Lord of the Flies) and burned them over an incensed fire, infusing everything with the devilishly smoked scent of hellebore, attar of roses and rue. He quoted freely in Latin from the Gospel of Saint John (1:1-5). "In the beginning was the Word, and the Word was with God, and the word was God. The same was in the beginning with God. All things were made by Him; and without Him was not any thing made that was made. In Him was life; and the life was the light of men. And the light shineth in darkness; and the darkness comprehended it not." And also, John (1:14): "And the word was made flesh, and dwelt among us, (and we beheld His glory, the glory as of the only begotten of the Father), full of grace and truth."

His methods, far from producing the desired result, seemed to have the opposite effect. She showed little or no aversion to replicas of the cross, or to *the sign* traced over her liberally again and again (*In nominee Patis, et Filli, et Spiritus Santi.* Amen), together with the ritualistic sprinkling of holy water. Curiously enough, she reacted emotionally to an image of the Madonna and when the bells tolled "Ave Maria," she cried on cue.

Fits followed ranting. Before her movements were curtailed and they tied her up, tied her down, Nina was prone to levitate from the bed, and falling backwards, to lie there as if dead. Future episodes of the mystifyingly dangerous aerial show then canceled, her seizing and fainting fits continued from time to time. Usually, they would revive her with vinegar, much as her late husband used to do. Once, though she was on the verge of being marinated like a pickle, she remained unconscious for what seemed like eternity. Everyone's drawers were in an uproar. The Laundress made a vapor by burning a piece of a man's shirt before her which made Nina open up her yellow eyes and scream—vomiting up shards of beach glass and sand pebbles, seashells and seaweed, seething a long stream of foam —projectily, a whole mouse, wadding; she coughed up a fur ball composed of enough angora wool to knit one very cozy sweater and a pair of warm stockings. Cleared of these obstructions, *The Voice* was unleashed. Screams segued into infernal noise: a charivari of howling, bellowing and roars to beat the band. The Devil chastised them with warnings to the effect that they had better leave him and Nina alone, especially when she was in one of her deep sleeps.

Max had him flogged for his troubles. And then he cast stones. In the life and death struggle for poor Nina's immortal soul, the forces of darkness seemed to be winning, and her body—the battleground—torn asunder. As Max prayed fervently over this broken-down devil's handmaid whose heart was barely beating, the Devil blasphemed. The room became fetid with the sulfurous stench of his breath, which wafted through the air like wind off flapping wings of bats. "Charlatan!" he growled at Father Max, "Whoremaster, beast master, ringmaster, slut!" He called him a harlot, a whoremonger, flimflam man. There was a clash of mythic proportions.

Max flew at him across the room in a rage. All the rules governing exorcism etiquette that he knew he should abide by went right out the window. He failed to strictly adhere to precautionary finger wagging (those mental sticky notes) reminding him of ways to maintain his sanity, remain invulnerable, steadfast, hang tough, come out with his faith intact, keep his cool, stay strong. It was unstoppable, like a plague or a snowstorm; he was as vulnerable as a once fixed star in the firmament. This inquisitor, so recently fond of conspiracy theories, had now witnessed apocalyptic visions which he would be loath to share. The Devil's mythomania, his clairvoyance, his uncanny ability to ferret out, point his finger at, put his finger on the pulse of a man's faults, foibles, incompleteness, his weaknesses, his *besetting sin,* and to blow it all out of proportion so that the tiny demons he had always wrestled with, the ones he prayed about or suppressed, reared their ugly little heads, becoming monstrous, perversions, travesties, the diabolical dreams of a megalomaniac.

Max, whose very own two hands closed around his sister's throat, tried to choke the Devil to death himself, shook it every way but loose until at last it seemed that he would succeed in separating it from poor Nina's body. She struggled, batted at the air, and swiped at things no one else could see. Flies with mica wings. An angel so beautiful the sight of it could stop a person's heart. And from the neighboring houses came the sound of children giggling in their sleep. Then her body hung limp like a rag doll, and she saw stars.

The very same stars Romeo would dare to defy; the same stars Bruno Falcone would swear on when they came for him in the middle of the night.

* * *

Felicitá slept like a baby while Bruno sat up, as was his habit, late, looking at the sky. He felt simultaneously both his weight and weightlessness, in his soul, a shrinking, a small hard tightness like a knot and expansiveness like air. A man trying to conceive the infinite, his soul yearning toward God. By now, the news of his discovery, his cosmology and philosophy as set down in a treatise entitled simply *"Pensieri per il Nuovo Mellenario*, Thoughts for the New Millennium," would have hit *Venezia* like a meteor, and its aftershock, co-disasters like an earthquake, like a tsunami, would have reached Rome. And he wasn't a bit worried. Not like they could call it a theory. No need for diagrams—though he drew them. The proof was there for all to see. The stars had conspired to prove him right; the forces of the Universe were on his side.

He looked through the open window at the lights as if they were jewels sparkling in the sky and looked at his new wife like a thief counting his treasure, a gift, pirate's plunder, because in his heart of hearts he doubted that any man deserved such riches and he felt fiercely protective, anticipating that his happiness might be stolen, taken away from him at any time. Somehow, he felt he had gotten more than he was entitled to, much more than his fair share, and he wondered, when he saw the soldiers barge through the door to arrest him, between *il noto e l'ingnoto*, the known and the unknown, given the chance, would he take back one single solitary word?

> Behold. I have cast the dice. I am writing a book either for my contemporaries or for posterity. It is all the same to me. I may wait a hundred years for a reader since, God has waited six thousand for a witness.
>
> —Johannes Kepler

* * *

The Contessa had the castle searched and the countryside gone over with a fine-toothed comb for her son and daughter-in-law who had vanished in the night without a trace, and would not ever have lost heart or hope though a thousand search parties came back empty-handed, and Perpetua, who could no longer bear feeling so utterly useless just sitting around twiddling her thumbs, rounded up Tiramisú and set out to find them on her own. She got plenty of hot tips; chased down so many leads that ended up nowhere, consulted the spirits of the dead, followed her heart, tracking footprints in the snow, hunting, sensing, roving, stalking, running; cried to Heaven until the trail grew cold. Circling back on her own tail, finally she was right where she had started before they had ever laid eyes on that castle, found herself down in the valley she wished they had never left in the first place. Her fairy-godmother get-up had gotten old by then; she no longer looked like Betty Davis as a spruced-up Apple Annie, but was decked out again in rags, beautiful dress changed into mourning clothes, black—bereft of magic, her hair a ratty come-apart nest. There was dirt underneath her fingernails, and she smelled like a stable when she stopped at the village well, weak and dying of thirst.

As she collapsed in a heap beside it, without a drop of desire ever to move again, she saw someone she recognized from the village, a woman named Tessie, famous for her expansive form and a talent for telling dirty jokes.

"Three nuns find themselves waiting at the pearly gates," said Tessie, ladling some water from a pail for Perpetua and helping her to drink. "Saint Peter says to them, 'I'm going to let you in—but before I do—you must think about whether you've committed any sins of a sexual nature and wash off those offending parts of your body with water from this well.'"

"The first nun delicately holds up a finger and dips it in a pail of water" (Tessie illustrated. Everything jiggling when she laughed, which was contagious.)

"'Okay,' says the second nun. Very reluctantly, she leans over the pail and rinses out her mouth."

"Last of all, the third nun," Tessie said, wiping water from her lips with her sleeve, "The third nun says nothing at all. She looks askance at Saint Peter, hoists up her dress (as Tessie demonstrated) and her apron in the air above her head and bending over for all the world to see, plops her *culo* right down in the pail of water."

The sight of Tessie laughing her ass off in a bucket made Perpetua laugh until her stomach hurt. She rocked, clutched her middle and wiped at the tears. "I'm crying," she said, having all but forgotten her despair.

No sooner had Tessie taken her leave, when who should show up to draw some water but Nina's laundress who just so happened to be out looking for a midwife (or she'd have to deliver the baby herself) when she stopped to draw water at the well, recognized Perpetua at once, and begged her to help. Sure, Perpetua would have known that bigmouth churl of a troublemaker just about anywhere by the snub nose and obvious bubble aura around her head, but since she had never actually turned down anyone in need of assistance, she couldn't start now, especially after hearing her shocking story in gory detail, and so consented to go along for the ride.

The Laundress washed Perpetua's clothes herself, fed her barley cake and tea before presenting her to the priests simply as a midwife, and under such extenuating circumstances, Father Max asked no questions, but bowed out gracefully with Donato from the chamber of horrors soon to be turned birthing room.

By the time Perpetua got there, Nina was more dead than alive. The poor woman might sooner be delivered from this world than deliver a baby, thought Perpetua, but she would do her best to save both the mother and her unborn child. She could tell at once that Nina's affliction was not the plague, nor did she need to be wrested from the grip of bad angels, but instead, from the stranglehold of her brother who, with his best intentions single-mindedly may have been responsible for dumping her at death's door, and in the short time Perpetua had to size him up, felt him to be evil incarnate. Best to be done here and be gone as quickly as possible.

The still fresh signs of Nina's ordeal were fairly easy to read, the telltale marks of scourging, stoning, and strangulation at the hands of that nutty inquisitor. First, she needed to cleanse the premises (the house and environs) possibly of evil, but most defiantly of cootie-bugs as it was pediculous—infested with lice, fleas and ticks, chinch bugs, chiggers, midges, and other household pests. She fumigated everything immediately, burned all the old bedding, bloomers, bonnets, ticking, especially sponged the goat shed where the vibrations she felt just in passing, were so intense, she knew in an instant that she had stumbled upon the hotspot: Here was the breeding ground where the blights were born.

The patient's overall measliness remained critical; her flesh cankered, her spirit soured, malignant, crabbed. She was obviously in a state of advanced vermiculation or to put it in lay terms, badly worm eaten, and whiffy. Even Perpetua cringed at the fantastic dimensions of the tapeworm she would hopefully expel, and thank God, she was an expert in the cure of cankerworm, administering a vermifuge as she intoned this supplication three times: "In the name of God I begin and in the name of God I do end. Thou canker-worm begone from hence, in the name of the Father, of the Son and of the Holy Ghost." Afterwards she applied a little honey and pepper to the afflicted parts.

They cut off her dreadlocks and shaved her head until she mostly resembled a martyr, nitpicking away. They hosed the whole place down with her in it, repeatedly doused everything in sight with disinfectant till it was clean as a church and reeked of lemon polish and wood soap, oil, incense, water, wine, salt: resonant with Marian prayers, an *ex voto* for the Blessed Virgin predominantly displayed above her head, and a circle drawn around the bed, until every last entity had cleared out in a mass exodus, from the choicest of rats and comeliest mice, right down to the piddling little circus fleas who bounced onto their backs, raising it all to the level of performance art.

Gratified by the way things had up to this point, Perpetua turned her talents to the next task at hand, which was to distill a potion of pearl dissolved in vinegar. This *salt of pearl* as it was called (as any good pharmacologist worth her salt knew) was a sure-fire cure for falling down desease or the convulsions and fainting associated with *malvita* (epilepsy) from which even an idiot could tell Nina suffered, and obviously had never accurately been diagnosed. This powerful unction was proven to purify, keep the body sound, and comfort the brain, the memory, and heart. Nina licked up the salty ears that streamed from her eyes, completely bewildered, but revivified in time to participate actively in the birthing of her baby (who obviously felt that this was as good a time as any to be born) as her water broke.

Perpetua was a good midwife—at one time she may have even been the best—but she wasn't young anymore, and after a hundred hours or more of labor, in the time between contractions, which seemed to be increasing instead of decreasing, she'd fall asleep, and in that respect, Nina screaming like a hellcat was a heck of a wake-up call. Perpetua sent the Laundress and the Housemaid out scavenging for herbs: for ergot to hasten and relieve the pains, for belladonna to inhibit miscarriage. She pulled open the drawers, doors, and windows, but nothing seemed to help speed up the delivery: clearly, this child was quite contrary, and when it finally decided to come into the world—it was ass backwards.

She brought the baby boy into the kitchen to warm him up and to purify him (little did she know that she was stepping on Father Max's toes, baptism being exclusively the province of priests) without delay, because time was of the essence in a case of an infant born feet first: just the type of tasty little morsel the Devil found so irresistibly delicious. Therefore, making an offering of the child as she held him over the fire, Perpetua gave him her blessing and the nickname—Felix.

The Housemaid, who was so young her breath still smelled of milk—knowing nothing of the old ways—happened on the scene in the kitchen, and catching Perpetua turning the baby over the fire, naturally assumed that she was roasting him alive, screamed bloody murder, making the Laundress rush in (as fools do) and start to scream because of the screaming. By the time Father Max sent Donato to see what all the fuss was about, Perpetua had already kissed the baby goodbye and was gone.

Traveling under the cover of night, sweeping her tracks from the snow with her broom, she followed the flight plan of all of the many other witches who had headed for those same hills.

I have gone out, a possessed witch,
haunting the black air, braver at night;
dreaming evil, I have done my hitch
over the plain houses, light by light:
lonely thing, twelve-fingered, out of mind.
A woman like that is not a woman, quite.
I have been her kind.

I have found the warm caves in the woods,
filled them with skillets, carvings, shelves,
closets, silks, innumerable goods;
fixed the suppers for the worms and the elves:
whining, rearranging the disaligned.
A woman like that is misunderstood.
I have been her kind.

I have ridden in your cart, driver,
waved my nude arms at villages going by,

learning the last bright routes, survivor
where your flames still bite my thigh
and my ribs crack where your wheels wind.
A woman like that is not ashamed to die.
I have been her kind.

—Anne Sexton, "Her Kind"

* * *

In the case of Perpetua, charges were leveled, testimonies
were given, and stories, essentially, were collaborated.

. . . I am a woman in a state of siege, alone

as one piece of laundry, strung on a windy clothesline a
mile long. A woman co-opted by promises: the lure
of a job, the ruse of a choice, a woman forced
to bear witness, falsely
against my kind . . .

—Olga Broumas, "Cinderella"

"Hah!" said the Laundress, extracting evidence of concealed
charms like rotten teeth from out of Nina's mattress. "*Ecco qui!* I
knew it all along," she exclaimed as she pulled out pins, needles
with threads of damask and sandal, fingernail clippings, bones, and
long strands of hair curiously wound together as proof that Nina
had been the victim of Perpetua's witchcraft. That was only after
they'd been interrogated, spilled their guts, and told Father Max all
there was to tell about what happened the night of the birth. How
while their heads were turned only for a moment, a bigheaded
bawling brat (much like the Duchess' howling baby/pig in *Alice in*

Wonderland), which looked more like a *bugaboo* than a baby, had been substituted for Nina's normal one. Everyone knew that witches sometimes snatched away beautiful mortal babies before baptism in exchange for their own offspring, sometimes conspiring with fairies, gnomes, demons, and dwarves, leaving ugly little changelings in their place. To round out the description of this wizened *fairy child*, the Housemaid added a horsy face, and a tail (as an afterthought), and the Laundress said "Wings!"—which was really a brilliant touch, and a realistic one, at that, if one was to swallow the rest of their story.

They claimed that as they stood by and watched in horror, that *witch-baby* jumped right out of Perpetua's arms and scuttered into the kitchen. It would have flown right up the chimney too, if Perpetua hadn't gotten a hold of it first, dragging it out by its foot (or little hoof, as the case may be), and, turning it three times over the fire, sacrificed its soul to the Devil.

The priests believed that Nina had been bewitched, leveling a charge of *maleficium* against Perpetua, which they based on the premise that power is a double-edged sword—*She who giveth is also she who taketh away,* and since Perpetua was the only one able to cure Nina, it made perfect sense to them that she must somehow be responsible for the curse that had made her sick in the first place. In other words, Perpetua's was a (*You're damned if you do, and damned if you don't*) no-win kind of situation.

Working backwards from this point, it was only a matter of time before the Grand Inquisitor jumped to the conclusion that she was also to blame for the blight, which had resulted in his brother-in-law's death, tracing the onset of the disease, without too much trouble, to his encounters with that wicked little granddaughter of hers—Felicitá. Nina, who remembered having tucked away in her bosom the memory of her husband's final act of indiscretion with that trick-turning goat-girl, pulled it out now like a plum, produced it for the court. However, she proved to have a memory like a sieve and when pressed, seemed to have forgotten more than she ever knew. Here's where the storytelling talents of the town *chiaccierona* came in handy.

Greatly exaggerelaborating, that *diseuse* of a laundress filled in all the blanks, copiously fleshing out the case with big fat lies until the dossier they had on those two witchy women could make Satan blush (as hunted outlaws go, Bonnie and Clyde were a couple of nancy-girls in comparison). Filled with seduction, sorcery (magic tricks), cursing—*malvita*, bewitching, plague casting, storm casting, hobnobbing with the Devil, and murder, it was heavy as a drowning stone.

And frankly, the Podesta coming back from the grave a là *Night of the Living Dead* didn't help Felicitá, or her grandmother's case, one little bit. Some dead people carry a grudge. They should (one would imagine) forget the past, live and let live, get over it. But they can't. They should be (one believes) above the petty concerns that monopolize mortal thoughts. Far from it! Most have made a mess of things and have ended up badly. This peevish lot of malcontents landing themselves in Limbo, in the no-man's land betwixt and between, wander around at loose ends, so to speak, knocking on Heaven's door.

"I was robbed, cheated, poor, cold, hungry, betrayed, murdered, boo hoo hoo." A big bunch of crybabies. Negotiate a peace? Forget about it—it's vendetta time! What they desire most is retribution, to settle the score; they're out for revenge, they want blood.

Processions of the dead were *de rigueur*, especially during the Ember days when the disinterred were known to wander the streets of the village, tired, homesick, and hungry. Loved ones opened their doors, left out offerings of food and drink and bowls of roasted chestnuts. In they would march, just like the Podesta (a bogeyman with a big stick up his *culo* that made him waddle like he was wearing a dirty nappy, padding in, in shaggy pajamas and slippers like a giant Telletubbie) and throw themselves onto their old beds, exhausted. At the sight of her dead husband, Nina's disequilibrium returned, and she got woozy, fainted straight away. Max tried to shush the other screaming ninnies and confronted the overstuffed Dipsy wearing a Podesta face mask he breathed through like Michael Meyer in *Halloween*—demanded in an oh-so-very-Scroogelike way to know what that *Scaramouch's* ghost thought he meant by barging in there in the middle of the night and scaring people half to death?

The Podesta stared at him with his unblinking googly eyes, flapped his arms and jumped up and down. Just then Max thought that possibly nothing would give him more pleasure than to grab a hold of that clown (*buffone*) by his stupid horn (which anyone could see was actually an antenna) and yank it right out of his big old puppet head. Then the Podesta, pointing at the video image of Felicitá appearing on his TV screen tummy like the witch's Dorothy trapped inside the crystal ball, began to name names. "Hctiw a s'ehs!" he giggled in falsetto and reverse so that Max had to put his ear up close to his immovable mouth in order to make out the muffled sound box quality of the words. "She's a witch! She's a witch!" he repeated in true Monty Python style—right out of the *Holy Grail*. Well, who could argue with that? After all, the accusations of ghosts are to be taken quite seriously, more to heart than last confessions, or deathbed wishes, even. With that, he had as good as signed Felicitá's death warrant, ordered her execution, and may as well have pulled the switch himself. From there on in, she was a living dead girl.

Having gotten that off his chest seemed to give him an appetite, which being dead and looking like some dumb doll, apparently, had done nothing to diminish, and when at last he had scoffed down the last bowl of Tubbie Custard, appearing to respond to the ring of some far away mobile, he waved bye-bye. "*Ciao*," he said, or "*Oaic*," rather, and shuffled off to join the other Dipsy, Laa-Laa, Tinky Winky and Po look-a-likes in the conga line of the dead. The last of their jiggling Tootsie Pop-colored *culos* went zigzagging off into the clouds to the beat of some distant hum.

They had found the scapegoats they'd been looking for in the form of an old woman and an ex-shepherd-girl—*ex silentio.* Max was hot to see Felicitá burn: particularly in light of the fact that he had just discovered the marriage tie that bound her to that *pazzo* Bruno Falcone. But here, in his mad rush to fry both that crazy priest and his charming wife, he was lagging seriously behind Rome. He could send all the *posse comitatus* he could muster up into the mountains with their burning torches and packs of bloodthirsty dogs to track down some ratty old scarecrow, but Senzagioa, the Pope's Cardinal Inquisitor, wanted her granddaughter, and the sling Bruno Falcone's ass was in belonged to him.

Like a dream come true, he finally held the fate of that arch-sinner in his hands. Bruno had been seized by the Venetian Inquisition and turned over to Rome where Senzaagoia now had him right where he wanted him. Imprisoned on a capital charge of heresy, he was bound in chains and thrown into the holy dungeons of Castel Sant Angelo, pinned to the crag (so to speak) and run through. *That will teach him to play with fire,* thought Senzagioia, stroking his pointy beard and walking away with an irrepressible jangling of keys like hollow bones. Each day the Cardinal Inquisitor came with his servants to interrogate him, and they applied their particular brand of torture until he was nearly dead—but then stopped just short of letting him die, with the relentlessness of Zeus and his voracious eagle.

And like Prometheus, that culture hero, fire-bringer, and champion against oppression, Bruno lay dashed in agony upon the rock, his body broken, flesh torn to ribbons. But his spirit couldn't be bound up by chains, his soul restrained, or his beliefs suppressed by the white-hot scourge of the church, the tyrannical rampaging of Rome—*Il Papa* and his power-tripping priests. And he told them so—time and again. Let them thunder, hurl their bolts of lightening, rock his world with the earth-shaking shenanigans of angry gods—but nothing could convince him to recant, and although he and his wife were now blamed for just about every evil under the sun: innumerable plagues, supernatural storms, and all sorts of aberrations in Heaven as well—nothing could compel him to give her up. The Holy Office was giving itself a congratulatory pat on the back for catching Bruno with his pants down, hand in the cookie jar (so to speak), and it was Felicitá who held the smoking lid. Yes indeeedee—the fact that (up until now) she had successfully evaded capture was chalked up to prove in no uncertain terms she was in league with Satan, and to make matters even worse, Senzagoia had it on good authority that that little witch was pregnant.

But for Bruno, it had become next to impossible to make sense anymore of their rhetoric, synonymous with the unrelenting pain and the confusion gathering in his head like—

purple haze all around
Don't know if I'm comin' up or down
Am I happy or in misery?
Whatever it is, that girl put a spell on me...

Don't know if it's day or night...

Is it tomorrow, or just the end of time?

... 'scuze me while I kiss the sky
—Jimi Hendrix, "Purple Haze"

* * *

Felicitá knew with absolute certainty the second her husband's heart stopped beating. She experienced his execution sympathetically and still lived to tell the tale, re-living the sequence of events (the beginning of the end), which was set in motion on the night the soldiers stormed the castle. They rushed into the room, upsetting the dressing table with its collection of bottles flown into a blizzard of broken glass like light shards, ice chips, splashes of lavender, rose petals, smashed scent pots, droplets of colored water. Her *corredo* tipped over onto the floor: spilled jewels crackled and sparked like firecrackers. They tore at bed curtains like pieces of sky, and the faux heaven painted on the ceiling came down around them too, with a crash of soldiers and falling angels. An ice fog, thick enough to make a smokescreen, crept in the cracks of windowsills and rolled through doors as they held Bruno back to get at Felicitá: casting away the sheets, clearing away bedclothes like cloud cover. They found the bed empty, but the mattress still warm where, they could swear, just a moment before she lay sleeping. But Bruno's voice had startled her from her dreams—shouting for her to get away, telling her to run for her life. And that's what she did, even as her heart cried out for him, filled with dread for the Contessa and for her sweet Tiramisú, nearly paralyzed with fear and guilt for abandoning her grandmother. Frantic, she spouted breathless prayers and did not look back, but like the goat-girl that she was, high-tailed it just the same. And because she was an expectant one at that, Felicitá fled to safety with the protective instincts of a wild thing—mother—just as fast as her little legs could carry her, back up into the mountains from where she had come, vanishing into the Val Camonica.

* * *

Still, she had never actually lived in a cave, Felicitá ruminated, taking stock of her new surroundings, trying to get a hold of herself. This surely was no castle, not by any stretch of the imagination, but was almost as good as the hut she had shared with her grandmother—without its small window, of course, and also without its fire, large cook pot suspended from the ladder that led to the loft, or bedstraw. Calling up those associations was like pouring salt on fresh wounds. Hyperbolically speaking, an unflattering light was cast upon her present circumstances, rendering them unbearable, and she swallowed hard as a huge lump formed in her throat. Fighting back crocodile tears as her finger automatically outlined the petal-like butterfly wings of the *Camuni Rose* petroglyph on the wall of her new home, tracing it over and over and over again till she began to calm down, the beauty and spirit of it filling her with a kind of peace so that she could even concede, before she drifted of to sleep, that as wookey-hole went, this one wasn't nearly so bad.

Each night before you go to bed my baby
Whisper a little prayer for me my baby
And tell all the stars above
This is dedicated to the one I love
                                    —The Mamas and the Papas,
                                    "Dedicated to The One I Love"

Into her dreams came her husband; she saw him as he passed through the piazza on his way to the Nona Tower (the secular prison across the Tibre from the holy prison of Castel Sant'Angelo), where they were taking him to await his execution. He fell on his knees before the statue of the angel. In 590 AD, when the plague ravaged the city, Saint Gregory the Great made a solemn procession, imploring the Virgin to stop it. Legend said that an angel appeared in the sky and, lifting its sword, alighted at the top of the Mausoleum, thereafter, called Sant'Angelo, as a sign that their prayers had been answered. A chapel was erected on the spot, and later a statue that commemorated the miracle. On his knees in the Courtyard of the Angel, in the face of what could only be considered a very serious miracle shortage, a veritable miracle crisis, really, Bruno Falcone prayed. He pleaded for his life, and failing that, he bargained for the lives of those he loved best, asked pardon for his sins and forgiveness for blasting his enemies, especially Senzagioia, who he'd sworn to see in Hell, and who, in turn, swore he'd see Bruno burn first—a drama which was about to be played out on the world stage, and to which history would bear witness.

Bruno Falcone was burnt at the stake in Rome in 1600 in the Piazza del Campo dei Fiori (Square of Flowers) with an iron gag in his mouth. This bridle, or heretic's fork, was a popular silencing device employed during torture so that sounds from the victim would not interfere with the conversation of the inquisitors. Popularized in Spain, it came in especially handy during the *auto da fé*—acts of faith (a regular Saturday night bonfire/marshmallow roast) when dozens, sometimes hundreds were burnt together at a time, and the sound of screaming tended to ruin the effect of the sacred music, spoiling the appreciation for the crowd. Bruno's bridle was created with special modifications designed expressly with him in mind. One long spike pierced his tongue and the floor of his mouth and came out underneath his chin, while another penetrated through his palate, its stem embossed with the retraction they had failed to get— "*Io abiuro*, I recant."

Into Bruno's prison cell came the hooded friars from the Company of Saint John the Beheaded as if they had been circling the Tower forever, swarming in the grey dawn like a flock of flying monkeys, and this was the moment they'd been waiting for all of their lives. He was completely at the mercy of the Dominican and Jesuit priests accompanying him in the tumbrel on the road to the square, making their last ditch attempts to get him to apostatize, to renounce the blasphemous beliefs he was apparently more than willing to die for, and in turn, perhaps, he might qualify for redemption, or to put it bluntly, he was going to a Dante-like Hell in a hand basket.

The wheels of the cart turned so excruciatingly slowly along the way that they may as well have been the wheels of the rack. The cart bumped and pitched over the rough stones of the streets lined with crowds of jubilarians who assailed the prisoner with invectives, as if he were a chained monster, and curses like a shower of confetti in a perverse ticker tape parade. The priests, mumbling maledictions and prayers, pressed images of the Pope, and the Virgin, and various other icons of the church towards him, but he would only cast down his eyes, close them or turn away, sick to death of their twisted party games. Then the crowd really got ugly. They flouted, jeering and demanding retribution—sent up cries of "Burn the witch!" all together in an impressive and, hitherto, unparalleled display of solidarity.

The hooded men stripped Bruno naked and led him frog marching to the stake. Lashing him to it, they recited a long and quite impressive litany of his sins before pronouncing sentence. These amateur theatrics entertained the throngs to no end. They especially loved the part when Bruno turned away from the crucifix thrust in his face, and there was all that chanting as underneath him, the faggots were lit, and in his eyes wide open like a Michelangelo, the embers kindled to a glow. They just ate it up. Virtually fascinated by the *spetacolo* of someone being burned alive, they were glued to their seats by the special effects of flames on flesh and bone, on the chambers of his heart, the sinews of his brain, the fire in his eyes, and snakes of long flaming hair. So mesmerized were they by the lit-up skull that they completely missed the moment of transmogrification when his soul exploded like a champagne cork that went right over their heads like a Roman candle. And God in his Heaven, who knew that sound (bubbles going up in a bottle of Asti Spumante, fizzing like Brioschi, Paaz Easter egg tablets dissolving in bowls of water and vinegar), the sound that a soul makes, better than any other sound in the world and could distinguish it from any other sound in the universe (from babies being born and butterflies, the birth and death of trees, forests, bugs, animals, plants, entire species, civilizations, nations, volcanoes, islands, ideas, planets, solar systems, Universes, tropical storms) waited for it. On cue, He swept through the firmament with His silvery white beard, flowing hair, and turbulent robes, the veined pink of cracked and peeling fresco. Down the Milky Way he plummeted, and through the vault of Heaven with all the high drama of creation and the Sistine Ceiling. He recognized Bruno at once, and as he weighed his life in the balance, snow fell softly in sync to the music in God's head like trembling bells, putting a damper on the pyres and festivities below. Then, with just a simple point of his finger, he picked the most fitting form of all (for all eternity) for a man like this (martyr, mystic, magician, cosmologist, prophet, star traveler, a priest of the sacred fire), and made him into a star. At which point Felicitá's dreams all turned to ashes.

Snow continued to fall on the burnt offerings, charred remains, and smoldering bonfires. Disoriented, the crowds scattered to the four winds, leaving the sanitation department to clean up the mess in the now deserted piazza. Bruno's body was taken down and suspended from the bridge of Sant'Angelo to the choreographed score of blowing snow as a reminder to those whose heads were filled with fluff or luminous ideas they might one day dare to manifest and share with the world. Hung upside-down, he swung like a pendulum in the ever widening arc of his feet trussed up against the sky, his arms sweeping over the river, his fingertips reaching for the watery reflections of stars, which, on the upswing, reeled through the empty sockets of his eyes, the spaces between bones, until he was just a blur, a streak of light like a fiery (albeit inverted) wake of a comet.

* * *

In the mountains, the snow was getting deep. Wolves howled in the night, incited by the smell of warm blood, afterbirth, sacrifice, a baby wrapped in swaddling clothes. The hem of Perpetua's black dress brushed against ghosts who swirled around her like mists, breathed down her neck; the fingers of shades touched her cheek like icicles, shadows whispered their dark, unwelcome secrets in her ear. She felt the wind brush like wings as she swept over the blowing snow (which wiped out the trail of her broom so that there were no tracks left in her wake). Swiping at the flakes in her eyes, she flew into the moonlight's high beam, following a star, in the path of *fiocco di lana*—flocks, and sheperds, *zampognari* playing their bagpipes, a procession of peasants, camels and Wise Men like old Befana. Unlike that folk witch (the mythical ancestress who according to legend, entertained the Three Kings and their entourage bearing gifts for *Jesú Bambino*, but when it came right down to it was just too busy sweeping her house at the time to strike out for Bethlehem until she saw the star and realized her folly. By the time she had baked some cookies and set out to find them, it was a case of too little too late: she lost her way and is still out there searching. Each year on the night before the Epiphany, she rides on her donkey or flies off on her broomstick, stuffing herself down the chimneys of children's houses like a Santy Clause, and cackling softly, fills all the stockings of good girls and obedient little boys with *caramelle*, or, for those who've been naughty, lumps of charcoal and ashes.), Perpetua held on for dear life: she hitched her broomstick to that comet's tail and never let go until she was within no more than spitting distance from the opening of the grotto.

The old woman was coated from head to foot with hoar frost. Snow hung in clumps from her black dress, from her kerchief, and white hair sticking out from beneath it. With icicles clinging to the tip of her long, crooked nose and dangling from the pointy end of her chin, she looked like a yeti, abominably frightful and frozen half to death. As she entered the cave, she found a miraculous manger scene, a *presipio* composed of two figures: Felicitá, posed on a mound of golden Lady's Bedstraw, the cloud of her hair spread round a snow-white face encircling her head like a halo, and an infant asleep in the hay.

Felicitá, startled at first sight by such a terrifying apparition, clutched her baby tightly to her breast and quickly backed up against the wall. When she heard the snow monster speak with the voice of her grandmother she thought she must still be sleeping, or otherwise seeing things, until the heat from the fire began to melt the encrustation of snow and ice, making her more recognizable, and Felicitá threw herself at her grandmother with all the joy of the reunion she had imagined in her dreams ever since they had been parted. Perpetua had to literally pry her granddaughter's arms from around her neck and discourage further displays of affection in order to keep her from smothering them all to death.

One day, not long after the disappearance of her daughter-in-law, and the news of her only son's death reaching the castle, the Contessa was out walking, and hiking up her skirts, trudging about the mountains, she considered her own mortality: it wasn't as if she'd been lulled into any false sense of security in these burning times, and, wondering what other tricks fate might play, she slipped and fell. After a short downhill sleigh ride on her backside during which her mouth opened wide as an airplane hanger, but no sound came out until she hit a big bump and then "Whooooooooooooo oooooooooooooooooa!" she said, like Santa reigning in his deer, bounced up several feet in the air and crashed down, sprawled out, a few yards off, in a great heap of snow.

Some day in the future, she would tell the story of how she'd been projected to that spot by some powerful force like a heat-seeking missile, and how, as she lifted her face from the snow and thanked her lucky stars that no one was around to witness her landing, something sparkled (in a bigger way than ice crystals have of sparkling) and as she reached out to grab it, felt that immediate sense of recognition, the rush of disbelief and joy which comes from the discovery of long and hopelessly lost things. It was the stone from her Byzantine cross, the one Bruno had given to Felicitá for a wedding gift—the one she never took off. The Contessa would tell them how she dug it out of the snowbank in which it lodged, chipping away with the care and practiced patience of a bone collector.

Donatella ran her frozen fingers over it gingerly, held it cupped in her hands like a baby bird; in it beat the heart of a homing pigeon. With no other guide, she set out immediately on a fresh expedition to search for Felicitá and Perpetua and conquering the mountain like the Bride of Mount Blanc, found them—just in time to ring in the new year. On the eve of the new millennium, they went outside at midnight, clanging and banging and hollering to chase away the evil spirits. Together they made a joyful racket, loud enough to wake the dead.

Candida, or Candy, with a perfect stork bite in the shape of a butterfly on her backside, was born on the eve of *L'Epifania*, the same night that the Magi, those astronomer-priests (Melchoir, Gaspar, and Balthazar) presented their gifts of earthy gold, celestial incense, and myrrh from beyond the grave to another baby born in a cave. The blessing was performed by her mother and grandmothers who prayed for protection and purified her with the *water of the bboffe,* baptizing the baby over the fire whose smoke rose up like prayers to the spirits of the ancestors. Bruno read the smoke signals, puffy white cursive crop-duster cloud-letters. Graffiti of fake snow sprayed twelve thousand feet high on the walls of Heaven. Love poem. The sky- written torch- song- cloud hung there, suspended, for the breath of a cloud-life on a clear day.

> Now, I'm gonna love you
> Till the heavens stop the rain
> I'm gonna love you
> Till the stars fall from the sky for you and I
>   —The Doors, "Touch Me"

then slowly dissipated. Letters became distorted, stretching out until they were less recognizable, nearly illegible, no more than wisps, disappeared, invisible, a blown away kiss, while *la Befana* flew off to Bethlehem, a small figure on a broomstick silhouetted against the moon, following the tail of a strange and compelling star.

Felicitá, Perpetua, Donatella, and Candida lived out their lives in the caves, ravines, and passes of Naquane, concealed in gardens of glaciated stone, swirling prehistoric mists. Over time their stories were chiseled and/or scratched permanently in the memory of the people like the leitmotif of roses, butterflies, sacred deer, warriors with shields and swords, wagons and wheels which adorned the walls of their sanctuary, the pictographs imprinted in the charged stones fixed blow upon blow. Together with the legioned souls of heretics who fled into the mountains to escape the madness of the witch hunts—persecution and death—to the people of the Val Camonica they became known as Anguane Women, protectors of the region's inhabitants.

* * *

"Although —" Sophia's mother instilled in her from the time she was still very small, tracing pictures in the palm of her chubby little hand. "Although no one has ever seen those women, you can be sure that they are watching, just as they have been for hundreds of years. As the spirits of those long dead witches fly over the valleys at night, Baby Sophia," her mother said, "you can hear their voices—if you stay still long enough and learn how to listen."

CHAPTER SEVEN

Women Who Fly

"And all the women that were wise-hearted did spin with their hands, and brought that which they had spun, both of blue and purple, and of scarlet and of fine linen. And all the women whose hearts stirred them up in wisdom spun goat's hair."

—Exodus 35.25, 26.

Women who dream have wings of their own.

—Jefferson Starship, "Women Who Fly"

Baby Sophia got a bad case of jet lag, the plane having encountered some serious turbulence. As a result, she felt as if her internal organs had been rearranged somewhere over the Atlantic; her stomach was in her mouth and her heart stuck in her throat when the wide body from New York to Malpensa was sucked up and dropped down inside a series of thunderclouds like a ride on the Coney Island Cyclone. Coming from behind the curtain, the voice of the pilot (a weak wizard) instructed the passengers to remain seated as long as the sign was turned on, and to observe the warning to not *fumare*. "Fasten your seat belts folks," he may just as well have said. "Keep those fingers and toes inside the car. Hold on to your hats. You're in for a wild ride!"

"Good grief!" Baby Sophia muttered, trying unsuccessfully to arrange herself comfortably in the bulkhead seat she had reserved, and to settle in with a new romance novel. The stewardess who, right from the start, reminded her of a french fry, pretzel, or a swizzle stick with an airline emblem in her starch-white shirt sleeves, straight blue skirt, patriotic colors, logo, light and airy as a straw, streaming up and down the aisles like the skinny stripe from a flag, now, after seven whole hours or so in the air, looked a little frayed around the edges, thought Baby Sophia as she wrested the blanket she had requisitioned out of the woman's hands. She desperately needed this additional cover in order to shield herself from the *corrente* that had been blowing steadily on her neck since they left the ground. The stewardess tried fussing futilely with the air condition nozzle one last time.

"That draft is going to kill me!" The plane gave a sudden, violent shudder; everything in the cabin was shaken up like tiny plastic beans in a baby rattle. Crammed-full overhead compartments crashed open and a Raggedy Ann tumbled down on Baby Sophia's head. Grabbing the doll by its little neck, she glowered into the black buttons of its eyes and thrust it at the woman sitting next to her who already had her hands full with the screaming baby she held on to for dear life. Her bracelets clunked together, especially the one with charms as big as bocci balls (most of the women wore all of the jewelry they owned when they flew, as well as a Fifth Avenue furrier's dream of fox stoles and white mink car coats: they strapped money belts bulging with lira notes to their thighs, hid trinkets in their girdles and the satin linings of Russian hats, and stuffed their brassieres with diamonds). Anyway, all of those charm and bangle bracelets made the most maddening noise. If this plane doesn't land in Milano any minute, Baby Sophia thought, I'm going to throw myself out the window. Instead, she ordered another soda, her eyes lighting on the propeller pinned to her air hostess' lapel as she filled the glass up with ice and cleared away the collection of miniature whiskey bottles (a fresh supply of which Sophia kept tucked inside her bosom and pulled out as needed). She fixed herself a highball. Baby Sophia wiggled her toes in the stretchy airline slippers, slid the elastic mask around her head, and pulling the spongy blue darkness down over her eyes she lost herself for a while in the time warp between worlds. Bunches of bracelets jingled like bells: somewhere a multitude of stewardesses were getting their wings, Baby Sophia sighed.

Decked out in their life vests, ripcords in hand, the passengers of flight 2378 from New York to Milan flung themselves out the emergency slide, barreling down like on a Shoot the Shute. "Look out! Get out of my way!" Baby Sophia yelled, launching herself out of the plane screaming bloody murder until she got stuck about a quarter of the way through and had to be rescued, taken away on a stretcher and off the runway in an ambulance. Later she was deposited (bag and baggage) on the platform of the Stazione Termini by a disgruntled minibus driver, after having been treated for mild shock and badly bruised knees at the local area hospital, which, according to her, amounted to the equivalent of Bactine and a Bandaid for the pain and humiliation she had suffered.

So it wasn't until the following morning that she landed herself in Sabbioneta, outside of her family's home, looking as if she and the house had been lifted up inside a cyclone and dropped down again in the midst of her relatives and their rounds of *saluti!* She exchanged greetings with her mother and with her father, her grandparents, all of her aunts, uncles and many minikinlike cousins, all asking about her trip.

"It was the flight from Hell," said Baby Sophia.

Baby Sophia looked past the children in their short pants and nightshirts and pretty, pastel party dresses who picked her pockets for the lollipops she always brought them, flocking around her like pigeons. "Where's Sabrina?" she asked. Everyone looked down at their feet except her cousin Maria whose gaze she followed to the pair of sparkly ruby slippers sticking out from beneath the house. Baby Sophia took a closer look and got a little green around the gills, she raised a cloud of road dust as she threw open her arms and yelled, "Where's my sister?"

"Sophia, what's wrong?" asked Sabrina, appearing suddenly, looking like someone had dropped a house down on her, but still Sabrina, just the same.

Maria ran over as fast as she could and snapped up those party shoes while no one was looking.

The family went inside and didn't resurface for days. "What do you think they're doing in there?" Maria asked her mother, faking concern for her cousin, when all she could think about was that maybe somehow things had changed for the better, which, of course, in her book meant that Joseph and Sabrina were not going to get married after all. There was a lightening in the air, the draught was over, the rain had turned the countryside green, fields of poppies waved their papery heads, rainbows of flowers bloomed like madness, spring was bursting out all over.

Baby Sophia was busy as a bee (that was the buzz) heating up the telephone lines and keeping the Western Union wires smoking. Rat-a-tat-tat-tat. The dish that Maria would have paid good money for was this. After days of racking their brains, trying to determine what was best for Sabrina's own good, her parents reluctantly agreed (caved in under pressure, really) to Baby Sophia's somewhat radical plan that a change of scenery might be just the ticket (as it was her business to know these things), and decided to let her go with Baby Sophia on a cruise ship to America. Which, as far as they were concerned, was about as bad as a slow boat to China. It might just as easily have been Timbuktú.

"*Pronto*. This is Sophia Sonnino from Sophia Sonnino Travel," she repeated so many times that after a while any member of her family could imitate her exactly, and mimic her, they did. "*Pronto*. Can you hear me?" After spending a lifetime on hold with reservations she called in some markers, pulled a few strings and in the end, she had accomplished the impossible. Like magic, she held the roundtrip cruise vouchers in her hand and then the only thing left for Sabrina to do was to pack her steamer trunk and head with her sister for England. Before the month was over, they would be sailing from Southampton for a voyage to America.

Sabrina was among the fifteen hundred passengers who died when the ill-fated luxury liner hit an invisible iceberg in the North Sea. She was drowned like an innocent witch (in the process turning the jeweled Byzantine cross, a family heirloom given to her by her mother as an engagement gift, into buried treasure), sunk to the bottom of the sea like a stone. The unsinkable Baby Sophia was one of the worst shipwrecks in history's seven hundred survivors, but unlike the buoyant Molly Brown, she was not then, nor would she be anytime in the near future, much in the mood for singing.

Grey skies are gonna clear up
Put on a happy face
brush off the clouds and cheer up
Put on a happy face
Take of the gloomy mask of tragedy
It's not your style
You'll look so good that you'll be glad you
Decided to smile!

—Charles Strouse and Lee Adams (lyrics),
"Put on a Happy Face"

After the disaster, she was so consumed with survivors' guilt she couldn't even return home to face her parents and their fathomless grief.

Her mother, Trinitá, known as Trinitá del Monte, of the Mountains, cursed the day all those years ago that they had left their home. To her way of thinking, it may have been an avalanche that caused them to move, but moving away was what had triggered all of the other disasters in her life. She truly believed that if they had stayed in Val Camonica, none of this would have happened. If they hadn't abandoned the village and the home her family inhabited for centuries, Trinitá, whose destiny it was to follow in the footsteps of her mother (renowned in her town as the local *strega* and reputed to be a *jettatore*—one who has the ability to cast the evil eye, the *malocchio*. Once she had cursed someone to death—), would never have lost sight of her power, and that would have made all the difference.

At night, she dreamed of snow. "If I've been buried alive once," she was famous for saying, "I've been buried alive a thousand times." She had the crazy eyes of an insomniac and never could get warm, not even in summer. During *Ferragosto*, she wrapped herself up in a shawl. And all through the winter, underneath her knitted dresses she wore striped woolen stockings and men's undershirts with layers of black merino wool sweaters piled on top—all handspun: her accomplishments as a spinner fueled entirely by her motivation to keep warm. She slept under mountains of blankets, bedspreads, covers and comforters, quilts, Afghans, and plaids. She was never without a hat, and never ever *sensa calzette*—without socks. Under the heavy linen sheets, she kept a *prete*. Each night, inside of this beehive-shaped wooden cage, she hung a pot of hot embers and covered it, shivering all the while she waited for the bed to warm up. She spent long hours huddled around the stove pot or with her head stuck inside the pizza oven, although she was not much good at kneading bread dough, pizza dough or pasta, at folding laundry, bed-making, checking her children's temperatures by touching their hot foreheads and feverish cheeks, or anything else that required warm hands. And under no circumstances were icy lips ever considered to be an asset. Fortunately, her husband had always given off enough heat for them both. Holding him was as close to warm as Trinitá would ever get.

One day, cold as ice and kneeling in the shrine before the statue of the Madonna, she squinted at the wall of votives, for tilting there among myriad miniature body parts: waxen, gold, and silver limbs, hands and feet, arms and legs, eyes and ears, bellies, breasts, faces and figures, lips and hearts, especially hearts, and among the many foundering ships nailed up by sailors who had survived disasters at sea, was a small representation of Sabrina's ocean liner, and Trinitá discovered that if she held her head at just the right angle when she contemplated this tiny vessel, she could keep it from appearing tilted.

The silver charm was cast on the day Baby Sophia and Sabrina sailed for New York, *Buon Viaggio*! As a sort of travel insurance, it was supposed to have kept them safe from *pericolo*—perilous storms and impending shipwrecks, pirates, and sea monsters who nibbled anxiously at the edges of the world. Inscribed like all ex votoes with the initials V.F.G.A. for the Latin, *Votum Fecit Gratia Accipit*, He Made the Vow and Received the Grace, it had half succeeded. Sabrina was gone, but Baby Sophia's life had been spared, and for that blessing, she would be eternally thankful. In gratitude she had spun the banner she was about to present to the Blessed Mother.

Trinitá blew warm air into her chapped, clasped hands, and white-knuckled her rosary beads while losing herself in the tangle of her offering's threads made from Sabrina's tulle wedding veil, her silk bride's dress—unraveled—flax sheets bleached silvery white (having been washed and laid out on the lawn in the moonlight to dry), clean linen, tablecloths, and the lacy nightgowns of her daughter's trousseau. All those strands of the past she had twined round on her spindle.

Once upon a time, her distaff was laden with clouds, with bats of carded silk amassed like snow, or wound with wool they were like the clusters of mist she gathered as a young girl, spinning, with her legs dangling over the side of a mountain: her spindle dropped down over the ledge, suspended in air. And sometimes it was the stuff of spells and enchantment, a witch's curse, the whim of an ugly gnome, and she was a poor princess or a wretch in a fairy tale threading yarn through her fingers, spinning stinging nettles into gossamer thread, straw into gold, until her fingers bled, and nearly imperceptible flecks of dried blood were woven into ivory nettle cloth as fine as cobweb.

The sound of her teeth clattering and her knees knocking together distracted Trinitá from her long string of prayers. "The carrying of the cross," she reminded herself, plaintively, fingering the sorrow like a tangled twist of flax, a silk waste salvaged from the spinning floor. Shivering out of control, she wrapped the prayer flag around her shoulders like a shawl against the blast of arctic air whirling in from a hole in the ceiling and suddenly in the shrine it began to snow, and the snow made her so sleepy that she had to lie down. She pulled the banner tightly around herself like a tunic, its gold braid and tassels swinging from her shoulders. Dedications to her daughters slanted across her chest: words in metallic thread, whipstitches, curlicues, swirls, looping like the writing on a beauty queen's sash, insignia. Sabrina and Sophia's baby pictures and small medals pinned there with pink faded ribbons commemorating both miracles and heavy losses. She pressed her forehead against the cold floor, licked the dark wet spots where snowflakes alighted on the stone.

Since it was common knowledge that Trinitá was already buried alive once etc., etc., etc., it came as no surprise to anyone when it happened again. Only this time she remained under the blanket of snow for a very, very long time. She slept through all of the First World War from which her once upon a time son-in-law Joseph finally returned safely, but three years late, delivered from the Dodecanese (Medeterraneo) where he had been a stranded castaway, marooned on one of its mountainous islets. She was blissfully unconscious throughout the courtship and on the day that he proposed to her niece Maria and was accepted. She remained completely in the dark throughout the whirlwind engagement of *i promesi sposi* and totally oblivious to the high spirits of the town on their wedding day as the fluttering satin ribbon of a wedding party wove its way through the fields toward the trellis tables, laid with cakes and confetti eggs on blowing damask cloths.

A spring storm made it impossible to prepare the night before, whipping through gale force winds and heavy rain. Hail pelted crops and fruit trees. It riddled the party streamers, which they had woven through the boughs, with holes like buckshot, turning their tissue-paper decorations (wedding bells and doves) into the mess of wadded up toilet paper made by goblins on Gate Night. The wind wailed like a banshee. It tossed up people along with farm animals and fences, and then dropped them back down again. A *contadina* said that as she was coming in from sweeping her terrace, she was tossed up as high as the moon, and countless witnesses swore that they had seen her silhouette thrown against the face of it. Everyone rushed to the church for holy water, which provided protection against the storm.

At seven in the morning, it was foggy and bleak. Rosa's bones ached; her teeth were set on edge. Adept at reading signs, she sniffed out the odor of ammonia in the sulfur-charged air. Rotten eggs, she thought crinkling up her nose at it. There was pee-pee in the wind. Someone somewhere had stirred up that tempest from a cesspit—some witch's weather magic to be sure. Come out come out wherever you are. Whoever this *tempestarii* was, Rosa realized, breathing an audible sigh of relief as the sun began to burn through the haze, clearly she had missed her mark.

Besides, nothing short of a tropical storm could have dampened Maria's spirits: her fidgeting, at the moment, making it impossible for her to be tied into her corset. She sucked in her breath until she thought she'd lose consciousness, held up her arms, submitting to the dress pulled over her head like a child forced to put on her nightie, not able to stand still long enough for her mother to sew one last stitch; she squirmed and squealed and was stuck with pins. "*Ecco,*" Rosa said finally, exasperated, as she smoothed the gown down over the girl's hips and straightened the tip of her veil. "*Meno male,* Thank God."

All that day Maria smelled traces of rosemary left by those hands.

Joseph detected it too, beginning his honeymoon the way he did, underneath that wedding bell of a dress, and for the rest of his life, he never could smell rosemary without thinking of Maria, and the reverse was also true. But at the beginning, even a breath of it in the air was enough to make him crazy, and at least a hint could always be detected in the fields of wildflowers and wheat, in the mulberry leaves and smoke from the rearing shed, and in the lofty heights of the barn. Consummate in every cherry, beetle wing, wisp of hay, barrel, and tangled vine. In every bottle of olive oil, put-up stores of pickles and jars of preserves, in every liter of wine produced, in the *marmellata* and soap there were traces of rosemary. It was like their silent wedding vow, unspoken yet inherent in the wind, in the sound of feeding silkworms coming from the nursery—like rain. The loosed floorboards creaked with it, the wedding sheets whispered; "I would die for you," the antique bedstead groaned.

Joseph had returned with a hazy memory of the war, the clothes he was wearing, and a conch shell he carried home with him in a sack—a *memento* of his adventures, the only souvenir of his years of wandering. It told her its secrets when Maria held it up to her ear, and it became a reminder of the time that she waited, long after everyone had given up hope. In his orchard, where in the past she had habitually hung around, languishing for him, she started to install herself in the topmost branches of the trees that became her watchtowers, her widows' walks. She focused on the vanishing point where golden field, blue sky, and river converged on the spot she expected Joseph would turn up at any moment; holding her breath for the telltale tip of white sail, staring into infinity. Sometimes, her eyes were tricked by seagulls; the sight of their wings stopped her heart.

The feathery down of dandelions, milk thistles, and butterfly weed, which made good stuffing for life vests and sleeping bags for soldiers, needed to be gathered, and she helped the women and children with that. Mostly milkweed silk was good for wishing on: Maria did her part to help the war effort by blowing those seeds like thousands of tiny parachute troops into the wind as she repeated the rhyme her mother taught her. "What's the time by the dandelion clock?" A deep breath. "Huff! One o'clock. Puff! Two o'clock. Puff!"

Rosa tried teaching her to knit the shirts and socks that would be sent to fight frostbite on the Italian front, but she could not knit anything up properly, her fingers, always in a tangle of needles and gnarly threads, were impatient, erratic like the wildly romantic, jagged rhythms of her heart, silk wastes. She spun daydreams like webs on the air. On closer examination of her knitting and her plans, she discovered there were flaws, snags; and she pronounced them full of holes. At night, she unraveled all the day's stitches and began again the next. As Shakespeare wrote of Penelope awaiting the return of Ulysses, all the yarn she spun "did but fill Ithaca (or in this case Sabbioneta) full of moths."

When the war was over, many marriageable young men came home and entertained dreams of a future with a girl like Maria in it. She had no shortage of admirers. There was an overabundance of suitors to whom she would not even give the time of day, brushing them off like flies—*mosche, zanzare*—myopic or farsighted: dreamy-eyed boys who hadn't two lire to rub together. But Signore Volpino—Mr. Fox, or Il Volpe—The Fox as he was called behind his back, the wealthy landlord, with only one eye to his credit, was the biggest best of all. A voracious gnat! *Insetto nocivo!* Maria hated the sight of him. And it wasn't petty or superficial; it wasn't as obvious as the eye patch, but that, put together with his greasy, tawny-colored hair and grizzly salt-and-pepper beard, painted the perfect portrait of a pirate, a thief and a plunderer, went a long way in revealing him for the barbarian that he was.

Though he may have looked for all the world like Hook, he was no safe Disney villain, no fanciful animation, grinning crocodilian time bomb sidekick and all—tictoc, tictoc. He was a sweet-talking *ruffiano* (who reeked of old spices and rum—yo ho ho) with the wiles and wicked appetites of the big bad wolf. *Papagallo!* Predator! A serial killer, whose wives had all died in childbirth when they themselves were no more than children. *Tutti morti.* In all three cases the midwife had arrived too late and so apparently had the undertaker, for no one ever saw the bodies. Each time, when the layers-out came, Rosa among them, the bereaved confessed to being so profoundly affected by the sight of his *Nocciola (Noccioline)*, her (their) splintered lips, her (their) eyes like two (six) dead stars—that he'd dug the grave(s) himself. He broke down and cried like a baby.

In a locked room, three little dresses belonging to the dead ménage, now hung in a row from hooks on a wall. Three pairs of dainty button-up boots lined up neatly underneath: inconceivably small like the costumes displayed in the Museum of Art, Madame Tussaud's, where tourists in modern times passed by and gawked at the diminutive proportions, impossible lengths, the sixteen-inch waists, doll-sized fans, and little white kid gloves which could conceivably have belonged to the white rabbit. The Fox was a serious collector.

One morning when he had been a widower for a year, he took his watch out of his waistcoat pocket, and deciding that it was time, began turning up at Rosa's doorstep (with spit-polished boots and slicked back hair) like a bad penny. He brought with him olive oil and wine, sometimes chickens or fresh eggs, five-pound boxes of *cioccolati*—cherry cordials, macaroons, and money that he presented to Rosa in exchange for having his fortune told.

Rosa washed the cards, she swirled them around, spread them out and gathered them up again to reform the deck. With her left hand she cut the deck in three, stacked the last cut pile on top of the first and the second on top of that. She fanned out the deck and instructed Il Volpe to choose seven cards that she laid out in the shape of a crescent moon on the smooth planks of the old farm table. Her fingers were so familiar with the timeworn cards that she could probably have read them blindfolded. At times like this, she almost wished she had no eyes to see with, certainly no gift of divination, no esoteric knowledge, and no window into his crooked heart. Well, what am I supposed to do? she asked in response to her own admonishments. She had to think not only of herself, but of Maria as well. They had to eat, after all, and besides that, a little tarot reading never hurt anyone. Even if she couldn't keep the Devil from her doorstep, maybe if she played her cards right, she might succeed in keeping him at bay, because it hadn't taken her long to grasp that The Fox's obsession for money mingled with his new obsession for her daughter was the reason behind his burgeoning interest in fortunetellers.

Like most self-made millionaires, Il Volpe was preoccupied with money: how to make it, how to hold on to what he already had, which some claimed may already have exceeded the national debt.

There were sacks of silver and gold in his cellar, it was said, side by side with sacks of rotting apples and barrels of wine—a treasure-trove. But as if that weren't enough, he still had to have more. Lucky duck, for him the war provided lots of fresh opportunities. The spoils were there for the taking and he had his feelers out, so it was no surprise that when a certain silk farm replete with vineyards, orchards, fallow fields, barns, coops, chestnut tower, mulberry trees, rearing shed, and an ancient farmhouse right out of a fairy tale, a smallholding which just so happened to fit in perfectly with his domestic plans for the future, went into foreclosure—its owner MIA and no one to pay the taxes—he was the first one on the scene with a pen and an open checkbook.

It got so Maria was pretty good at avoiding him; she could usually see him coming and hightailed it out of the house. If she didn't disappear in time (which happened periodically), she made no effort to disguise her feelings; she simply wouldn't talk but remained stubbornly silent throughout his long and painful visits. She became so good at posing over her knitting (finishing a sweater for Joseph before he came home) that after a while she began to believe it herself, and with a million-miles-away look in her eye, knitted as if her life depended on it.

One day Rosa had her carry a basket with a custard and *una noce di burro*—a knob of butter and some honey for Zia Anna who was home sick in bed. The old aunt lived in a *casupola*, a tiny cottage on the edge of the wood that bordered Joseph Batista's land, and although someone had plainly posted a "No Trespassing" sign, it was a lovely spring day and instead of going straight there, without dilly-dallying, as her mother had told her to do, she took the path through the woods and stopped to pick some poppies that caught her eye.

Lo sai che i papaveri, son alti, alti, alti
e tu sei piccolina
e tu sei piccolina
sei nata paperina
che cosa ci vuoi far?

—*Presentata da Nilla Pizzia,*
Festival di Sanremo del 1952

she sang to herself. She had just gathered up a fistful of flowers when she heard a bustle no more than one hundred paces to her left, the sound of snapping twigs, of branches breaking underfoot and quickly hid herself. From her covert behind the tree, she caught the flurry of The Fox's split coat tails, and the shadowy weight of the girl he was dragging through the woods by the hair like a sack of sweet potatoes. Maria clapped both her hands over her mouth to keep from screaming. She had no idea how long she stood there without moving—seconds, minutes, maybe, until finally, she just couldn't stand it anymore and dashed out from behind the tree.

"*Bu!*" said The Fox as she hit the ground running, stopping her dead in her tracks.

Hey there Little Red Riding hood,
I don't think little big girls should
Go out walking in the spooky old woods alone
You're everything a big bad wolf could want.
Owwwwwwwww!

—Sam the Sham and the Pharaohs,
"Li'l Red Riding Hood"

When she came to a featherbed on top of an enormous pile of chestnuts, Maria, all dressed in white like a bride, was a bleary-eyed wreck, achy all over. She had the mother of all headaches, which was not surprising considering the size of the lump on the side of her head. It throbbed when she tried to move, and the slippery mounds of chestnuts she lay in made struggling counter productive, like drowning in quicksand, or one of those blow-up carnival attractions for kids filled with brightly colored balls that you can't climb out of: the harder she tried to get up, the more she slid indecorously around until she'd exhausted herself, sat there helplessly, and cried.

Having gotten that out of the way, she began slowly but surely to sort herself out. One by one, she picked up the nuts and threw them aside. They did slip down again like grains of sand but, after what seemed like an eternity, she had cleared a spot big enough to stand in, making it possible to see out the window. The main house was in clear view, the sight of it confirming what she already suspected—that she was a prisoner in the chestnut tower on Joseph Batista's farm, and she didn't need to see The Fox leave through the front gate to remember the nasty disposition of her jailer.

For the time being, at least, she was left to her own devices. She paced the tiny floor space of her prison. She sang herself songs. She was a pale apparition in a wedding dress with wild auburn hair—startling—like she had been caught up in an electrical storm or struck by lightning—very Bride of Frankenstein. It was caked with blood, entwined with bits of twigs and leaves, ladybugs from the forest floor, and there were strange scratches on her dirt-smudged face and legs and arms. Though she looked ready to haunt a house, she was not likely to scare away any of the neighbors: the place having been deserted for years now, as far as anyone knew. They hadn't a clue that Joseph Batista's property had recently been sold out from under him, that Signore Volpino was about to become the new *padrone*—and it was moving day.

Maria, tired of counting chestnuts ("one thousand, one thousand and one . . .") and of gazing out the window like a trapped princess in a fairy tale, waiting to be rescued by knights or princes (she had no brothers), and playing I spy ("I spy with my little eye something that begins with the letter C), happened to spy a rather large, humped chest. She blew off the dust and tried to lift the latch, but, of course, it was locked. Luckily, someone had left a crowbar close by, and with that, she managed to jimmy it open.

The dress she unfurled smelled of camphor, which had kept out the moths, and the airtight trunk apparently had spared it from the ravages of time because, aside from a few snags, some rust-colored stains (an especially large one in the middle of the shoulders), and a few tears, the fabric was remarkably well preserved for being three hundred years old or more. It was, in fact, the most magnificent dress Maria had ever laid eyes on; certainly, the heaviest and the hardest to put on. She wished she had a mirror so that she could see herself all dolled up in that yellow velvet, decked out in silver chains and ropes of pearls. A star shaped pin gleamed from her breast as she held out her arms to admire the gold sleeves. The silk whispered as she spun, kicking up straw, particles of dust, and feathers in the air around her: dust motes danced; mice chased off into the corners to hide.

Then suddenly she stopped. Remembering herself and where she was, she continued to sort systematically through the chest with the hope of finding anything at all that might help her. Inside she found jewelry and dried flowers; silk wastes were tucked away with the bones of small animals. She took them all out and examined them carefully, but any kind of answer continued to elude her.

What remained were notebooks, a collection of at least two dozen, all written in a curious left to right hand, illegible, and in the same brown ink. Pages and pages filled with sketches of water and wind, wavy grass, flowers, nests, eggs, bridges, hands and feet and faces, cocoons and caterpillars, all sorts of mechanical things. Maria rubbed her eyes, there was only one notebook left to look at, but the daylight was nearly gone, and without a candle she had to hold the book right up close to her face. Even then the drawings were barely discernable: insects, bats, butterflies and moths, dozens of studies of wings: aeronautic drawings, skeletal renderings, flying machines and men with wings spread across the pages with all the strangeness of prehistoric birds.

The light failed. Maria lay on her featherbed and stared into the gathering gloom up above, where a spider was spinning in the air, until she fell asleep. The first thing she saw in the morning when she blinked her eyes open was the finished web, which would have seemed just like any old web except for the fact that it drew her attention to some sort of contraption hanging nearby that she hadn't paid attention to before. After several tries, she got it down, and by that time, she'd managed to figure out that it was a woman's petticoat hoop (or giant bee skip, bell, or birdcage). That was how (as she later told everyone) she got the idea and hatched her plan.

Out of all those tiny bird bones, fossils and flowers, jewels and wedding clothes, Maria made an effigy of herself as The Fox's bride-to-be and set it up at the garret window. Out of the wicker and ribbons of the hoop skirt, she fashioned an armature of wings that she strapped to her back. Then, she covered herself in honey (the only thing left from her basket), slit open the mattress, rolled herself in white goose feathers, and looking like a fantastic bird she made her escape. In her disguise, she even succeeded in getting by Signore Volpe, who had been making trips back and forth to the house all day long with his baskets filled with gold and the touching mementos of dead girls. She made certain to fly by his blind side and counted heavily on his being convinced by the sight of the grim bride doll she placed at the window.

That should have been the moment when Joseph Battista, returning with his kit bag like brave Ulysses, instantly took stock of the situation, and with the instincts of the woodcutter, picked up his ax to chop off the wolf's head. This, however, was not a fairy tale. When Joseph did finally return home a full three days later, he found his house tied up like a present in yellow florescent plastic ribbons of police tape, and there were holes all over his property, which made it look as if some monstrous dog had been madly excavating for lost bones. Bones were found. The bodies of five women between the ages of fifteen and twenty were sent off in little Zip Lock bags to the crime labs in Milano where the forensic anthropologists and odontologists had a field day, as did the homicide police (who had assembled one of the largest task forces in history), forensic physiatrists, and newspaper reporters.

They learned more than anyone ever needed to know about how those poor girls died and at whose mercy. They had a complete identikit of their killer—unfortunately, not a soul could testify to his whereabouts, as no one had been made a party to his travel plans. The girls' families all got together and offered a reward for his capture, or any information leading to his arrest. He was a man with a price on his head, a bounty hunter's dream, and a target for avenging angels: inspiring a wave of vigilantism that would see no equal until the *Summer of Sam*. There were sightings in London, and as far away as the Bronx, New York people cried wolf.

The night Maria wore the bird suit and made it safely home to her mother, they phoned the police, who set out on a manhunt with their torches and their blood hounds under the light of the full moon. But it turned out to be nothing but a wild goose chase as they circled around after their own tails and barked up the wrong trees. One of the dogs did pick up a scent in the woods, and they followed the trail for about a mile, tracking it to the end where they found only a wolf's den—an empty one at that. Signore Volpino had disappeared underground, and would no doubt one day resurface, assuming a new identity somewhere in the Bahamas where he might reinvent himself, taking up most likely where he'd left off on another trip down the aisle with a pink-dyed carnation stuck inside his label, his furry tail itching to free itself from beneath the coat flaps of his rented tux.

* * *

Raise high the roof beam carpenters. Like Ares comes the bridegroom, taller far than a tall man.

—Sapho
— J.D. Salinger, *Raise High the Roofbeam, Carpenters* and *Seymour: An Introduction*

The bridal party, and guests of Maria and Joseph's wedding, lit on the tables in the meadow like white moths and pretty painted butterflies carried on the wind with the sound of the church bells, blowing sunlight, and clouds with silvery linings. Her great aunt, Zia Trinitá, slept soundly through the whole affair and through the next nine years of the couple's marriage while they prayed and waited and all but gave up hope of ever having a child until they were finally blessed with a beautiful infant daughter. It was at this long-awaited child's naming day that she resurfaced. They were never quite sure how she picked that particular day, August 1, to rear her ugly head.

Following the ceremony there was a fine feast with food, wine, and music. When it grew dark, bonfires blazed in the fields. Everyone for miles around was invited to come: family, friends, the parish priest, and the baby's godmothers—Rosa, and Joseph's sister, Dorotea (A.K.A. Arcangela, who had not yet taken the veil). Everyone that is, except Zia Trinitá who hadn't been seen in ages, and was all but forgotten. Well, she showed up anyway (uninvited, just as the guests were about to sit down to eat) and was more than a little ticked off at having been dissed. She made quite an impression—what with the shock of seeing her after all those years and appearing all decked out in black and apple green. She was remarkably well preserved; a little pinched, but other than that she hadn't aged a day.

Maria couldn't apologize enough or do more to welcome her aunt. They made a big to-do rearranging everyone to make room for her at the table. They poured her a goblet of wine and put together a place setting complete with gold charger, fancy dish, and dinnerware—but try as they might, they couldn't dig up an extra knife. Trinitá, imaging that this was just some other kind of slight, bitched and complained under her breath, as she bit down on the pink, sugar-coated Jordan Almonds.

When the last of the guests had added their money to the already bulging white satin *boosta* bag and collected their *bonboniere*—confetti wrapped and tied in pink tulle and ribbon with the baby's name, Lea Battista, and the date—1 *Augusto* 1934—Trinitá, who had barely spoken a word to anyone all night, got up from her chair, and crossing the room slowly, she made her way over to the innocent baby's bassinette. The air was so thick you could have cut it with a knife like the layers of christening rum cake. You could hear the tension: the sound of someone at the end of their rope, a boat straining at its moorings, the tightening of a saddle, a groan, a broken vacuum cleaner belt and the burning smell of rubber. Everyone held their breath as she bent over the sleeping baby and secretively whispered some terrible prophecy in her ear.

"Dream on, Dearie," she hissed through her teeth. "The Cannibal Queen is firing up her cookpot, and a kiss with the patience of a sinister spindle has been gathering itself in the dark for a hundred years. *"Arrivederci!"* she waved as she headed for the door and the company breathed an audible sigh of relief, all except Rosa who had the power to see what others could not, and shuddered inwardly at the sight of the rosy piece of fruit plopped atop the white crocheted wool of the christening blanket Trinitá had spun like fate through trembling fingers, and understood how all through those cataleptic years, she had been polishing up that poison apple heart. The gift tag read "Let the fairest have it!"

Since the godmothers had been waiting for just the right moment to give their gifts, both Rosa and Dorotea agreed that now was the time to give the baby their presents and bestow their blessings. They hoped to prevent the party from ending up on a sour note, and to try to dispel the breath of spoiled fruit that Trinitá had left in her wake. Tainted ribbons fluttered. Roses bloomed wild: their suckers spreading like forest fire. Thick, tangled canes with salient thorns formed an impenetrable wall. Pink flowers opened in the night like a profusion of stars, their musky fragrance mingling with the smoke of charred spindles heaped onto bonfires. Suddenly everyone was drowsy and couldn't wait to get home to sleep in their own beds.

"Rubbish," Rosa wanted to say to Trinitá. "You have no power here. Be gone, before someone drops a house on you too," just like Glinda warning the Wicked Witch of the West with a seemingly effortless, mechanical sweep of her magic wand for effect. But that would have been sheer bravado. Clearly, they were in big trouble, considering the fact that Trinitá's mother had had the ability to murder someone with just some well-aimed spit or a sideways glance. The power of words spoken by someone who knew how to use them could weave a spell—like the one Trinitá just leveled— that could take lifetimes to play itself out. *Absit. Omen.*

But as the years went by and Lea grew from that baby girl of sugar and spice variety into a young woman who was both beautiful and good, outstripping all of her family's expectations, they could almost have given up the need to know what evil Trinitá had dreamed up for her all those years ago.

A quiet child, and cautious, Lea survived the early years with just one stitch. She proved to be so careful they could trust her to collect chicken eggs without dropping a single one and to safely keep a silk moth pouch sewn inside her undershirt. She never went in water over her head or wandered off far enough to cause anyones alarm. She kept strictly to the paths she knew, woodland rides, picking flowers and berries only at the margins of the forest. If the thought ever occurred to her to venture out into the woods alone, she never did act on it, stopped in her tracks by one of a million proverbs such as "*Il lupo perde il pelo, ma non il vizio*, The wolf changes his skin, but not his habits," in the voices of her mother and grandmother warning her away from the company of wolves.

In winter, she wore either a white *cappucio*, or a red riding hood, and in summer, a straw hat shaded her face, protecting her perfect skin from the damaging rays of the sun. She washed with the milk and honey soap Rosa made her. Without complaint, she allowed her mother to brush out the long thick ropes of her hair and replait it again each morning, careful not to stare too long at her own reflection in the mirror (or else, they warned, she'd see the Devil), and not to make funny faces (which she was continually reminded, might incite angels to fly overhead and make a little girl stay stuck that way forever).

She was a mother duck to Lavinia and then to Gabriele who toddled after her as soon as they were able, traipsing through the heather, and splashing around in rice paddies, plash, puddles, and fields of sugar beets on their way to play house or school. Lea, being the oldest, was always the Mamma or *la maestra*— the teacher with a long thin ruler who wrote lessons on the blackboard with squeaky new sticks of chalk, gave out papers, conducted spelling bees and graded tests. Inevitably, Gabriele would cry, unable to stand the pressure, and Lavinia misbehaved in preparation for her education at real school with nuns who she would be shocked to find had none of Lea's pretend impatience, her angelic face, or pockets filled with foil stars. Tough, but fair and lavish with praise, she gave out so many gold stars (which Lavinia and Gabriele liked to stick all over themselves) that on a really good day they glittered in the field like small constellations, or dancing on the way home in the dark, like fireflies. She routed out pretend places on made-up maps, pointing emphatically with her stick to faraway kingdoms called Kasbah, Citadella, Camelot, and the vale of Avalon.

Lea's fairy tale world became even more colorful in 1940 once she'd learned the new marching-off-to-war lingo. Imaginatively assimilating images of Wolf Cubs and goosesteps, it wasn't long before she existed in a Galapagos-type Wonderland, a Looking-Glass world filled with Looking-Glass creatures worthy of Queen Alice: one where foot soldiers ran through the wood, tripping and falling over one another until the ground was covered with little heaps of men and then their horses.

At school, air raids forced children into bomb shelters where Lea huddled with Lavinia and the others, covering her ears. She imagined fighter planes called Fiat Falcons and Kingfishers, Herons, Storks and Seagulls, Sparrowhawks, the Kangaroo and *Gobbbo Maledetto*—the Damn Hunchback bomber clamoring into the skies of war-torn Europe.

> Charley, barley, buck and rye,
> What's the way the Frenchmen fly?
> Some fly east, and some fly west,
> And some fly over the cuckoo's nest.
>
> —Anonymous

Allied planes roared over Italy like the Lion and the Unicorn fighting for the crown. Bombs fell; Lavinia cried. The White Knight and Red tumbled onto their heads as they fought over her like Alice, and Lea wondered over the rules of battle, trying to make some sense of the existential, riddling madness of Red and White Queens.

> "To the Looking-Glass world it was Alice that said
> 'I've a sceptre in hand I've a crown on my head.
> Let the Looking-Glass creatures, whatever they be
> Come and dine with the Red Queen, the White Queen, and me!"

And hundreds of voices joined in the chorus: —

"Then fill up the glasses as quick as you can,
And sprinkle the table with buttons and bran:
Put cats in the coffee, and mice in the tea—
And welcome Queen Alice with thirty-times-three!"

"'O Looking-Glass creatures,' quoth Alice, 'draw near!
'Tis an honour to see me, a favour to hear:
'Tis a privilege high to have dinner and tea
Along with the Red Queen, the White Queen, and me!' "

Then came the chorus again: —

"Then fill up the glasses with treacle and ink,
Or anything else that is pleasant to drink:
Mix sand with the cider, and wool with the wine—
And welcome Queen Alice with ninety-times-nine!"
                                —Louis Carroll, *Through the Looking Glass*

Rosa died in her sleep before Italy's final liberation in the spring of 1945 while SS units were wasting the countryside. It was April, the same month Mussolini was murdered by three soldiers— in fulfillment of the prophesy, and his body hung upsidedown from the girders of a filling station in the Piazzale Loreto, Milan. His mistress, Claretta Petacci was strung up beside him.

Clara's dress hung down exposing her undergarments, and a British commander of an armored car that drove into the square, seeing this, climbed down from his car, mounted a pair of steps which stood near and pulled up the woman's skirt fastening it round her knees with his webbing belt. The crowd howled at him but he paid no attention. The armored car drove nearer with machine guns swinging down to discourage any ambitious hooligans who might interfere.

—Alan Forrest in H.V. Morton's *A Traveler in Italy*

The very same Italians who had once gathered in crowds all over the country to hear Mussolini's speeches, crying *"Vinceremo! We will conquer!"* tore off their emblems and squashed them under their feet like bedbugs, shouting "Death to Mussolini!" Not so long before, Lea stood in a piazza among hundreds of people including schoolchildren in Fascist uniforms: in black shirts and berets, with red neckerchiefs tied around their throats. In their hands, they held out their piggy banks for their leader, the *Duce*.

"Fratelli d'Italia," his voice boomed from the balcony above, filling them up to busting with emotion—the power of his words.

"Duce! Duce!" they cheered, saluting. *"Si! Si! Si!"* All those arms like thousands of uplifted wings, a storm of blackbirds about to take flight. Startled pigeons went up like smoke. In evidence everywhere, the *fasci* insignia caught the light: "One out of many" it stood for, like a medal or a diploma: a ticking heart time bomb from a wizard in the land of *e pluribus unum*—Oz. Next stop Wonderland.

Lea's life was brimful of magic, practical and otherwise. The veil between worlds was blown bubble-thin. She could reach through with her hands, find the underleaf places where butterflies deposited their clutches of dusky rose eggs, her delicate fingers swirling the water where dripping prince-frogs surfaced to cough up the lost gold orbs of princesses at their feet. Saints trembled in the tall, marshy grass that rustled with their sweet breath: Teresa with her tumult of rose petals, storm of butterfly eggs released in mid-flight, Saint Ambrose and his bees: the air hummed, warm like honey, subdelirium, a restlessness like silk moths spinning, the Madonna's voice like the sound of heavy sheets on the line.

What could they want with a girl like me in the middle of nowhere—on the cusp of a bombed-out star? she wondered, the summer she spent on her back in the fields reading *Lady Chatterley's Lover,* pondering the city's ancient walls wedged into the vineyards, a world crawling toward the aftermath of war as she sprawled out, knees scraping the sky. Her legs, spread like angelwings opening to the warm sun, brushed against crepe paper orange and black petals. Just another poppy to the honeybees and butterflies with their compound eyes detecting motion, the patterns of flowers, the proximity of a mate; long tongues discovering the minutest traces of sugar, like love. She lay still as a dead leaf, safe from sight-hunters, highly cryptic.

The world, her mother and grandmother never failed to warn her, was a dangerous place, full of death traps, the trawlers and nets of butterfly catchers, flying arrows, cages, and poisoned bait. Rosa had done her best to keep her precious Lea safe with rituals for protection, prayers, potions, amulets and spells, red threads and tiny bells tied into her clothing, ribbons woven in her hair. Sometimes she wore so many charms that she jingled when she walked like some pagan princess. Her room was a temple where a sisterhood of saints, stuffed toys, and baby dolls were piled on her bedspread, stacked sky high in corners like totems. Relics littered bureau and bed table altars; dresser scarves and scatter rugs covered the places where white Carrara and pink Verona marble was burnt by the dripping wax of church candles and matchsticks whose smell permeated the space like the interior of a shrine, or a tomb.

If only they had known what form that crazy spinning woman's curse would take, if only it were possible to give that dread a name, a particular pathology and a face, then things would have been so much easier—as uncomplicated as the pragmatic sanction that all the spinning wheels in the kingdom should be burnt up. And though, over the years, she had used all of the powers of farseeing, intuition, and divination that she could muster, still, she missed it altogether. If Rosa had been able to predict the future accurately, she would have known for sure that unlike the enchanted princess whose peril would come to her from a splinter in some flax—in Lea's case it was not simply spindles and poison she needed to worry about—but the Prince, and that predestined, antidotal kiss.

CHAPTER EIGHT

Filhas de Santos
Daughters of the Saints

Lea tilted her head slightly and turned her neck to one side, listening like an owlet perched up in her lofty tower to the tinkling of bells. Silvery bells. A falconer's bells lifting into the high, cold air. Feathers fell around her. The sound of wings flapped overhead; mice ran off into the corners to hide as a small hawk flew in through the open window and perched as if it had always meant to do just that. Lea, wearing long stands of Renaissance jewels and the fancy old gown she'd played dress up in from as long ago as she could remember, spread it out around her like a gold cloud which trailed over ancient traces of chestnut dust on the floor littered with pledgets, owl pellets, and the bones of trapped birds. But the falcon settled itself in the trusses, studying her surroundings and looking at Lea with dark, piercing eyes, wings lifting up behind it like a cloak, seemingly undisturbed by the rustle of pure silk or restless bird souls.

She ate some berries, still surprised at having found so many—white and red berries in the snow on the edge of the winter woods. Her fingers burned from the cold when she picked them. Thorns scratched her skin, stuck like ice splinters where glaze-frost covered tangled canes and snow bolls bloomed pruinose from the insides of pericarps, shimmering like silvery pussy willow in the thin pale sunlight; frazzle. In her chest, her heart felt cold as glass. With the fringe of her white shawl pulling in the March wind, and her feet numb from standing in the snow, she picked enough to fill her basket, carrying it back with her to the tower where she popped the berries into her mouth one after another like frozen Bonbons. The icy berries made her wince as they slipped between her lips and teeth. Too hard and cold to bite, she rolled them around on her tongue until they thawed, became warm and squishy and the flesh melted away, leaving only traces of tiny seeds, like sins— bittersweet. In no time at all, she had nearly emptied the basket.

Beside her lay her broken comb and old hand mirror edged in roses. She picked them up, wiped smudges from the misted glass with her gold sleeve, clearing away clouds formed from her smoky breath breathed into the tower's chill air, and saw, reflected back from the cracked, peeling silvering, a fairy tale girl—desperately beautiful. She had Lea's raven hair, translucent skin over which a blush spread, staining the alabaster apples of her cheeks, pouty, berry-stained pillow lips, and big, dreamy bedroom eyes. She could see snow falling through the window behind her and caught sight of a boy about her age with coal black hair complete with a kiss curl, and a *scarlatto* shirt (something gold glinted like miniature streaks of lightening, incandescent, the burst of a flashbulb going off in daylight, scent of burning, melted filament) thrashing his way towards the tower. It was her sister Lavinia's new "boyfriend" battling the thick rose hedge, wielding a rather large stick like Lancelot's sword.

Her dilated pupils made her look as if she were in a trance: the eyes of an acid-queen, a dreamer focused on some illusory thing (a fairy spindle, a colored thread, a comb, a poisoned apple), an imagined kingdom, at once beautiful and terrifying. She'd never been there before, but still, she was familiar with how the sunlight spilled like gold onto the stonewashed floor. She knew the shadows and every door to every room except for the forgotten one where the old spinning woman waited in the dark. Her whole life she had been moving toward that inevitable wound, enchanted sleep, storybook prince: searching out the castle, the witch, the point of the spindle. Suddenly Lea felt impossibly tired; the air filled with the scent of almonds; her heart beat the slow, hypnotic pulse of a butterfly that had eaten too many spoiled berries, and she wound herself into an embowered sleep where dreams were spun like flax around the promise of a kiss.

Antonio Carabello bit his bottom lip until it bled. He was out hunting with his hawk, flushing the field of brown grass, bushes, and thick briers when a gust of west wind whipped under its wings and lifted it into the air like a small black kite. Squinting into the blowing snow, he searched the sky for the sight of wings, held up his leather-gloved fist. I must be dreaming, he thought when he saw the falcon fly into the window of the tower he hadn't even noticed until then, hidden as it was by the fog, a tangle of wild vines, storks' nests. It reminded him of the *castelo* in Praia do Forte. That ruined castle, overgrown with wild grasses and weeds and the nests of *tuiuiú*, jabirú storks, tumbled down amidst palm trees and a view of the blue-green sea—an image surreal as a tropical Macbeth. There's a castle—

> There's a pasture in the countryside I used to call my own
> There's a natural pillow for my head, the grass there's overgrown
> I think of that place from time to time when I want to be alone

It's been a long way from anywhere
Like Heaven to your town, this town
— James Taylor, "Anywhere like Heaven"

An air of make-believe pervaded the place and in the impenetrable silence, a strange feeling like longing crept over him as he struck with his stick at the great twisted branches interwoven with brier, thick honeysuckle, and thorny eglantine, following his heart as if he were part of a spell.

The Carabellos had once lived here for centuries. That would account for the strong affinity he felt for a country in which he had only planned to spend a few months, he thought. That, and the fact that his father had described Sabbioneta so many times over the years. Antonio could easily picture the setting with its silk farm, gold fields, city shaped like a star, the *campo santo* with the heavy iron gate and the tomb of a sixteen-year-old girl. His father must have told them the story hundreds of times—how that beautiful young girl was murdered by her own father to keep her from marrying a boy he disapproved of, and how he, Amadeo, then not yet seventeen himself, ran off to fight in the war, how he never could get the image of that churchyard out of his head, how at night he dreamed of ghost moths, and how when it was over, he didn't return home at all as was expected, but left instead for Genoa where he hopped on board the first steamer leaving for South America.

* * *

Subcontinents drifted, iceflows slid into melty seas where sirens wailed a spellbinding lament, their liquid voices lolling sailors who, like Odysseus, stopped up their ears with wax, lashed their bodies to the masts to keep from flinging themselves over the sides of their ships toward that fatal embrace. Harpies hovered: caretakers of souls, featherbreasted women with wings and itty-bitty birdy feet to carry off the bodies of the dead. Mermaids sunbathed on the rocks, kelp drying in their flowing hair like flowers, the tide lapping at their fishy tails, bare arms, naked breasts, salty skin, pooling in the hollows of their slick bellies—and the Fata Morgana—that old sea witch—still rose like a mirage out of the fog in the Straits of Messina.

Such storms were encountered off the coast of Brazil, Amadeo could swear that all of the witches in the world had raised the tempest by dumping the contents of their cauldrons into the sea, and then they must have thrown their hair in for good measure. He countered them with the sign of the cross and clung on to his St. Christopher's medal for dear life, but it soon became obvious that every *tempestarii* that ever existed conspired to see him sunk, and inevitably he was—shipwrecked on a reef near Salvador da Bahia de Todos os Santos, washed up in the Largo de Sant'Ana.

It happened to be on February 2, one of the most important nights of the year for the *Candomblistas* of Bahia celebrating the *Festa de Iemanj*á, *Mãe e Rainha das Águas,* Mother and Queen of the Sea and of all o*rixás* (gods and goddesses). In Rio de Janeiro, they celebrated on January 1, millions of Brazilians gathering on the beach to bring in the New Year, and in coastal towns and cities all over the country people paid homage to Our Lady of the Waters. Followers kept icons of Iemanjá (dolls dressed in robes the blue and white colors of the goddess, ceramic mermaids, and/or plaster figurines of the Virgin Mary) on their home altars. In veneration of her feast day, pilgrims, dressed in white, carried statues into the street and walked in an imposing procession to the sea. Devotees threw gifts of jewelry, perfume, mirrors, and fruit into the waves.

They whispered their prayers to flowers, which were sent out on little boats, asking for her guidance and protection, praying for good luck, good health, good fishing. Hundreds of stems and lit candles were stuck in the sand: votive offerings from talc-y beaches sprinkled with sea foam and champagne.

Baranhas, Bahian women, wearing traditional dresses and turbans of white wrapped around their hair, waded into the ocean as the sun set. The *mãe de santos,* mother of the saints, the high priestess, lighted candles and initiated *filhas de santos,* or *abian*—daughters of the saints, priestesses who, in a rite of purification, had their heads immersed in the water and were ordained.

At midnight, they launched a small fleet. Everyone watched as the painted boats decorated with flowers, candles, and figurines of saints were pushed out to sea, and waited for the goddess to manifest her powers. If all the boats were overturned, it was a sign that she had heard their prayers, accepted their offerings, and promised good things for another new year, which they brought in with singing and dancing and drumming until dawn. They drank champagne and ate watermelon in her honor. The *mãe de santos* blew cigar smoke in the faces of anyone requiring her blessing: displays of fireworks exploded in the sky, cinders and ash and pieces of light fell into the sea like stars.

In the Largo de Sant'Ana, pale blue and white flowers floated out onto the bay for Iemanjá. Rosalinda Álvarez waded in with her own bouquet as the water lapped at the flouncy hem of her skirt, wet her white underpants (which always had to be new for feast days and New Year's Eve; this pair with red embroidered hearts for luck), and the fringe of the shawl her mother had bought for her along with the sweets from the market in Marachal Deodoro—Rosalinda remembered—the stalls with handmade laces for sale, amulets, animal teeth, a plethora of potions, hundreds of small glass bottles of perfume dangling from cords clinked together as they caught the light. There were candles in shapes of human figures and skulls, and the sight of dead snakes in jars made her stick close to her mother as they passed them on their way to the stall with the *figurinhas* art. Among the ceramic saints and *orixás*, Rosalinda's mother found the loveliest clay figure of Iemanjá holding her mirror: with bare breasts, flowing hair, long flippy tail—a beautiful mermaid. She pinched open her small purse and fished out the coins one by one, and after overseeing that the fragile piece, which would become one of her favorite things, carefully wrapped and tied with string she placed it gingerly in her sack. Rosalinda clung tightly to her mother's arm as a passing stranger brushed by and she felt the clamminess of his sleeve, not so much afraid of thieves or thugs as aware that mercreatures liked to walk on land, especially on market and fair days, and were easily spotted because they dressed like peasants and the left sides of their coats were always soak and wet.

Slowly, they wound their way through the wealth of junk and treasure in the *feira do troca-troca*. *Carrancas*, carved figureheads posed for effect among pots, leather handbags, and straw baskets to the hype of the Brazilian rag merchants, *sulanqueiros* selling their scraps of clothing and the rhythm of the *Zabumba* drum bands accompanied by the *pífanos*, vertical flutes. Stopping to buy sweets they listened to the singers and street poets perform the *literatura de cordel*, literature of string, popular writing sold in little pamphlets, politics and plays hung from fair stalls like the handmade laces and bottles of honey-colored perfume, poems and miracles fluttering in the warm tropical breeze. In Rosalinda's memory, the air smelled like sugar and coconut milk.

At the lacemaker's house, the sun filtered through fine Renaissance lace cloths strung out on long clotheslines: slices of filé clouds, sheer veils, translucent sheets of sky: light. Lacemaking, she had learned, was brought to Brazil by the Portuguese women from the islands of Madeira and the Azores, who settled on the northeast coast, and on the island of Santa Caterina in the south. Their husbands, fathers, and brothers were the fishermen who made the nets the women decorated with delicate flower patterns and geometric designs. "Where there's fishing, there's lace," she recalled, while her thoughts became entangled with the delicate webs of a trousseau tablecloth and the white filé lace shawl her mother held up to Rosalinda's lovely copper-colored skin.

It was a place of miraculous transformations. As the sun set the world was alchemically altered: sea, sky, and sand turned to silver, and fishermen became the silhouettes of angels casting their wide nets into the air. They pulled wisps of cirrus out dripping from the liquid sky onto the sand and hauled them back home. Black angels—arms brimful with heavy white clouds: cumulus amassed on a stick carried like a catch shouldered by two hunters, or, dragged behind them, the sodden nets trailing like water-laden nimbus.

* * *

The ruffles of Rosalinda's dress, the fringe of her shawl, and long loosed ropes of her hair floated up around her momentarily in waves, Medusalike. Her white cotton shift sank down and wrapped around her legs, trapping tiny sea creatures: glowing shrimp, shells, particles of sand, sparks. Iridescent fish darted between her thighs awash with the cold light of brittle stars; luminous jellyfish clung; mollusks emitted luminescent clouds. All around her the sea foam bubbled, effervescent. She pulled strands of seaweed from the long tangle of her hair and picked a shell out from between her toes—a small smooth shell—the kind the *mãe de santo* told fortunes with at the *Jugo de Búzios,* Casting of Shells. In the *terreiro* or *casa-de-santo*, sixteen white seashells were cast onto a white towel spilling the secrets of saints, intentions of the gods. That the goddess of the waters was the girl's own *orixá* was clearly written in the stars, the *mae pequena* had said. The sea gleamed in the blue-green light of Rosalinda's eyes. It was evident from the whirls of her fingertips, pearly pink crescents of her nails, lovely arms, long legs, and sleek brown feet right down to ten perfect toes where her fishy tail might've been: water baby, beach bunny, Gidget. She looked like the billboard ad for Johnson's Baby Oil, or Coppertone: a girl just emerging from the waves, trailing a towel, surfboard, and seaweed, surrounded by sea foam and by the scent of roses. Her life force was governed by the ebb and flow of tides, the pull of the moon. Iemanjá, who attended from the day she was born, would watch over her throughout her life—a protectoress, patron saint, a queen of saints like the Virgin Mary pictured on prayer cards—pale blue cloud, halo of stars, constellations.

As for her future, the face-up and face-down configuration of seashells, with smooth edges filed so that the serrated sides appeared to reveal the teeth in these miniature mouthpieces of the *orixá*, told the *mae* that in Rosalinda's life there would be miracles. "Miracles," she had said, as Rosalinda looked back into the dark brown in white white of the priestess' eyes— "Miracles and ordinary things."

* * *

Rosalinda turned the smooth shell repeatedly in the palm of her hand, put the little mouth to her ear and listened. She heard the voice of the sea trapped there like a genie in a magic lamp, message in a bottle. The voices of the crowd became increasingly distant as she swished around, drifted further, without realizing it, down the beach from the singing, her attention caught by the firelight on the boats, reflections of candles, small mirrors floating by on the bay. The plankton, which in the daytime tinted the surface of the water pink, glowed weirdly at night, millions of them lighting up, just then, as something—a ship, a fish, a manatee, peixe-*boi* (cowfish) maybe—something made a wake, churning up water like a child on a Styrofoam kickboard. She spotted a fin, a tail, a mermaid making waves, "*Nossa!*" It was *Iemanjá* rising out of the sea, and clinging for dear life to the goddess' flanks was a man.

"*Aiuto! Aiutomi!*" he called.

"*Socorro!*" she called. Cries for help attracting the attention of the crowd which reacted pretty much as if they were in the scene from *Jaws* when someone sees fins circling, yells, "Shark!" People were panic-stricken, screamed, ran out of the water pal mal, or off in the general direction of Rosalinda who, in the meantime, did the first thing she could think to do under the circumstances—she tossed out a rope of her hair.

> Can't you feel 'em closin' in, honey?
> Can't you feel 'em schoolin' around?
> You got fins to the left, fins to the right
> And you're the only bait in town
> —Jimmy Buffett, "Fins"

Although having a man wash up in their bay, albeit on the back of a goddess, drew quite a crowd (was treated as nothing more than a curiosity by some, terrified others, and was hailed as a miracle by many, if not most, of the pilgrims who witnessed it), historically, it was not unprecedented. The Brazilian waters were filled with the flotsam and jetsam of European flotilla following in the wake of Amerigo Vespucci, the Italian navigator who sailed into the Baía de Todos os Santos on November 1, 1501, and christened it the Day of All Saints. Rosalinda herself descended from the Portuguese, Diego Álvarez, the sole survivor of a ship headed for the West Indies wrecked on a reef near Salvador in 1510. *Caramuru* or "Fish Man," as Álvarez was called by the Indians of Rio Vermelho who saved him, lived twenty years among the Tupinambá and married Catarina do Paraguaçu, the daughter of the most powerful chief.

The first night after his ship went down, Amadeo clung tenaciously to its splinters, to hope and to sleep. It was not until he awoke the following morning that he realized he was adrift at sea, buoyed up by a mermaid, carved figurehead, seawoman! *"Maria di Legno,"* he laughed aloud, recalling the fairy tale in which the Princess successfully escapes from her father by walking over the waves wearing a dress made of wood. Never having seen the fantastic figures created for carnival in Brazil, Amadeo had no way of knowing that his "Wooden Girl" was no angel, ship's *carrancas* or the saint from a church, but a giant mermaid, a symbolic representation of Iemanja from a parade float. But just then, he wasn't making any fine distinctions. Mermaid, goddess, blow-up doll, *Madonnina*, saint! *Che mene frego*! What the . . . do I care! He hopped on board her back, threw his arms around her neck, wrapped his legs around her flanks, and planted a big, wet, salty kiss on the top of her beautiful head, trembling uncontrollably.

Who knew how long he drifted, floating and dreaming of land? "Until I saw the lights," is how Antonio's father always told it. "And I took hold of a tow rope thrown out to me, which was your mother's hair, soft as silk, strong as hemp, and pulled myself in."

"He was more dead than alive," his mother liked to add without any attempt to conceal her conceit for having saved him, for all of that hair, every last strand of which she still retained, wound around and around and around in her white bandana.

And it was the color of sky in Rosalinda's eyes—of sea, of butterflies, it was the iridescent blue of morpho wings he pulled himself toward, into, out of: falling, he'd say, more deeply, he believed, than any man had ever fallen before, or flown.

Inevitably, at the end of the story of how he was shipwrecked and saved, Amadeo would tell how he was swept from the sea with no more than a pocketful of drowned silkmoth eggs and the dream of starting a silkworm farm in Brazil, where he met and married Rosalinda Álvarez, the beautiful daughter of a wealthy butterfly farmer. "Dreams do come true," he never forgot to add, ever after.

Rosalinda and Amadeo remained passionately devoted to one another and to the goddess whose miraculous intervention had literally brought them together and without which, Amadeo, they were certain, would surely be dead. As soon as they were married, they built a *barraca* to house the statue and placed her on a high altar, but the cult of the Wooden Madonna spread faster than you can say "jungles burning," and so many people came from everywhere to worship at the tiny hut that it was always near to bursting, endlessly necessitating the creation of bigger and better sanctuaries. So eventually, a basilica was built around her with beautiful floors of *azulejos*, the blue Portuguese tiles set by Amadeo himself, and a wall so full of silver and gold votive offerings that not even a fricative *f* could escape from the tight spaces between them because of all the miracles that followed.

As to her provenance, according to popular accounts, the image had been stolen from the carnival parade two years earlier, sambaed off and then abandoned by the revelers, a band of men dressed like Bahian women drinking *pinga* and playing merry hell. She was then hauled away by street children who, while weighing the market value of mermaid flesh pound for pound, were spooked by some weird noises and ditched her on the steps of the nearest church, where she would likely have amazed the poor woman who swept the steps in the morning if it weren't for the fact that a strong wind had come up suddenly in the night and lifted her far off into the hills of Bom Jesus. For a long time, she was lost in the jungle and forgotten, until some barefoot hippies happened upon her— high as kites. They were five Americans, just kids (four guys and a girl) who had met up in Arembepe Beach and were hanging out together stringing beads and braiding their hair—stringing beads in their hair: they played guitar and sang (the girl, it was said, had the voice of an angel, wings hitting air). When they left, they carried the image out of the jungle with them and were on their way back to civilization, maybe even returning to the States, when their boat was lost and so was the icon. Somewhere between Ipanema and the crowded curve of Copacabana Beach, she tumbled into the waves and didn't resurface again until she turned up afloat in "Salvador da Bahia de Todos os Santos, in the neighborhood of

> Largo de Sant'Ana, where Yemanjá, Our Lady of the Waters, dwells."
> —Jorge Amado, *Dona Flor and Her Two Husbands*

> *La niña de madera no llegó caminando:*
> *allí de pronto sentada en los ladrillos,*

viejas flores del mar cubrían su cabeza,
su mirada tenía tristeza de raíces.

Allí quedó mirando nuestras vidas abiertas,
el ir y ser y andar y volver por la tierra,
el día destiñiendo sus pétalos graduales.
Vigilaba sin vernos la nina de madera.

La niña coronada por las antiguas olas,
allí miraba con sus ojos derrotados:
sabía que viviamos en una red remota

de tiempo y agua y olas y sonidos y lluvia,
sin saber si existimos o si somos su sueño.
Ésta es la historia de la historia de la muchacha de
madera.

The wooden girl did not arrive on foot.
She was suddenly there, resting on the tiles.
Ancient sea blooms covered up her head.
Her gaze had all the sadness of roots.

There she stayed, looking out on our lives,
our comings and goings, our crossings on the earth,
and the day slowly shedding all its petals.
She watched over us, unseeing, the wooden girl.

Maiden garlanded by ancient waves,
there she would watch us with her ruined eyes,
aware we were living in a far-off web

of time and waves and water, sounds and rain,
not knowing if we were real or if she dreamed us . . .
—Pablo Neruda, "The Wooden Girl"
from *Absence and Presence*—Translated by Allistair Reid

* * *

An intense fog, characteristic of the marshes in winter, had engulfed the "castle" tower that morning. Antonio could almost swear that Hero (the falcon last seen flying through the brush) had been swallowed whole before he heard the sound of bells, spotted the tips of pointed wings as the bird zoomed in through the window. Some other guy might have been daunted by the challenge of penetrating that protective cover; the ancient hedge of wild roses formed a virtual wall with monstrous canes and thorns so grotesque they could easily have sliced a man's flesh to ribbons, but not Antonio, who approached it like a champion in Nintendo, a knight-errant in a game of questing gods.

Inside the tower, where the girl lay sleeping, pale, and still as death, it was quiet as a tomb, and just as cold. Antonio beat his hands against his arms to warm himself while his eyes slowly adjusted to the gloom and his breath provoked the candle flames flickering in the chill and fog that crept in all around, frothy white, and in the effete sunlight, straw-colored like champagne. Something bubbled. There was a yeastiness in the air, the smell of fruit esters, and he was overwhelmed by the heady scent of old roses, oleander and plum, apricots, hints of wormwood and wood smoke, of toast both buttered and burnt, dark things in a ferment, familiar yet unidentifiable. Something wicked spinning itself in the dark crepitated, unraveling.

He reeled toward a nearly imperceptible jingle like broken glass, a soft sweep of feathers across his cheek; the sound of blowing snow; silk. The air stirred with the movement of wings as Hero returned to his leather-gloved fist. Antonio fettered her, slipped a small black hood over the bird's head, then saw the sleeping girl and trembled: touched by the impossible beauty of what (this lover's game, dream date) he believed she was capable of scaring up. "Lavinia?" he called completely in the dark, unaware that it was Lea, that he whispered seductively, irresistibly to illusions. "*Bellissima*," he sighed to the conjurer of shades of mauve and gold, a mirror image, trick he was drawn to—the long shadows of lashes on her cheek, her complexion like moonstone, the dark ravel of her hair, the dangerous proclivity of her mouth—rose red; a magical color tempting as maraschino cherries—a bite of something poisonous.

> Romeo and Juliet
> Are together in eternity . . .
>
> Like Romeo and Juliet . . .
> We can be like they are
> Come on baby . . . don't fear the reaper
> Baby take my hand . . . don't fear the reaper
> We'll be able to fly . . . don't fear the reaper
> Baby I'm your man.
> —Blue Oyster Cult, "(Don't Fear) The Reaper"

* * *

Lea was late. When the moon rose and fell and rose and fell again without a speck of blood in sight, first she took the Fifth, and then she gave it up—if only half-heartedly. Was she just being evasive they wondered. Artfully cryptic? Or was it simply a case of mistaken identity? Was she triable? Accused of impersonating her sister, in her own defense, Lea argued she hadn't set out to deceive. She admitted that when Antonio called out to Lavinia (as he said he had, swearing up and down. "*Ti giuro!*" he repeated over and over and over again), she had simply been unresponsive. In answer to her sister's fervid "How could she?" Lea's reply was a dim "I don't know."

"*No lo so,*" she sighed.

"*Bugiarda*! You big fat liar!" Lavinia cried, believing she might die of a broken heart; drink hemlock. Wouldn't they be sorry to see her dead? she mused with a drama queen's flair, imagining their pitiless grief and mentally arranging her lovely corpse like a dress-up doll a lá Snow White, Evita, Judy Garland encased in glass until she got bored of lying there beautiful but lifeless and so envisioning a less passive role for herself, she inspirited new scenes of spite, all with a "Just you wait!" kind of a theme. For the most satisfying scenario, she had now developed mental shorthand—she was the queen (cruel or beneficent, depending on her whim) in the one she liked best which began with her sister clapped in the bloody tower, standing before her for sentencing, or sometimes with her head (Blindfold? Or no?) already on the chopping block, the black-hooded *boia*, the blade of his executioner's ax glinting above the prisoner's scrawny little neck while all the people in all the kingdoms in *all the mornings of the world* held their collective breath.

Joseph would kill her if he found out, Maria thought, seriously entertaining the possibility herself before remembering that women who slept in glass houses shouldn't throw stones, or more to the point (in her case), women who cast spells—she quibbled, giving her head a shake, impatient with this bent of hers for mixing up metaphors with recriminations at a time like this when so much needed to be done and pronto. So, gathering her wits about her, and taking the few spare lira she had stashed away in an underwear drawer with the corsets and brassieres she couldn't stand to wear, off she flew like the wind to a chapel in the countryside where she succeeded in having the banns read so fast that it made all of their heads spin.

Silk was special-ordered from Mantua. Yards of ice-blue silk for Lea, lengths of steel blue, and electric blue for Lavinia, cobalt, sheer and whispery as butterfly wings, the azure of sky, powder blue, or baby blue for bridesmaids, robin's egg for flower girls, and the palest duck shell green crêpe de chine for Maria. Bolts of bridal white tulle and wedding veil, which arrived like chrysalis, upright mummies delicately unwound from sheaths of papyrus, crinkly tissue, wafer-thin as the covering on Torrone candy, whiter than the shells of confetti they uncased with strands of crystal beads and glass tubes filled with tiny seed pearls, dragées, cards of chantilly lace, buttons, and eyehooks, and spools of silvery threads.

Maria, tape measure draped around her neck like a noose, peered over the rims of the glasses pushed down toward the tip of her nose for weeks. Lack of sleep made her face white as dressmaker's chalk, puffy as a pin cushion, prickly as a porcupine, and they soon grew used to her talking with a mouth stuffed with pins like quills; she clicked like a thimble and snapped answers with her scissors at the air as if it were full of loose threads.

While everyone else in the house slept, Maria never let up on the pedal: completely focused on the task at hand—sewing machine, spinning wheel, spinning nettles. She leaned into the light of the small bulb that cast its halo on the top of her head, made a pool of the silk puddled on the floor like moonlight on a frozen lake, skillfully maneuvering the fabric beneath the needle, nailing a perfectly straight seam with the precision of a skater tracing over the ice: endless distances swept in her wake as icy silk pushed through metal teeth like blades—sparked. Shavings sprayed up in the dark—blown glass threads, pinked frostwork, snapped-off scraps of snowflakes, frozen bits of lace. Maria stood up, brushed herself off and shook out her arms like the Snow Queen spilling snow from her sleeves: Mother Holle shaking out her mattress. Flurries, turning from feathers into skeins of geese as they fell, settled on the frozen lake like a warm blanket of snow.

Lea helped with the finishing work: lace trim, eyehooks, appliqués, and buttons all the way down the back. She did most of the hand beading on her own gown, sewing on thousands of Austrian crystals, beads, sequins, dragées, and seed pearls by hand. That dress— heavy as chain mail; white armor. Pins and needles, needles and pins sharp-pointed and fine flashed in the air, cast nearly invisible stitches with glistening threads. Predictably, one pricked her finger like a thorn. Three drops of red blood fell onto the dress, sprinkled the snow-white silk stained now like wedding sheets from long ago, bloody linens flown from out of balconies and windows, or strung up on windy clotheslines like sanctimonious flags. Inklings of blood, reminiscent of lost butterfly islands, of bleeding hearts, of hearts that fluttered, or buds tightly clenched, of cherry pits, wild strawberries, plums, windfall, or the dropped petals of blousy roses, bloomed. *Nel tempo quando Berta spilava* . . . Once upon a time . . . wedding sheets blew in the windy sunlight emblazoned with small pink stains, a coat-of-arms like gilded Madonna lilies on the pure white standard of a saint, unfurled. Lea dozed off; the work dropped into her lap.

When at last the dresses were done, the girls were fitted and turned round and round like so many jewelry box ballerinas until

Maria couldn't see straight enough to thread another eye, her back ached and she found it next to impossible to get up off her knees. "I wish that your grandmother were here to see you," she sighed, becoming uncharacteristically maudlin; tears welling up at the sight of their images reflected back from the full-length mirror like sugarplum fairies in a dream of the "Nutcracker Suite." Lavinia, looking every inch as beautiful as the bride-to-be, but feeling mean as an ugly stepsister, groaned, while the lovely Princess Lea waltzed around like Cinderella herself to the wedding song the bride and groom would dance to.

Fly me to the moon la la la la la la la la

La la la la la la la la la la la la la!
In other words
La la laaaaaaa

In other words
Baby, kiss me
                              —Frank Sinatra, "Fly Me To The Moon"

And the other shoe dropped! Left with no alternative but to indulge in her new favorite pastime, Lavinia invented clever and ever more satisfying scenes of torture and recompense. In a highly polished Dr. Zhivago-like daydream, she is a beautiful, romantic, impassioned peasant-girl on the side of the Russian Revolution. Poof! Poor Lea is turned into Princess Anastasia and banished to Siberia. "What now my love? La la la la la la," she hummed, while slipping slender gold-embossed ribbons (Lea and Antonio, 24 *Giunio*, 1955) and miniature plastic doves around clutches of white rice and confetti in snow-white tulle. In the distance, wolves howled.

Invitations were sealed with honey-mustard colored wax, marked with a B, and posted. Trays of cookies arrived from Zia Monica or "Auntie Nun" as they were in the habit of calling Dorotea, the Abbess Arcangela, by way of Father Rosario with her regrets and gifts of tatty—*chiachierino* lace from all of the cloistered sisters at the convent in Palma with their prayers, *in absentia*.

The reigning Maid of Honor tied a red bandanna around her forehead and took to her bed with a vengeance, while the bride's other attendants were busy planning Lea's wedding shower, making no effort to tiptoe around Lavinia as they deviled eggs and floated a frozen fruit ring—pleased as raspberry sherbet punch to be meeting, shopping, and deliberating over important decisions regarding cream puffs, canapés, the corsage (orchid, camellia, carnation, rose? Regular or wrist?), and the appropriateness of gag gifts such as edible underwear and inflatable zebras. The shower was a huge success. They managed to totally waylay the bride-to-be who was so tickled pink they could have knocked her over with a feather even before she got just as pickled as everyone else due to the disproportionately large quantities of Spumante continually being poured into the punch bowl. Subsequently, all pretenses at being ladylike were dropped; decorum flew right out the window as Maria (who was in rare form) told a whole slew of dirty jokes, all of which featured figs and/or donkeys and had them laughing hysterically like a bunch of hyenas. Upstairs in her room, Lavinia screamed, covering her face with her pillow.

Lea's lovely head, on the other hand, was crowned with a paper plate halo for a hat onto which all the trimmings from her shower of gifts were attached: an Easter bonnet, rain hat gone mad, a regular riot of ribbons and bows raised high as the tiers of her wedding cake. Surrounded by her presents, she sat on the carpet with legs splayed, spaghetti straps slipping from her shoulders.

In a fair imitation of a Mona Lisa smile, Lea looked out from behind the pastel veil of streamers curling around her face like the aurora borealis; two crepe paper Pentecostal doves alight in the palms of her hands as she smiled for the camera. Posed on the faded floral Aubousson, she was an Arabian princess on the edge of the magic carpet, a May, Homecoming, or Rose Bowl Queen: an American Beauty blooming wild. A feathered Brazilian priestess high atop a Carnival float, a Madonna, a saint, a little bride doll for parades, feast day processions.

The days slowly stretched toward solstice, Saint John's Eve, the longest day of the year, just cause to celebrate the death of winter, the victory of light over darkness, warm over cold, good over evil, and life over death; in modern day Sabbioneta, one thousand nine hundred and fifty-five years after the crucifixion of Christ, it was the feast day of the Baptist, Saint John the Beheaded, which happened to fall, by chance, on the same day as the *fiera*, or annual church picnic. Following ten o'clock mass, the priest led a procession to the firelighting ceremony. With prayers and incantations, he kindled the first fire and then it was time for the festivities, and on with the show. This was it—

In a fallow field over which wildflowers (especially poppies in scarlet and gold) and weeds had had sovereignty for centuries, on Midsummer Night's Eve a play was enacted, a very old pantomime, the ancient tale of the Sleeping Beauty, with a twist, as it was not the Principessa but the Principe D'Azzurro, or the Blue Prince as Charming was called in Italy, pretending to be asleep, the one who will never awaken without a kiss.

Little girls sat in clusters, sacrificing wildflowers to wreaths and daisy chains, or using them as magical props in their fortune-telling games. "This year? Next year? Sometime? Never? He loves me? He loves me not?" they asked, plucking the petals of ox-eye daisies one by one. They tore out fistfuls of grass with their eyes closed, wild posies of daisies and Queen Anne's lace, tussie mussies of champagne and caviar dreams: the number of daisies in the bunch divining when they were to be married. And they wished like crazy on dandelion thistle—thousands of powdery puffs blown into the wind that played with the edges of older girls' dresses like blousy magnolias, ruffling their petals as they tossed about the question of "Who will marry Roberto?" Hovering over him like a cloud of moths, the hems of their cotton shirt-waist dresses flew up, hit the air. Talc-y wings, in shades of apricot and light peach, blush, ivory, pale brimstone, clouded yellow, bath white, dappled white, and Adonis blue, sunny and damp and blowing in the field, released the scents of licorice, honey, citrus, myrrh—old roses.

A storm of powdery thistle settled on the sleeping prince. He tried not to twitch—pollen tickled his nose, he had to pee, grass pinched through his freshly pressed dress pants and starched white shirt, which was getting sweaty and wrinkled—the last detail registered only by his mother who was otherwise beaming at her boy, the light of her life having his day in the sun.

Among the weeds, Roberto lay still as death and waited, focusing on his breathing, the nearly imperceptible rise and fall of his chest. He tried to concentrate on keeping his eyes closed, his eyelids from quivering. Getting married was the furthest thing from his mind. He had had enough of having to feign death, or even sleep for that matter. Was it possible to be any more restless? he wondered. Had anyone anywhere ever been this wide-awake?

At last, one of the group came forward or was pushed; "Let me guess," he thought, believing he could tell by the cadence of their voices, the others' teasing, *her* breathy laugh—the sound of a girl with the wind up her dress.

"It's me," she announced with a whisper: Marina with her lapis lazuli eyes, her golden hair spilling across his face, lips that broke the spell with a honeyed, hypnotic kiss.

The audience clapped against the background of a ruined tower, white sails tilting.

White paper plates, party napkins, *crescentine* with *prosciuto di Parma*, salami and cheese—*parmaginano*, cakes and wine were unpacked from picnic hampers spread out on the lawn festive with summery dresses, pony rides, beribboned babies, piglets, Billy goats, little lambs, and calves about to be branded. Under a striped, orange awning were several tables with food for sale: sausages spiced with fennel, *struffoli* (golden dough-balls dripping with honey, sprinkled with nonpareils), *canditi* (candied fruit on a stick), *granita di caffè* and flavored ices, baskets of cherries, peaches, pears, *Brutti ma Buoni* cookies (Ugly but Good), jars of lavender *miele*, and *marmelatto*. Children nudged each other out at the table with bunnies for sale, baby chicks, and a box of FREE KITTENS beside the busy raffle booth where for a chance you could win a brand new *televisione* (RCA Victor), a set of linen sheets made by the nuns, crocheted toys, a real suit of armour, a victrola (RCA Victor), or long-playing records.

"*Non toccare! Non toccare! Non toccare la robba! Via! Basta!* Stop it! Keep your hands off the stuff. *Per l'amore di Dio!*" The grownups yelled in exasperation at the teenage girls who were all over the record albums. But they couldn't care less, being young, and apparently crazy. Wrapping their arms around the albums and closing their eyes, they laid the faces of their record idols flat against their own and kissed their cellophane wrapped-like-candy lips. Behavior which made envious, spiteful boys behave badly, and left others, like Gabriele (aspiring singer, still a soprano), starry-eyed, wannabe Sinatra, wonder what it took to make girls swoon at the sound of his voice, to try and figure out why they fainted at the very sight of him, and to picture his (Gabriele's) own perfectly handsome face (okay, so maybe his nose was classically Roman) on album jackets and the covers of teen magazines. From that day on, he became a little dark, a little mysterious. He smoked cigarettes and drank martinis. He always wore a sport jacket, his eyes were shaded by the turned-down brim of a hat, and he never ever missed an opportunity to sing before a live audience or mirror.

In any event, it was the big prize, the grand prize donated by (Baby) Sophia Sonnino Travel-in-the-Bronx, a forty plus day cruise for two—Genoa-Naples-Gibraltar-New York, which created a virtual feeding-type frenzy.

Baby Sophia, who had spent months trying to settle on just the right one from among the six picks of transatlantic ships, and having a special knack, managed to procure a first-class cabin on board the Italian flagship Andrea Doria, a luxurious liner which (along with the Cristoforo Columbo), was one of the premiere cruise ships built after the war. Rivaling the American Constitution and the Independence, it was the fastest and grandest in the Italian merchant marine, capable of carrying four holds of cargo and three passenger classes including celebrities and movie stars the magnitude of Mr. Clark Gable and Elizabeth (it-was-touted) Taylor across the Atlantic! Italy was extremely proud of her flagship, and, rightfully, so was Baby Sophia: marketing master, travel agent extraordinaire acting as ambassadress on the ship's behalf—blowing her own horn.

And she threw in one of her very own handcrafted broomsticks for good measure.

Following the drowning death of her sister, Baby Sophia, taking a badly needed hiatus from the travel business, took a job as a reenactor (demonstrating the art of broom making) in an historical village in upstate New York. She became quite an expert, and even wrote a book on the subject, for which she earned the reputation as a leading authority. Everyone in the family, albeit the town, had at least one of those broomsticks propped up against a wall somewhere, stuck in a chimney-corner, closet, or shed, that had been sent on some occasion as a gift from Baby Sophia: that is until her head was turned by a handsome, door-to-door Fuller Brush salesman named Henry. "Excuse me Madame," he had said, and Baby Sophia, answering the bell, was unable to resist (his scent of bubble bath, sandy blond hair, his smile—teeth white and straight as Chicklets, trim, clean nails, baby blue suit) his suitcase full of brushes and combs, catalogues of bright cleaners, and bought a whole slew of new mops, shiny dustpans, and enough broomsticks to pepper the sky with witches. They got married, bought a house in the Bronx with multiple broom closets and bedrooms, baskets, cupboards, and drawers for babies, which began with the birth of the twins, Lizzie (as in "Dizzy Miss") and May. Many more followed, and they were christened— Argentina, Arosa Sky, Arosa Star, Columbia, Guadalupe, Medina Victory, Olympia, Queen Anna Maria, Santa Maria, Saturnia, Sylvania, Queen Federica, Vulcania, S.S. Italia, Margarita, Liberté, Flavia, Marianna, Oceana, Independence, Golden Moon, Andrea Doria, and America. The boys—Cristoforo Colombo, Giulo Cessere, Michelangelo, and Raffaelo. And the baby—Brittania.

Baby Sophia was busy booking passengers for her brand-new travel business by day and making babies at night. She was exhausted but happiest in the evenings when she lined up her whole fleet for their bread and bubble baths, put on their clean pajamas, combed their hair (each with their own comb), read them all stories and sent them to bed (in spring she washed all the combs with a special brush and soap and laid them out on the windowsills to dry in the sun).

Her favorite holiday was Easter. They made quite an impressive sight as Baby Sophia in her Easter bonnet, Henry in paisley tie and polyester, and all the children, including the newest arrival (in the Perego covered with mosquito netting) dressed in sailor suits and ties, paraded down the street to the church, the blue ribbons from the girls' straw hats fluttering behind them.

Her finest hour was when she took her entire family on a trip to Sabbioneta, and along with a suitcase full of souvenir tablecloths and sheets, brought her mother back to live with them in the Bronx. She only wished her father had lived long enough to see his grandchildren, and to share the comparative luxury of their new *villa*. Trinita's moving in with them exasperated the crisis of space: either they needed to move, or one of the children would have had to sleep hung up on a hook on the wall—and all, except Michelangelo, refused.

Immediately upon receipt of the letter requesting that she donate a trip for the annual church picnic, she picked a ship, booked a cruise, procured a first-class cabin, dinner seating at the captain's table, a complimentary bottle of chilled champagne, fruit basket, and Perugina chocolates for the pillows. She didn't even send her secretary, as was usual; Baby Sophia herself went down to the docks at 48th street to pick up the tickets. Though it was hard for her, she couldn't trust a mission as important as this to just anyone.

The sight of the harbor still made her sad, reminding her of Sabrina whose spirit found a voice in the sound of an ocean liner's whistle. The steamer's black funnel became the perfect symbol for loss, as were the streamers and confetti tossed from the passenger decks, falling like snow as the ship pulled away with its precious cargo of family and friends, bearing little sisters towards invisible ice sheets. If Baby Sophia had been interviewed on *Inside the Actor's Studio*, to James Lipton's question, "What sound do you love?" she would have answered, "A baby crying." And in response to "What is the sound you hate most?" she would have replied, "There is no sound in the world sadder than the blast of a ship's horn."

* * *

Chance books sold out like hotcakes; there was still a line winding out the side of the tent when megaphones made the announcement to "Let the games begin!" Competitors and spectators alike went off to the boxing ring, bacci courts, bingo (*la tombola*) tables, or playing fields for mock battles, tugs of war, and tennis tournaments. They ran a steeplechase (on horseback) over the countryside, and held rolling races with melons, rocks, round wheels of cake, cheese, and hard-boiled eggs. They threw balls and hurled javelins and discuses in the face of the sun. Archers aimed their pointy arrows in flight shooting, fleet shooting, and freestyle contests. By early afternoon, the air was thick with smoke from guns firing opening shots, bonfires, branding irons, toasted marshmallows, hibachi grills, and dead heats.

The bell rang for the main event. The boxers getting ready to battle it out in the ring put on their gloves: the contender, Antonio Carabello, in white satin trunks, pitted against a young prizefighter from Verona, Eugenio DePiero, defending his (two-year) regional heavyweight title.

Lavinia noticed her sister among the ring of spectators but couldn't bear to stay and watch. She had spent the better part of the morning with a book, picking pollynoses, black slugs, and winged seeds out of her hair, preferring to while away the hours underneath a shady tree in the society of impulsive gods and dead poets—

> Bring me my bow of burning gold!
> Bring me my arrows of desire!
> Bring me my spear! O clouds, unfold!
> Bring me my charriot of fire!
> —William Blake, "The New Jerusalum"

chain-smoking and waxing poetic. "Bring me his testicles! Bring me his bloody head on a plate," she thought, flashing Antonio a look as he adjusted the mouth guard and had his gloves laced up. She folded a stick of Doublemint gum in her mouth with an "If looks could kill . . ." glare before storming away. It was her turn to man the kissing booth, and she went off to her station to do it with a vengeance. But she soon got puckered out and packed it in early, going home, with that now famous pout of hers, to sleep alone in her own bed.

When every last runner from every last race finally collapsed across a finish line, when last bells rang, and last rounds were called, score cards counted and judges' decisions were final, winners were declared and ribbons and medals handed out accordingly to the victorious and myriad runners-up, Antonio, who had put up a good fight until the end, was still standing after five whole rounds in the ring with the reigning heavyweight champion. They handed out the gold and called the winning raffle numbers. Antonio collected his tickets and went out drinking with his friends.

Lea was ecstatic that they were the winners of the coveted cruise.

Everyone else danced around the bonfire as it blazed late into the night. Some jumped through in the train of Roberto and Marina, crowned king and queen with lacy wreaths wound with meadowsweet and living vines (which, one day would be replaced in favor of paper crowns, but not yet), who clasped hands and leapt, vanishing for an instant into the purifying flames and thick clouds of smoke.

Ranchers plunged in and pulled out their burning brands. Children finished ducking blindfolded for apples, placed the pips in the fire to see whose love was true, then sat roasting the apples along with frankfurters, melty s'mores, and anything else they could think of stuck on the end of a forked stick. Later, they caught fireflies, played a game of tag aptly called *Witch in a Jar*, and finally, in the true spirit of the season they ran all around the fields, barns, and porches yelling "Fire! Fire! Burn the witches!" Fortunately, it was just a poppet, a stuffed doll sacrificed in the stead of a real flesh and blood old woman who once had that honor in the dark recesses of the long ago forgotten. Nevertheless, as they watched things burn, some felt the stirrings of the ancient rituals, small reminders like the stiffening up of joints, an arthritic ache in their pagan bones. Plumes of purple smoke curled upward around the moon, still green wood smoldered; gnarly and knotted seasoned branches crackled. Splintered spinning wheels and broken bedposts spit embers into the sky studded with clovelike stars. The air was spiced with apples, marshmallows, beef franks, and burnt effigies. The thorny canes of old roses and burning spindles banked while revelers danced in the midsummer night's moonlight, gloriously aglow, around the fire.

As they looked up and lay back on their blankets in time to watch the fireworks, the fairies were coming out to have their field day; witches were hard-pressed to find an empty lawn chair. Wraiths of the living appeared unexpectedly. Creatures of the night: revenants, spirits of the dead, and all sorts of supernatural phenomenon materialized from the mists and marsh fog along the river's edge, by streambeds, canals and locks, on fields covered with dew, damp banks, deep wells. Drenched in moonlight they popped up dripping in the rice patties: apparitions with lost fingers, dank hair, dresses draggled as they waded through wet reeds. Swampy things with skin transparent as tadpoles in amphibious shades of green thinly stretched and cold like that of frogs kerplunking all around in answer to their croaking coughs.

* * *

At home in her room Lavinia closed the shutters, sighed, and went to bed, while Lea lingered outside on her own balcony battling insomnia. Technically the shortest night of the year, the summer solstice seemed like an eternity to the sleep challenged. Her mother blamed it on the anticipation of her wedding day combined with the night's festivities. "Too much excitement! Too many cakes!" Maria said, as she went about making her boiled milk and honey and filling a piping-hot lavender-scented bath. She poured water over her head from a chipped white Paterino jug; the heavenly steam wafted over everything, softening the too poignant edges of reality. All worries would be washed out of her hair—along with bits of flax, feathers, lamb's wool, goat's hair, thistles.

She tried to settle down, but too many things conspired to keep her awake: there was the sound of Maria at the sewing machine (a few last-minute stitches) stopping and starting, her foot rocking the treadle, the sound of the wind blowing, boughs breaking, tiny nests falling down out of trees toppling their cradlefulls of tiny eggs and nestlings, or it may have been the fluttering of the impossibly small hummingbird heart beating a hundred and sixty beats per second inside of her. In any event, it was too noisy, too windy; it was too hot to sleep. She tore open the shutters to let the breeze in and lifted her night slip, allowing the moonlight to spill over her skin like cold milk, collect in the buttercup of her bellybutton as she smoothed her hand over her slightly swollen abdomen, trying to soothe the worst case of butterflies in the history of the world. Plus, her bed was full of posies and crumbs from the cupcakes she herself had helped to bake and hand out at the fair. These little treats and tuzzie muzzies believed to be wish-fulfillers when tucked beneath the dreamer's pillow succeeded in filling her head with tousled thoughts and her sheets with petals and flower seeds, traces of hundreds and thousands, and crumbly angel food cake.

Too old for stories and bedtime bears, she recited the rosary instead, and even though she knew somehow lullabies never worked their magical spells when you sang them to yourself, she tried anyway. "Sleep baby sleep, the father watches his sheep," she sang, counting little lost lambs like Bo Peep. She rattled off a litany of her favorite fairy tale destinations on her pink, white, and powder blue beads: Agrabah, Camelot, Los Angeles-California, Kissimee-Saint Cloud-Cuckoo-Land, Munchkinland, Never Never Land, Wonderland, Oz . . . like a prayer. Imagining kingdoms in a tangle of butter cream and poppy-print sheets whisking her away to faraway places—not here—every night like a thousand and one others.

She fussed with her flowery quilt, shook it loose, kicking up a storm of roses and downy feathers till it trailed off, spilling its precious cargo of petals onto the floor where they pooled in the velvety dark like a dry moat of tears, like the long ropes of her hair she let down like Rapunsel, a ladder for witches, entangling princes. By the side of her bed a rose garden bloomed, her Baby Dolls snagged, her flesh bled on salient thorns.

"Matthew, Mark, Luke and John, bless this bed that I lie on . . ." she recited. Lying awake as midnight chimed, she popped out from under her covers, moaned like a miserable cuckoo clock and ducked back in again. "What's the time by the dandelion clock? A deep breath. Huff! One o'clock. Puff! Two o'clock. Puff!" Pillow feathers floated through the air like downy thistle. Only once before that she could remember, had she been up all night, and that was when she was eleven and plagued with a bad case of the chicken pox. She woke up itchy, clawing and scratching like a madwoman, infecting the blisters that had been so carefully pointed out with fingertips dipped in Calamine lotion until she was polka dotted like a soul riddled with sins. The pink stuff stained the sheets; its chalky scent crept under her skin, which would one day show the devastation from the scabs, they warned her, if she continued peeling them off like button candy. She pictured the scars, the pitfalls, and pockmarks: a moon face whose mottled surface she explored with her hand, sweeping over rills and ridges, shallow depressions, rubble, basaltic regolith. Measuring the effect of gamma rays, the radiuses of warts, memorizing faults like a topographer, fitting her fingers into its shadowed craters (like the wrinkled face of the witch as she flew by), familiar wounds; the scattered scars of new impact.

The gauzy curtains and mosquito netting sighed. The wedding dress and veil hanging from the bedposts lifted in the wind like a bad haunting. "I give up!" she moaned and, yanking the bed curtains aside in surrender, Lea tiptoed over to the balcony barefoot, her sheet trailing across the floor like a slackened sail, and climbed out over the edge. The trellis swayed beneath her, already overstressed from its ancient entanglement of honeysuckle vines and the weight of full-blown roses. She looked down only once before her feet touched the ground, cool as a web dancer, tightrope walker, Queen of the high wire, trapeze artist, the aerialist she had so often pretended to be that she could scramble up and down any ladder in her sleep, fly with her eyes closed.

She lay down on the lawn where in the morning they would discover her sleeping soundly on her sheet bleached white from the dew and midsummer night's moonlight, the long stem of a pink rose stuck between her toes.

In the meantime, Antonio was out drinking with his buddies at the local bar. His second cousin Marcelo, who was best man, took the honor very much to heart, arranging to surprise him with a giant cake with a stripper in it. Countless mushy toasts in Antonio's honor were proposed until every last *gocchietto*, drop of Grappa was drunk. It was in the wee small hours of the morning that all the groomsmen blundered home singing a medley of chantey songs like Sally Brown and Santy Anna and ending with Barnacle Bill. "I just got paid, I want to get laid," their voices reeled as they went off their separate ways, homeward sailors, in search of their own beds. Everyone except Antonio, that is, who, having thought up a heroic plan, tied his red signature sweater around his neck, and went off half-cocked in the general direction of the Battista Farm. But balls of steel and heart of a Jedi Knight notwithstanding, he'd had way too much to drink, was drunk as a skunk, in fact. Not even Superman or a sober Wookiee space pilot could have navigated his way through that marsh fog by moonbeam. Flying way too high at first, and then way too low, he attempted to leap across a spring in a single bound, making a serious error in judgment, a miscalculation in regard to the garden wall. He ricocheted off, really, broke his nose and hit his head as he tumbled head over heels into a tangled bed of climbing roses, wild mint, and fennel with a crash of mythic proportions.

Lucky to have landed face up rather than down, lying there in a blue funk with an unobstructed view of the sky gave him a whole new perspective. A world of possibilities that might not otherwise have occurred to him presented itself. He saw stars; signs. The existence of space aliens, for example, enthralled him for some time. He threw up. Contemplated *The Meaning of Life, The Effect of Gamma Rays on Man-in-the-Moon-Marigolds,* and *The Mighty Power of Hercules Against the Lunar Men.* Mostly, though, he thought about Lavinia—how he had screwed up royally. He was filled with remorse and longing, and he felt lost suddenly, remembering how far away he was from home: overcome by the very sound of the word.

"Home," he whispered to himself over and over, and wondered if he was ever going to make it home again. Then the word home, and doggies, and snow, my baby, hushabye, rockabye, sheep, gypsy, highway, sea, sky, sleep—scrabbled about in his head, configuring themselves into images of freight trains and sails, ships and galloping horses, and into clouds of dust and steam billowing backwards. He heard the echo of hooves and mournful whistles as he strung together cowboy songs, poems, and lullabies.

Goodnight, you moon light ladies . . . Deep greens and blues are the colors I choose, won't you let me go down in my dreams?

—James Taylor, "Sweet Baby James"

Waking up looking like roadkill, Rocky Raccoon, the Italian Stallion after fifteen rounds in the ring with Apollo Creed, he swallowed hard with an audible "Gulp!" The comic book balloon floated above him like a blown glass ball, followed by a "Hiccup! Hiccup! Gulp!" Flies buzzed all around. His hand automatically went up to his pounding head where he was alarmed to discover a lump the size of a coconut, and winced. Shutting out the pain that shot red-hot daggers into his swollen, bulging eyes, he caught sight of something blue slipping in through the trees.

The fever of wings that beat in his brain lifted him high into the malarial air above the marshes. Flecks of blue fell all around him, the iridescence of blue morphos glittering like shattered church-glass. Pieces of sky fallen to earth. *Azuejos*—blue tiles framed in his father's fingertips as he knelt on the sanctuary floor fitting them to-gether like a puzzle of Heaven. It was the blue of Rosalinda's eyes. *Fitas*—wishing-ribbons tied around his mother's waist, spun the color of miracles, dangling in the brackish pool of tears collected at the foot of the Wooden Madonna, gilt-edged fish darting in the grot-to between her toes. It was the crash-blue of Lavinia's kite tumbling out of the March sky the morning that he met her. One moment, the cloth was laid flat against the sky with a slapping like sheets on a windy clothesline, cross-sticks visible through sheer silk diaph-anous as butterflywings straining across the sun, and then a split second later it fell, blew with wild abandon across the frozen canal to his feet: tail and string tangled in the frozen reeds, caught on the laces of his hunting boots. When he looked up, there was Lavinia, cheeks flushed, breathless from chasing it down. More beautiful than any matinee idol or movie star. A Bridget Bardot! he thought when she was near enough that he could detect the warm scent of Merino wool, to see the looping letter L embroidered on her sweater—a Lollabrigida! And, maybe, just because it was almost spring, or because of the way that the sunlight reflected from her hair, he'd had to fight the impulse to kiss the top of her head as they bent down simultaneously to pick up the blue pieces of the kite. Electrostatic shocks discharged—*Snap, Crackle, Pop*—at the touch of their fingertips, and the air smelled of lightning storms, elemental.

In a letter Antonio had written to his mother and father that same day (a letter Rosalinda kept tucked away in a trunk with photographs, a lock of his hair, wind-up toys, trinkets, tin soldiers, silver spoon and rattles, brush and comb, teething ring, bitty scraps, christening dress and baby clothes, first tooth and training shoes, bibs and childhood treasures like *jacaré* teeth, small shells, and his collection which included a Kup Surat or Messenger Butterfly from the Malay Archipelago where the people believed it carried spirit-thoughts on the wind), following terms of endearment, between outbursts of poetry and a request for traveling money, there was a breathless account of his meeting with Lavinia, although Rosalinda and Amadeo got the sanitized version (rated P for parents) from which sex, of course, was censored entirely. In the deleted scene, entitled "The Abandoned Windmill," Antonio and Lavinia *throw cap and bonnet over the top* when they're caught in the sudden downpour and duck into the derelict windmill, wet and tentative as Brad and Janet. Fits of kissing and tricks that would have been a tribute to the decadence of *Rocky Horror* compete with the storm for attention: lightning crashes, thunder rolls and sails spin wildly in the lusty wind that Antonio alluded to in his letter. "*O vento está bem forte.*" Wild doves released into the well shaft go off like a hundred slow speed shutters. All uplifting arabesques: a blur of pale wings and soft lavender-blue underbellies light up the moody darkness like the Dutch white and Delft glazes of a Vermeer. Fat round raindrops plump metronomically in the flood-pool Lavinia and Antonio have made on the floor. At the end of the letter, he quoted a few of his favorite lines from the Brazilian Romantic poet, Castro Álvarez, and finally, postscriptum, he exhaled, "I have found the girl that I'm going to marry!"

Antonio and Lavinia had made love with some new twists and in some extreme settings literally hundreds of times since. "*Cazzo!*" How was he expected ever to guess that it was not Lavinia but that seriously possessed sister of hers, that crazy Lea, impersonating her look, her clothes, pretending to be her asleep that day in the tower. The two girls bore such an uncanny resemblance to each other right down to the dimples and dark mole just above the upper lip, a charm which, in Lavinia's case was genuine, and in Lea's case—counterfeit (a cosmetic dot, penciled-in beauty mark); sometimes it was virtually impossible to them apart.

Lavinia and Lea, like most of the Battista women, had a talent for mimicry and loved to play dress up; putting on military uniforms, they posed for pictures as Italian soldiers donning fake mustaches and smoking illicit cigarettes. They danced the way gypsies danced with roses clenched in their teeth. They performed T*he Greatest Show on Earth,* converting the tire swing into the high trapeze. "Ladies and gentlemen, *Signore e signori—ecco presentarsi ora al vostro giudizio, in una esibizione tutta grazia e ardimento. I più celebri trapezisti del mondo,*" announced Gabriel, as Lord of the Ring and lion tamer. "The

sensations of the ages—in ring one—the beautiful Bird of Paradise—
Queen of the flying trapeze—the daring—the incredible—the death-
defying, fearless and peerless—Lea!" (Or Lavinia as the case might
be.) They fought for center ring, flying through the air in cotton
candy-colored tutus without safety nets. They paraded around like
circus people, Queens of Sheba: two of a kind like Patty Duke and
Cathy, Mary Kate and Ashley; reduplicative.

* * *

"I do not know whether I was a man dreaming I was a
butterfly, or whether now I am a butterfly dreaming that
I am a man."

—Chuang Tzu (399 B.C. – 295 B.C.)

Antonio heard wedding bells: their toll exactly like the one
fabled to announce burials at sea off the wild coast of Devil's
Island, the sound drawing sharks. On scaffolds hundreds of feet
above the rocky shore, prisoners served their sentences trapping
elusive butterflies. The female morphos (with their enormous blue
wingspans and bad eyesight, who rarely, if ever, came down from
their high canopy above the tangled jungle) were irresistibly and
fatally drawn to the simple scraps of blue paper lure like poisoned
ribbons, which they perceived as attractive males.

He spotted Lavinia, wings fluttering hypnotically through the
air, and flew towards her. Thunder clapped and lightning struck as
he tripped and fell, losing consciousness.

Hey little sister what have you done
Hey little sister who's the only one
I've been away for so long (so long)

I've been away for so long (so long)
I let you go for so long
It's a nice day to start again (come on)
It's a nice day for a white wedding
It's a nice day to start again.

There's nothin' fair in this world
There's nothin' safe in this world
And there's nothin' sure in this world
And there's nothin' pure in this world
Look for something left in this world
Start again

It's a nice day for a white wedding

It's a nice day to start again
It's a nice day to start again
It's a nice day to start again

—Billy Idol, "White Wedding"

CHAPTER NINE

Butterfly Gods and Honeymoon Wings

While you are away
my heart comes undone
slowly unravels
in a ball of yarn
the devil collects it
with a grin

—Bjork, "Unravel"

"A sad tale's best for winter."

—Shakespeare, *A Winter's Tale*

Snow had begun to fall. Huge hypnotic flakes flew into the windshield of the cab Alex took home from La Guardia Airport. He watched, mesmerized, as snowflakes landed, lingered for a moment, pressed against the glass like lacy moths, melted, and were swiped away. His leg ached from being cramped up in the cab after the long flight from Los Angeles, and from the wound, still new, which ran the length of his thigh. Stitches were laid down across it like train tracks, miles of railroad ties, strings of electrical wires studded with stars.

Scottie, the driver, lit up a cigarette, striking a match in the dark after offering one to Alex from the slightly crumpled soft pack of Marlboros he was generous enough to share on the ride back from Queens. "Vietnam?" he asked in a voice like Braveheart's which made it sound *so* beautiful, as desirable as a tourist destination, popular resort: someplace people went to on purpose with their string bikinis and bottles of baby oil to work on their winter tans. "Miami?" "Mexico?" "Aruba?" "Bahamas?" he could have substituted just as smoothly. "Was it hot?" "Did ya pack yer bathin' suit?" "Find any girls over there?"

They cranked open the windows covered with condensation from the cold, the snow, and their breath as the fan of the heater blew on high with a broken defroster, and clouds of smoke filled the air. Snow crystals flew into the high beams of the yellow cab and scattered out from the back lights, dirty icicles clung to the chrome fenders and dripped from the tail pipe emitting silvery-black fumes of exhaust, streaming a fiery tail of flicked cinders and ash and lit cigarette butts that threw sparks as it sped over the Van Wyck Expressway like the burning dross of a comet.

Scottie adjusted the heater vent and messed with the radio, pressed the silver buttons, switching from ABC's *Solid Gold-Golden Oldies* to CBS's Bruce Morrow; *Cousin Brucie* who announced the *Top One Hundred* hits of 1972, had reached number 9—Looking Glass with the hit single "Brandy (You're a Fine Girl)".

". . . dy wears a faded chain made of finest silver from the north of Spain, a locket that bears the name of the man that . . . loves." while on WNEW FM, Allison Steele's sexy voice was spinning out rock songs like a spell. Alex fine-tuned it in, getting rid of the static. "I was soaring ever higher." Shutting his eyes, he dozed off, dreamed, as always, that he was flying, B-52's raining *Christmas bombs* down over the city for twelve days. Thirty-six thousand tons of bombs dropped like storms of insect eggs laid in midair. Their wings raining blood. Russian-made surface-to-air missiles—SAMs assailed them all around, planes were hit, went down, the world exploded—a little at a time. Circling back, fields and villages rushed out from far below. The smell of fires, jungles burning, violent poison, apples, and burnt almonds filled the air just before the crash, just before they flew into that cloud of butterflies: his plane meeting the path of their mass migration. He woke up, tried to blink away the snow falling in front of his eyes as the blizzard flew at the windshield like tens of millions of wings.

"That was Kansas," the *Nightbird* whispered. He was almost home.

Christmas kitsch covered every house on the block; his was trimmed with strands of colored seven-watt bulbs stapled along gutters, under eaves, and around doors and windows. They were wrapped around the wrought iron porch railing, strung to the boughs of clipped hedges, topiary bushes, and evergreens, and they wound up the tall columns of cypress spaced out around the nativity in the center of a neat rectangle of lawn. Up on the rooftop, a sleigh was tied down with old Santa and all eight tiny reindeer plus Rudolph, his red nose glowing. Plastic poinsettias and a huge red bow decorated the spotlighted wreath that hung from the storm door, and he could see the tree lights blinking through the parted drapes of the living room window. His homecoming seemed surreal, weirdly strange and beautiful.

He stepped out of the cab and stood on the slippery sidewalk with the help of his cane. "It's just for show," Alex said, but Scottie grabbed a hold of the duffle bag and helmet Alex had taken home as a souvenir of the war and walked him to the door anyway.

"Is there anyone at home?" Scottie asked. "Can ya get in?" Because aside from those strings of tiny lights twinkling on the tree, the house did look dark inside and deserted. No one answered the bell, but Alex knew better than to think the house could be empty.

"They're probably all sound asleep," he said. "I can get in through the back way."

Boughs of old roses, tangles of jasmine and wisteria, fruit trees, forsythia and sweet brier weighted down by clinging snow and ice hung everywhere. Alex cleared away the drooping vines with his cane as they passed through an arbor and along the cement path bordered by chain link fence to the garden. It was silent except for the blowing snow, the occasional car that could be heard driving through it from the street, the muffled sounds of traffic in the distance, and Scottie, whose whistling *Dixie* fizzled out like a Roman candle as soon as Alex pushed open the iron gate.

"My grandfathers in the salvage business," he offered in explanation of the courtyard that looked like the ruins of some enchanted kingdom, a place out of time. A cherub fountain had frozen in midstream. A Palladian image of Athena, a vestal virgin whose protective gaze and proximity to the kindling had procured her the title Our Lady of the Woodpile, watched, unblinking, from behind the snow falling over her face like a veil. A Bobolini Venus in white Carrara marble was juxtaposed to the clothesline that intersected the property, where washing (and sheets respectively) in warmer times was pinned, stretching between the long poles from one corner of the yard to the other. Broken church windows leaned against dormant chestnut and fig trees like mummies wound in sackcloth and string. Weeds poked through the sadness of empty panes, the tracery of a gate; gothic doors guarded by a pair of sleepy lions with great jaws, who yawned, open-mouthed. Gutters and winged gargoyles spouting ice hunched beside the perfectly still wings of Victory, of griffins and limestone angels. Wooden columns rose among vines that climbed the flanks of Leonardo's horses and a winding stairway. A two-hundred-year-old chandelier, bird feeders and birdhouses were suspended from old magnolia, mimosa, dogwood, and cherry trees branching out over birdbaths, an empty aviary, rabbit hutches and vacant cages, assorted saints, martyrs and masonry stars, slabs of marble and granite, piles of cobbles and antique brick, dated cornerstones and garden urns made of zinc, cement, iron and wire filled with dry nests of moss, garden seats, milk pails, watering cans, wine barrels, olive jars, a mercury glass gazing ball, patina pig and rooster weather vanes. Among the legs of wrought iron tables, filigree chairs, and rust benches were scattered ducks chased by a yapping dog beside frogs, turtles, flower and fruit baskets, a maiden pouring water from a pitcher, two of the four seasons, a girl with a thorn, a mermaid and a merman, a ship's figurehead, and a baby angel puckered up to blow a kiss: its hands cupping empty air like a prayer. There were pairs of faded pink flamingos and white swans sailing on a sea of snow in the moonlight. Frozen in an eternal embrace were Cupid and Psyche, and Venus and Adonis. They had been there—locked in each other's gaze for as long as Alex could remember—always that fathomless reach, that profound silence in the space before their lips would touch; and time stood still with the promise of a kiss.

Alex looked up at the vines that climbed the wall of white stucco and stone, to the second story, where he thought he saw something tremulous through the shuttered glass, like torchlight burning in the window of a tower. He found the hidden key underneath the milk box and opened the door, flicking on the switches to the porch lights and strings of plastic lanterns strung across the framework of grape arbor that cast a pink, yellow, red, green, blue, and orange distinctively sixties-colored glow.

Scottie put the duffle bag and helmet down in the hallway and patted Alex on the shoulder. "I'll be getting back now," he said, before he left like the White Knight at the end of his move.

"Thanks a lot," said Alex.

In the empty cellar, even the fire-breathing furnace was still. He recalled how he and Bella had tiptoed past, trying not to step on its make-believe tail, pretending not to wake the sleeping dragon. Together they had played at Tarzan and Jane, King Kong and Fay Rey, Franky and Annette, Dudley Do-Right (of the Royal Canadian Mounted Police) and the lovely Nell Fenwick, before Bella wised up enough to rebel against bondage, being tied up to trees and railroad tracks, always having to be the one to be saved, and so they joined together as secret agents, earth defenders, avatars of Mothra. No terrible roars just then, no man-eating tigers, wrathful Kong, or the scorched radiovores that childhood memories were made of.

The sound of his cane echoed as he went up the stairs; his boots stuck to the freshly cleaned checkerboard linoleum as he crossed the floor of the kitchen. From above the sink, the light of the florescent bulb bounced off the polished chrome of the faucet, chair legs, and rim of tabletop (a field of white Formica flecked with silver), and the handle of the Frigidaire. On the door, a collage of newspaper stories, photos and headlines were sprinkled like sheets of dirty snow among the bevy of clean white cut-paper flakes —"Christmas Bombing," "Journey to Jupiter," Nabokov's interview in the *The New York Times Book Review*, dated January 9, 1972 (Israel Shenker, quote: "What struggles these days for pride of place in your mind?" Nabokov, quote: "Meadows. A meadow with Scarce Heath butterflies in North Russia . . ."), "Nixon in Moscow," "Renaissance flights." There was a clipping of his grandfather driving his white horse and carriage through Central Park in the snow—the stuff of fairy tales.

"So, the Wicked Old Witch is dead at last," he said out loud when he saw the prayer card with a picture of Our Lady of the Snows, lifted it up to see whose wake they had gone to and when: "Trinitá del Monte," he read upside-down, and an *Ave*. Alex knew the Battista family history, hagiography, genealogy, and mythology as well as he knew his own—and Zia Trinitá was legend. Anything bad that happened in the family was automatically attributed to Trinitá. They blamed her for inclement weather, flight cancellations, turbulence, accidents, electrical failures, burnt cookies, curses, storms. They claimed that she could cast spells, control the elements, change fate with no more than a sideways glance, with ill-wishing, with just a few well-chosen words, and that she had been so jealous, vindictive, miserable and mean throughout her life *that* (they liked to say) *one day she was going to die of spite*.

What actually happened was this: It had been a particularly cold winter and she was old by anyone's standards, despite being as well preserved as a wax figure. They propped her up by the chimney corner (like one of Baby Sophia's broomsticks) with her homespun, spindle and distaff, in a chair by a roaring fire, which was lit twelve months out of every year. There she sat in her black bombazine dress, swaddled in layers of soft warm woolen blankets like a cocoon. Sophia took better care of her mother than if she were a baby. Her tussah-like hair was always neatly combed and never allowed to stick up all over her head like some kind of crazy person. She clipped Trinitá's thick yellow fingernails that had the propensity to grow long and pointed and her toenails too, which would curl like those of a Chinese empress if she were left to her own devices. She moistened her dry lips with Chap Stick and rubbed Baby Lotion with lanolin into the crepe paper folds of her skin. The effect, unfortunately, was none-the-less horrific, especially where small children were concerned. Alex, for one, would never forget having to visit.

He remembered watching in astonishment as Bella ran and climbed right into her Great Auntie's lap (like she had been waiting on line to see Santa Claus at Alexander's), sticking herself with the point of the distaff as she did. "Ouch!" she cried, rubbing the spot where a welt raised on her bare thigh like a sting from a mosquito bite.

"*Attenta Bella Mia*! Be careful My Pretty One." Trinitá said, as though she had never heard of the proclamation against spindles. "*Io stava filare.*"

Bella recognized the word from her grandmother's stories. It meant:

"Once upon a time. . .. *Nel tempo che Berta filava* . . . In the days when Berta spun." Fairy tales always began that way.

"*Dammi un baccio*, Give Zia a kiss," she instructed Bella who threw her arms around the old woman's neck and kissed the fuzzy cheek offered her. "Now go and play," she said, shooing her off to run and chase chickens in the yard with her many, many, many, many, many minikin cousins. A brand-new box of sixty-four Crayola crayons with built-in sharpener, and Lennon Sisters coloring book lay abandoned on the carpet: Peggy, Dee Dee, Kathy, and Janet posed in party dresses scribbled over with sugary pastels: Apricot, Carnation Pink, Bittersweet, Periwinkle. Their eyes flooded with Prussian Blue. Their skin—Beige. Their lips—bright Magenta.

"*E questo, da dove uschita?* Where did this one come from?" Trinitá asked when Alex was scooted out from behind the sofa by

Baby Sophia who had just run back from stirring sauce on the stove, judging from the wooden spoon she held, still practically dripping, in her hand.

"This is Nick's grandson, Mamma. Remember Nick? Maria and Joseph's landlord," she said, waving the long implement in the air over his head, her fuchsia fingernails curling around the handle. She wore a Hawaiian kimono-style muumuu with black- and strawberry-colored hibiscus and palm trees on sailboat grey. Her arms unfolded like a bat's wings as she gave the spit in the fireplace a turn. Alex had never seen another, even close to the size of that hearth: big enough to belong to a race of ogres he thought, picturing them in the cavernous recess behind Baby Sophia where fiery salamanders, snakes, and lizards leapt up around a black pot of roasting chestnuts, and a very large goose, cooking. "*Fee-fi-fo-fum! I smell the blood of an Englishman. Be he alive or be he dead I'll grind his bones—*"

"Heh?" said Trinitá, startling Alex. Since her eyesight had gone bad and she couldn't hear very well either, she said "Heh?" to just about everything.

"*Come ti chiami?*" she asked Alex.

"I'm Alexsss." Alex stuttered for a split second, remembering not to use either the English form or the Russian, Alexei Nikolayevich III, but to say his name in Italian. ". . . andro Sperano," he added for the sake of clarity and in hope of speeding up the interview. It was hot as hell in the room and the air smelled of warm wool, of roasted meat and chestnuts, of burning. The fire crackled and Alex coughed, choking on the smoke.

"*Vieni qui*, come here so I can see you better," she said, reaching out for him. Her dry bones cracked, the rocker and bare floorboards creaked and groaned. Alex felt the tips of her fingers dig into his arm like icicles until she had pulled him closer, and he was standing right under her very long nose, close enough that he could see the whiskers and hairy mole protruding from her pointy chin. "*Come sei bello*, Alessandro. Bello. Bello. Bello. Bello. What a beautiful boy you are," she said, touching his blond hair, looking into his luminous grey eyes. "*Sei anche bravo*? Are you good as well?" she asked, her voice dripping with honey enough to trap flies.

"*Si, Senora*, most of the time," he answered as honestly as he could.

"Sophia, what treats have we got to offer these *good* children? *Caramelli*? *Qualsiasi biscotti*?" she asked her daughter.

As if by magic, Sophia produced a basket filled with freshly baked gingerbread men.

"*Ecco*! Have a cookie?" Trinitá said. "*E prendi uno per la bambina.*"

Alex hurriedly chose one for himself and one for Bella and then left as fast as he could without running. He looked back only once and caught sight of Trinitá ready to bite the head off a gingerbread boy.

As the years went by, she sat closer and closer to the heat of the fire. One night when there was no longer any hope of getting warm no matter how many blankets or cords of wood she called for, or how much she stoked and prodded the logs from her rocking chair, a clump of wood slipped from behind the blackened chain link screen and tumbled out burning onto the stone hearth. Trinitá tried pushing it back into the grate with her poker, but in leaning forward a little too far, she lost her balance and fell in. Covered in all that dry wool she was devoured by the flames in a matter of seconds. It took twelve days to put the blaze out completely. Everyone got out in time, but as a result, Baby Sophia could no longer bear to live in the

Bronx and moved her family to a brand-new house in the suburbs with a winding staircase and central vacuum cleaning system.

* * *

In the freezer, a bottle of Gordon's Vodka was nestled in a bed of snow. Alex considered it for a moment, but closed the door and pulled a bottle of milk out from the refrigerator instead. A sheet of translucent glassine over creamy velum shivered: a cut paper butterfly in the upper left-hand corner was the messenger of this wedding invitation from the Battistas' granddaughter.

Mr. and Mrs. Antonio Carabello
request the honour of your presence
at the marriage of their daughter
Lady Bird
to Pedro Angel Garcia
on Sunday, December the thirty-first
Nineteen hundred and seventy-two

(Apparently, they were to be married at the Álvarez place, which was pictured on a postcard from Maria and Joseph—a pastel pink plantation house, palm trees and a skyful of Brazilian blue morpho wings bordered by a painted frame of jungle vines behind a very large banner that read Butterfly Farm.)

Salvador da Bahia de Todos os Santos
Brazil

If he could have been party to the post-its on Lavinia and Rosalinda's refrigerator, he would have seen the final lists (resulting from thousands of hours of party planning: figures, calculations, crunching numbers) of the many hundreds of guests, tiers on the cake, tons of fireworks, magnums of champagne, bushels of flowers, favors, and masses of morphos. In anticipation of the wedding ceremony (which by this time had already been concluded), cages of white netting were suspended from the trees like strings of lights while the bride and groom recited their vows:

> The island dreams under the dawn
> And great boughs drop tranquillity;
> The peahens dance on a smooth lawn,
> A parrot sways upon a tree,
> Raging at his own image in an enamelled sea.
> Here we will moor our lonely ship
> And wander ever with woven hands,
> Murmuring softly lip to lip,
> Along the grass, along the sands,
> Murmuring how far away are the unquiet lands:
> How we alone of mortals are
> Hid under quiet boughs apart,
> While our love grows an Indian star,
> A meteor of the burning heart,
> One with the tide that gleams, the wings that gleam and dart,
> The heavy boughs, the burnished dove
> That moans and sighs a hundred days:
> How when we die our shades will rove,
> When eve has hushed the feathered ways,
> With vapoury footsole by the water's drowsy blaze.
> —William Butler Yeats, "An Indian to His Love"

And three hundred humming butterflies had waited for the kiss to be released.

* * *

Two flight schedules were stapled together. The sheet on top (Maria and Joseph's) had the return date, 3 JAN 73, circled. The bottom one (belonging to Gabriele) had the flight highlighted in florescent yellow.

Nothing tasted better than cold milk right from the bottle, he thought, as he took another swig and wiped off the milk mustache with the back of his hand. A girl's bebop skirt flew up in the air on a flyer from the social club advertising the New Year's Eve gala featuring The Earls, a local oldies band. It was attached to the fridge with a neon flower magnet and a note that read: Ma, *mAma* (in Russian), I'll be back around two. Call if you need anything. Happy New Year. Sweet dreams, Priyatnyh *snOr*! I heart U—Teresa.

If nobody was at home except for his grandmother, then Alex knew exactly where she'd have to be. He turned the key in the lock to the Battista's apartment and climbed the dark, narrow stairwell to the top floor. Everything was still as death. Only the sound of his ascent, of his own heart beating, disturbed the stricken silence. Silver dust motes were suspended in the light that crept beneath the door, and he pushed it open slowly to find his grandmother fast asleep among the fringed and faded cabbage roses of the armchair and crystal decanter of cognac beside the bed where she dreamed of Siberia, of witches and winter palaces; in the distance wolves howled. Her little dog, Jimmy, made soft whimpering sounds at her feet. Struggling, she tried to call out. "Baboushka, wake up you're dreaming," Alex said. But nothing short of a small Revolution could wake her now. She tucked her chin back into the white fur trim of her robe. A book of fairy tales had fallen from her lap, fluttered down onto the pink shag carpet and rested there, mysterious: open, its almond-green stained glass covers seemingly illuminated from within like the much sought-after wings of a Spanish Moon Moth.

Everything in the room had remained exactly the same way as he remembered it: Barbie bride doll, Patty Play Pal, Chatty Cathy and Betsy Wetsy (like a weeping Virgin, the tracks left on her plastic doll's face, evidence of the manifestation of real tears), bug-eyed, bright-haired trolls, Disney musical jewelry box and all. He lifted the lid, releasing the fairy-sized princess and her miniature prince who, joined by their tiny, white-gloved hands, whirled round and round to the "Sleeping Beauty Waltz."

I know you I walked with you once upon a dream . . .

Yes I know it's true,
that visions are seldom what they seem.
But if I know you, I know what you'll do
You'll love me at once the way you did once upon a dream.

On Waverly wallpaper, characters from *Cinderella* were depicted among pink tracery and small roses bordered by scenes of Cinderella approaching midnight. A clock-face, made of pieces of wings, pinned down exactly the number of minutes mounting toward that hour. There were only two. The unusual gift was one of the many marquetry items fashioned from blue morphos like those raised on the Álvarez farm. Others included frames, pictures of parrots, beautiful-winged birds and pretty scenes. In one, a woman wearing a lovely dress wanders through a garden beneath a sky made entirely of iridescent, peacock-blue wings. Butterflies and moths too numerous to mention, of every size, color, and description, with wings pinned, partially parted, or spread fully—frozen in mid-flight—filled cases and glass domes displayed on the walls and atop furniture.

Her lovebirds, named Olive Oil and Popeye (for obvious reasons), a gift from Antonio, slept in their covered cage with heads under wings like doves. Once, Bella loved those birds more than just about anything in the whole wide world and the feeling was mutual. On the day they arrived, Popeye said *"Ti chiero"* in such an uncannily believable, disturbingly real imitation of her father's voice, it seemed as if he were truly there shaking his tail feathers and looking out at her from those little parrot eyes, that she had been inspired to say "Papá" for the very first time. Olive Oil, who said *"Io ti amo"* sounding more than just a little bit like Lavinia, learned to repeat *"Ya tebyA lyublyU"* from Anastasia like an amorous Russian, and had absolutely nailed "I love you" in Bella's voice as soon as she had learned to speak. *He* recited Neruda's love sonnets (ten), flawlessly, in Spanish.

> Yo no sabia qué decir, mi boca
> no sabia
> nombrar,
> mis ojos eran ciegos.
> y algo golpeaba en mi alma,
> fiebre o alas perdidas. . ..

> I did not know what to say, my mouth
> had no way
> with names,

my eyes were blind,
and something startled in my soul,
fever or forgotten wings . . .
　　　　　　　—Pablo Neruda, "La Poesía" *Love, Ten Poems*

Gabriele coached him until he could croon like Sinatra, and Nick taught him Poe's poem to his immortal beloved Annabel Lee, which Popeye recited so beautifully—Nick broke down and sobbed like a baby every time. She quoted Lord Byron. They both sang "Fly Me to the Moon."

It was hard to believe that once upon a time two little lovebirds made such a mess and commotion with their antics that they drove nearly everyone to distraction, and though they were once so fluent in the universal language of love, they now no longer made a peep, never breathed a word, not a trill: not the smallest smack or the tiniest peck, not a single solitary sound had slipped out from their cage since the day Bella had fallen—asleep.

In the antique white and rose French chiffonier (painted with panels of children and a parrot, a blue sky, the water, a castle on an opposing hilltop, flowers, exotic birds, and trees), if he were self-punishing enough to look, Alex knew he'd see the pink polka dotted hatbox still containing the shattered wand and the small set of wings his friend was wearing when she fell. A few loosed feathers, a spec of down drifted in the (same flash that he had seen from outside the window) light of the picture tube, the television tuned in to the *Lawrence Welk Show*. Alex remembered the Saturday nights when they had danced a polka or waltzed around the living room as happy as one of the Champagne Ladies, or Cissy King dancing with Bobby (or Mr. Welk). Bubbles filled the air, and they—effervescent, sang the song at the end he used to know by heart.

. . . dreaming dreams . . . building castles high. . .
. . . born anew . . . a butterfly.
Daylight is dawning . . .

When shadows creep, when I'm asleep
to lands of hope I stray . . .

I'm forever blowing bubbles, pretty bubbles in the air.

But that was a very long time ago—

He flipped through the stations out of habit, leaving it set to Dick Clark's New Year's Eve debut at the celebration in Times Square. The sound of the crowd was like the wind, a storm brewing, the rushing of the sea. The surge filled the screen in which the city, decked out in its glitzy bow tie of Times Square, 42nd Street, and lights of Broadway, displayed its show posters and lofty billboards above the slick sidewalks. From the Imperial Theatre neighboring the Music Box, the iconic face of the waif Cosette hovers like an angel as seen through a virtual storm of white glitter. Alex gazed into the television tube as if it were a crystal ball; it was one minute to twelve. The disco globe gleamed above the city like a poison apple heart. Time caught in an hourglass. Outside, beneath the icicles and a silent moon, a Madonna buried knee-deep, blinked imperceptibly behind a lacy veil, reminiscent of her feast day procession and the blizzard of confetti that flew into her face as they carted her through the town between old tenements. Flakes fell fast, big, and soft as feathers from the Snow Queen's sleeves, or, as if, Mother Holle's lazy daughter, resolving to shake out her mattress at last, had tossed the ticking and all of her bed linen in for good measure, and it settled in heavy sheets: white blanketing the whole world.

Suffocating snow, drifted against the frosted panes, swept into the room when Alex opened the window, sighing deeply with relief at the cold gush of air. The nearest pair of wings shivered. He looked down at the crystals, spilled over from the sill, and pictured shards of glass sticking up from the rug on that very same spot. Once when she was still small, Bella had shattered one of the display boxes with what Alex considered at the time to be an overabundance of empathy toward an insect, albeit a very rare and beautiful one, but still—

"It's just a bug," he had told her.

"No, it isn't," she insisted. "It's a flutterby!" And proceeded to break the case with her Playschool hammer as she sang "Twinkle Twinkle."

"Twinkle twinkle little stah how I wonder what you ah. Bunka bug the world so high like a diamond in the sky twinkle twinkle."

The *bug* in question, a birthday present from her father, was a Giant Blue Swallowtail. From the book *Butterflies of the World* Alex had read aloud.

> Giant Blue Swallowtails are one of the great rarities in the African forests. The males are easy to observe when they land on the damp ground of clearings to drink; the females, however, stay some sixty feet off the ground in the treetops. They are so elusive that their existence posed a real enigma to naturalists. Despite numerous expeditions, no butterfly catcher was ever able to snag one in a net until one specimen was finally discovered— not in a damp equatorial forest, but in Paris, in the collection of a leather merchant, where the precious female lay under glass . . .

Alex, somewhat older and wiser, knew that Bella's experiment could only end badly, and although he tried his best, no amount of scientific reasoning in the world (or graphic reminders of how she was *going to get it*) could talk her out of it. Predictably, there was no *happily ever after*. The second that the glass was shattered, the butterfly was reduced to dust and an inconsolable Bella, to a damp heap of tears.

For the first time since he'd entered the room, Alex noticed an album, "First Take," on the stereo turntable, slipped down over "Dream Palace" by Troika, Prokofiev's "Cinderella" and "Scheherazade's Fantasy". The television had drowned out the sound of the needle scratching— stuck. He lifted the arm and carefully set it back down again into the dark band at the very beginning. The disk revolved, the record label (with its letter A and a fan) spinning like a pink spot on a ringed planet.

> The first time ever I saw your face
> I thought the sun rose in your eyes
> And the moon and the stars were the gifts you gave
> To the dark—

The haunting sound of the song, the singer's voice stirred up the past in the same way sunlight disturbs golden motes of dust. The memory of the accident came to him like a vision in a dream during regular rituals like his morning shave and at other times as surreal as flying above the clouds. And along with it came the all too familiar and overwhelming feelings of grief tinged with guilt and regret. "Some *earth defender*, some *big hero* you turned out to be," he'd say to his reflection in the steamy mirror as his razor cut a wide swath through scented clouds of shaving cream.

"Instead of playing around that day at the station, you should have protected her."

He envisioned Bella standing at the top of the stairs. A doll-sized beauty in somebody's old communion dress altered to fit—trimmed in gold, fur, and frothy white. A "fairy princess" with a fairy crown: plastic dime store tiara, a halo gone slightly askew spinning around her head like a constellation, and (feathers sewed onto her) angel's wings. She starts down behind him, above him, her dress bunched up in one hand, in the other a stick they'd spray-painted submarine grey, topped with a glue and glitter cardboard star, and she's laughing at something he has just teased her about. "Poof! You're a frog," she says, waving her magic wand over his head like a little witch. An approaching train makes the earth tremor, Godzilla on the loose with sharp teeth and claws, pointy scales, terrible roars, and metal screaming. The sci-fi soundtrack swallows words alive, a little girl's sentences whole. Her lips form an "O" as a hot blast of wind lifts up her dress, her arms reach for something or someone to hold on to, her glittery wand falls to earth in a meteor shower. Feathered wings beat against the air like glass. She hovers in Alex's recollection, a stage angel in the school's Christmas pageant or a Madonna's feast day procession, suspended precariously above the podium by a rope; the cable snaps like a glistening thread. Feathers fall around him. Flurries start; ice splinters enter his heart.

> And the empty skies, my love,
> To the dark and the empty skies—

Snowflakes, like a sprinkling of magic stardust, swirled in through the window with the wind that turned the pages of the fairy tale on the carpet.

The Princess was "carried into the finest apartment in [the] palace," and "laid upon a bed all embroidered with gold and silver. One would have taken her for a little angel, she was so very beautiful; for her swooning away had not diminished one bit of her complexion; her cheeks were carnation, and her lips were coral; indeed, her eyes were shut, but she was heard to breathe softly, which satisfied those about her that she was not dead. The King commanded that they should not disturb her, but let her sleep quietly till her hour of awaking was come."

—Andrew Lang, "The Sleeping Beauty in the Wood." *Blue Fairy Book*

The tulle netting, gathered in the coronet above her head and pooled on the floor around her white work quilt, drifted. The wind ruffled the delicately trimmed sleeves and princess neckline of her white satin gown, the *nun's lace* edges of her pillowcase, and stray gossamer wisps of her hair black and shiny as ravens' wings, which Teresa had freshly washed, set in rags, combed, and accessorized with a New Year's Eve tiara. Banana curls tumbled over the case in waves all the way down to the corsage ribbon and sixteen sugar cubes tied around her wrist. Her face was white as snow. The apples of her cheeks faintly blushed with pink. The color of her lips matched the sweetheart roses that filled a bedside vase. A comb and 19th century hand carved Florentine, Italian Black Forest-type hand mirror rested beneath it. As he had done a million times in the past, Alex held it up before her. Over the few tiny pinpricks of dust mite flaw to the old silvering, her breath barely misted the pristine glass. He laid his head on her heart, listening with the heightened ausculatory powers of an auspex for the faraway, nearly subliminal sound of birds, and with the practiced patience of a prince whose kiss has been gathering itself in the dark for a hundred years, his mouth touched hers: a kiss that fell on her silent lips softly as a feather; the breath of a snowflake. Tears stung his eyes like slivers of glass, remembering how she had once wept for a butterfly dreaming of lost wings—

> The first time ever I kissed your mouth
> And felt your heart beat close to mine
> Like the trembling heart of a captive bird—

while Bella dreamed of air. Lifting. Falling. A blue Brazilian sky. Tiers of wedding cake clouds. Of vows being spoken.

* * *

The priest asks Pedro Angel Garcia, "Do you take Lady Bird to be your wife?" The butterfly cages are opened. The groom who is called sometimes Pedro, but always Angel by Lady Bird who he calls Flor (her real name Beija-Flor means hummingbird in Brazilian), thinks about the underwear she has bought. How she'd unraveled the white floss from tissue to show him the red heart with the words, *Just Married* (in red for good luck) stitched across what little there was of the backside.

"I do."

Silky wings brush his face.

They flutter around Flor's bustled, trumpet line gown: attracted by the shimmer of pink and hand-beaded flowers on rum pink silk satin organza. They light on the pearl and diamond choker, the petals of the bride's bouquet, the four handmade silk satin organza flowers attached to the veil that Angel lifts.

"You may kiss the bride."

Her fingertips tremble through his black hair as he holds up her veil. Their lips reach for one another through space and time. Her sweep train tosses up into the sugar-and-spice scented air. Clouds of butterflies lift. His tails, her dress—threaten to fly. They kiss, hovering in midair among blue shimmering and iridescent wings.

Maria and Joseph, and Rosalinda and Amadeo kiss, congratulating one another to the recessional fanfare of the "Bridal March" from Mendelssohn's "A Midsummer Night's Dream."

Antonio kisses Lavinia, as the two hundred or more electric blue butterflies take off into the treetops. He traces the outline of her mouth: the shape of long wings beating so slowly that they appear in an instant and then just as suddenly seem to vanish into thin air. Opening and closing, appearing and disappearing. Dazzling as jewels. For Antonio, that color blue (for lack of a better word) fit the memory of Lavinia's bridesmaid's dress so precisely that he could've had shoes dyed to match the gown: its torn hem like a simple paper lure attached to a string he chased after one morning when wedding bells tolled and he went flying (hurt and nearly blind) towards it through the trees—that shred of blue silk the color of wings and sky. All around him, pieces fell to earth.

Butterflies brush the tilted rim of Gabriele's hat as he warms up with the band, going over the lyrics of "Volare" he has been requested to sing. "Da da da da da da da da da da da da da, Da da da da da da da da da da da da da. Da da da da da, da da da, *dal vento rapito, e incominciavo a volare nel cielo infinito* . . . in his head." Bridesmaids flutter around him, sipping drinks through straws, flirting. They sweep by in their sherbet-colored dresses, the tulle, tissue-thin as butterfly net, catches sunlight, and he flirts back. But the air is filled with the scent of *Brazilian Dreams*. The pastries baked with coconut and sugar remind him of Ambrosia salad, pineapple and oranges, whipped cream, and the sweet, impossibly soft, white powdery scent of Teresa, who buys bags of mini-marshmallows and toasted coconut flakes at the A & P and then stores them in her pantry drawer.

Flower girls in petal skirts and fairy wings feast on almond-filled swan favors and candy necklaces. Lady Bird has given them all *At-Choo* wands with the inscription "And then bubbles blew all over the land, hatching dreams," engraved in their silver rings. They blow bubbles and chase them along with the last of the butterflies (of the same brilliant iridescence) as they alight from the tiers of wedding cake covered in fondant icing enscripted with *Happily Ever After*.

Angel's brother Tadeo emerges from the flock of white groomsmen to give the toast with a *love is good and life is long and two are best together* kind of theme but almost forgets his speech, dazzled by his lover Javier's eyes. After "Volare," the wedding song the bride and groom dance to, Tadeo and Javier and the rest of the wedding party join in to "This Guy's (This Girl's) in Love With You" by Herb Alpert and the Tijuana Brass and then all of the guests join in to the strains of "Samba Pa Ti." As he kisses the satiny bend of Tadeo's neck, Javier thinks—he is even sexier than Tom Cruize as the Vampire Lestate, or even his very favorite North American actor Johnny Depp—especially dressed in drag—unless, of course (and for a moment he entertains the possibility), he were to get decked out as a pirate of the Caribbean. Before night falls, no one (man or woman) would argue the point, as they watch him dance the Samba like a Bahian woman with a fruit centerpiece balancing on his head.

"What's that?" Lavinia yells in Antonio's ear when a small voice like the thrum of an insect competes with the music for attention—one of the flower girls runs towards them, her wings flapping in the wind like a larger-than-life angel with some really big news. "Telephone!" she says. "Someone named Alex calling from New York!"

"Bella is awake!" Antonio shouts before he has even replaced the receiver.

The band yells, "Meringue!" Everyone drinks too much *caipirinha* and joins the longest and most highly spirited conga line ever to wind its way through a wedding, wielding tropical fruit, delicate flutes or whole, gold-leaf-embossed magnums of champagne down to the beach (Rosalinda—the bottom of her mother-of-the-groom mermaid dress—damp and trailing in the talc-y sand, sea foam, and champagne—past the flowers and candles. Lady Bird—silver slippers dangling from her hand behind Maria, Joseph, Lavinia, Antonio and Angel and Gabriele) to watch the fireworks, eat watermelon, and smoke cigars. The *mãe de santos* blows smoke in everyone's face for good luck.

An explosion of champagne corks competes with a pyrotechnic palm tree for attention. Sparks fall into the sea like stars.

As the family heads for the airport, the guests call it a night, clutching tokens of wedding cake they take home to dream on, and sleepily gaze at the sudden flurries in the butterfly snow globes they are given as favors. Just when their release seems more dream than substance, the real butterflies are making the long flight from Brazil, north, by way of Rio de Janeiro. The pilots of small planes see blue lights in the forest's emergent layer high above the hills of Bom Jesus; a UFO fleet is reported over Buenos Aires. For months afterwards along with the usual, both the National Weather Service and NUFORC are flooded with reports of blue angels, blue snow, and sightings a little stranger than your typical signs: flying saucers tossed across the night sky like skipping stones, or extraterrestrial dross. "It looked like a very fast-moving star very high, very high. It did not leave a trail of light; it did not land or fade. They were extremely high in the air; they were high as any star."

That night, tens of thousands of New Yorkers are unable to sleep as their heads fill with wild things, a host of imaginings that make the long trek into Manhattan on their way to the Bronx like the migrating morphos fluttering in unison, simultaneously taking flight. Blue splashes up against the skyline, huge wings reel, circling skyscrapers: Above Houston Street, they lift like smoky clouds, settling in the Village like snow. The air fills with the beating of wings, the quickening of a thousand hearts; studios are quickly overrun. They rise above the city streets, landing on rooftops, startling the feral pigeons (poor dirty-things) who leave them room in roof gutters, and stop just short of warning them about the dangers of aerial antennas and power lines, glass buildings that look like the sky, and cats who sleep on fire escapes: Instead, they tuck in their heads and shut their eyes, cooing as hundreds of butterflies begin to deposit their eggs in chimney corners and roost in the eaves.

In midtown, swarms sail over the skaters in Rockefeller Center, circling the rink, the angels, clearing the top of the tree. By the time Nick and his date Louisa (a widow from Fort Lee) leave the Plaza, butterflies are balancing on the rims of pineapples or, settling on top of pink paper parasols, they dip their long proboscises like sipping straws into the mai tais at Trader Vic's. A few fluter overhead as Nick hands Louisa up into a carriage: after all the years of driving a hansome cab, he has never once ridden in the back—taken a romantic ride through Central Park during winter in the snow.

The swarm follows the scent of ambrosia salad to the social club where Theresa is thinking about Gabriele (the wind up her swing skirt) as she dances to "Fly me to the moon." Down the block the lovebirds sing "Baby kiss me" while a virtual blizzard of butterflies breaks through the glass and fills Bella's room: the wind from their wings turns the pages of the *Blue Fairy Book*.

And now, as the enchantment was at an end, the Princess awaked . . .
"Is it you, my Prince?" she said to him. "You have waited a long while."

On television, Times Square is shaken up like a blizzard in a snow globe. Confetti cannons explode. Cheers rise up from the crowd; the cacophony of noisemkers and strains of Old Lang Syne swell with the blasts of ships' horns from the harbor, the crescendo of music and canned party sounds. Tons of glitter and balloons drop when the disco ball falls at midnight like the final curtain at the landmark performance of *Les Mis*. "Ten! Nine! Eight! Seven! Six! Five! Four! Three! Two! *One*! *kiss and suddenly nobody else will do*," as strings of Cosettes dance in the famous *Chorus Line* wedge exactly like in the *New York Times* ad display artwork. All the people in all the kingdoms in *all the mornings of the world* kick up their heels. Assembled with their broomsticks, clean up crews dressed in white coveralls wait in the wings like bands of angels for the halting mixture of swirling snow and magical party dust and butterflies to settle, while in Bella's room the last refrain in one final flurry of syllables escapes from the stereo turntable.

> I thought our joy would fill the Earth
> And last 'till the end of time, my love,
> And last 'till the end of time
> And last . . . 'till the end . . . of time. . ..

EPILOGUE

Madonna of the Sheets

Cercare salvezza nella fuga
Seek salvation in flight

—Anonymous

Baby look at me
And tell me what you see.
You ain't seen the best of me yet
Give me time I'll make you forget the rest.
I got a story and you can set it free
I can catch the moon in my hand
Don't you know who I am?
Remember my name

—Irene Cara, "Fame"

The sheets at Santa Maggiore were stripped. Not just from Lea's bed, from which the obvious signs of birthing had been delicately handled, the linen laundered, but from all of the beds all over the convent. The secret was out—vows or no vows—once the word of Lea's ascension spilled over the cloister walls it spread like wildfire throughout the religious community, the island, Italy, Rome—the world.

The beautification took a little time. Several accounts of the event were recorded by the Curia, and the lives of those who gave witness, similar to those touched by angels, like lottery winners, were changed forever. Testimony was given by two of the sisters of the convent, who while picking some vegetables from the garden before matins, looked up into the sky and saw what they had as yet been unable to say out loud—but had thought, and subsequently had sworn to on paper in a document which has since become part and parcel of the Vatican Archives—describing (and here the language was a little vague)

> . . . the somethingessence of a bird of fantastic proportions, the tumult of white robes; wings. A flurry of feathers. An angel-girl with the face of their Lea, hovering like the Holy Spirit.

It had been difficult to see in the blinding light, they attested—like the light of the sun turned up higher suddenly, or like the light of a spaceship landing—not that they could've known anything about that and crossing themselves in a panic had fled toward the dormitory doors, spilling apronfuls of artichokes and prickly pears onto the ground as they ran.

The Devil's Advocate had a field day.

Vittorio and Ginetta, who had spent the last moments before dawn extricating themselves from each other and the interior of his Penin Farina, found themselves suddenly with the police, gearshift bruises and tell tale bench marks still on their impressionable faces, smelling strongly of lovemaking and leather. Ginetta fidgeted with her short, tight skirt as Vittorio told what they saw through the steamy windshield. Regrettably, most of what he said was lost, since his non-ascribable talent for gesturing could not be captured entirely on paper, but should have been recorded on film, i.e., camcorder. Ginetta listened and concurred enthusiastically, and sometimes when it seemed that Vittorio's thoughts were irretrievably hung up in midair/-sentence, she chimed in to supply the missing component.

Only a little less colorful, slightly more sedate presentation was repeated for the record in Rome: the two witnesses having since had to answer to their families—Ginetta's mother, and her father, in particular, had been overly zealous in his quest for the truth, especially in regard to his daughter's close encounters in the pre-dawn when she was supposed to be at home, asleep in her own bed. But to their credit, the two cleaned up nicely. Even the D.A., it seemed, was not immune to their charms. While His Grand Inquisitiveness made the sisters visibly tremble, strict adherence to their story obviously shaken, when made to see in the Devil's eyes those ancient instruments of torture that exacted confessions, tore the truth (the boiling cauldrons of oil, the red-hot pincers, the rack) limb from limb, flesh from bone, from the Hell-bent on their own destruction, these mindblowing antics had little effect on the young lovers. They would not buckle under; even with the most rigorous tests of their credibility, their story did not alter; their faith was never shaken. They stood tough: arm in arm, hand in hand like early Christian martyrs thrown to the lions. He saw the purity, the cool clear light of conviction in their eyes and watched it spin and dance around their beautiful young heads. By the time they were finished, Lea Battista was well on her way to blessedness.

But, while it was the testimony of the two sisters, and decidedly that of Vittorio and Ginetta that helped her procure a halo, it was the street vendor, a hitherto poor and rather worldly pigeon-seller named Umberto Manna, who made her an icon. On the morning that Lea took to the air, never to be seen alive again in this world (although, of course, she had appeared in visions to a few, or a multitude, or she could never have been made a saint), Umberto Manna served as her safety net, her cushion.

According to the story, Umberto Manna had stooped to fasten the strap of his sandal on the cobbles of the square, but because the droning of the wind had made him "stupid," it took a moment or two before he noticed that something was hanging like a luminous cloud, or so he thought at first, watching it swirl and spread above his head until he realized, as he stood there affixed and amazed, that he was looking up the wedding dress of the loveliest creature he could ever have imagined. He threw open his arms and ran about the piazza beneath her like a circus clown with a safety net calling for her to come down. "*Ciao bella*! Hello Beautiful!" he shouted.

"Come down! Please! *Salta giù*! *Ti prego*! I'll catch you! *Op là hup*!" When suddenly and without warning she went off like a giant firecracker, exploding like a cloud, like a fluffy down pillow, like an enormous party favor. Bits and pieces of white shrapnel flew everywhere: cloud-shards, scraps of lace, particles of veil, a blaze of confetti and pigeon feathers, pearls, sequins, and beads bursting, splintered like the shattering scatter of a star.

Silvery dragées spilled from the sky like hailstones, went pinging across the pavement. Debris settled everywhere: a thin film of powdered sugar; dust. And the air was not filled with the sulfurous smell one expected from fireworks displays, gunpowder, storms, exploding brides, but reeked instead of burnt almonds, of broken eggs and vanilla, the tangible essence of *rose e limone*, of marzipan paste angels and mounds of pigeon poop. The latter, droppings from the birds that had spontaneously begun to fill the sky, sprung, it seemed from the last spewn, airborne bits of Lea Battista. Umberto

Manna collected the refuse, catching the birds to fill his cages; there were pigeons enough to sell forever, birds without end. "Amen! It's a miracle," he yelled, falling to his knees, his lips pressed to the empty piazza, which he cleaned as best he could, sweeping all of the scraps up off the dusty paving stones into an old pillowcase. The sack was then delivered into the trembling hands of Mother Arcangela and the cloistered sisters of Santa Maggiore who would press and paste the miniscule remnants into tiny black folders along with likenesses of Lea to be sold as holy relics.

As the Lea cult grew and grew and they ran out of these *pezzettini,* little pieces, they scraped her sheets, tore and shredded them into millions of fresh souvenirs of the miracle, and when that supply was depleted, they found more. Once they resolved that "sheets" collectively, held the possibility of having been slept upon or slept beneath by Lea Battista during her stay at Santa Maggiore, all linen was considered sacred; no sheet was safe. The linen closets were emptied, laundry bins and hampers ravaged. All the beds in the convent were stripped.

The pilgrims flocked to Palma, to the convent where Sister Lucia, sorely missing and mourning her dear, sweet apprentice, still saw Lea, her face dusted with powdery white icing sugar, lick a finger dipped into snowy peaks of whipped icing, test a fruit filling on her tongue, brush away a loosed wisp of curl with the back of a buttery hand—beating eggs; folding. She felt her sometimes: Lea's touch guiding her old woman's hands when they were too unsteady to trim the edges of a citron-filled heart with lime-green marzipan thread or to pinch rose petals out of creamy pale pink paste: a lamb or angel's eye askew just a little from her fingers' slight *tremare.*

Sister Lucia could feel Lea's presence when she was close: sense it with her whiskers. It filled the air with her essence—*rosa e limone*, expanding in the emptiness like a thing unfolding: its wing's breath pulsing—brushing her cheek, whispering in her ear as the fantastic colors of marzipan swirled, and cakes and pastry (*dolce*) were magically turned out like a dream of the *Nutcracker Suite*.

"The bread of angels! The best cakes on the island! In Italy! In all of the world, maybe!" people said. And the sisters' heads spun to the motion of the revolving metal drum as the turntable spun out sweets to throngs of the anxiously devoted.

Sister Nicola (*di Bari*), who fashioned statues of saints from wax that looked like marzipan to grace the home altars of wealthy local ladies, began at once on a likeness of Lea. She rendered her all dressed in white with an exuberance of flowers issuing from the wedding blossoms in her hair and cascading down to the bridal bouquet clutched in one hand, or vice versa. In the open palm of the other hand were cradled two small white doves. But it was the bare feet that made them sorry—touching something in the too-easily-accessible and all-too-vulnerable Italian heart. It had just their right mix of religious feeling and other-worldly flavor: a personification of youth, of feminine beauty, of unbearable loveliness, of passion, penitence, of suffering and the Italian penchant for melancholy, for mourning, longing, and love, and the promise of transcendence she held in her hand—the possibility of miracles. Together with an untimely death, she was the most romantic vision to come out of Italy since Juliet.

Because visitors might not go beyond the grille to enter the cloister, the statue was removed to a nearby church where old women with rheumy eyes, clutching their beads to their breasts, came to pray for the things old women prayed for, and young girls brought their charms, trinkets, love letters, and locks of their lovers' hair. Because of this, Lea came to be known as a Patron Saint of

Women, but especially of Brides—of *Spose* everywhere. They brought her pieces of wedding cake and bridal wreaths: spilling their prayers, like clutches of confetti tied in tulle, where they lit candles at her feet for the things young girls dream. And, so, it was also said that she visited them in wedding chapels and in windy churchyards, appearing auspiciously (on the breezy vistas of springtime when flowers were in bloom) to a young girl with wind up her dress, or in the bedrooms of the brokenhearted where she had been invoked, or drawn by little groom's cakes and relics slipped beneath pillows wet with tears—she comforted them with crumbs to wish on and brought hope through the power of the scraps of her sheets tucked beneath their heads.

Outside her window at Santa Maggiore, Monsignore Valentino still sought her face behind the grille, now nearly covered by the thick wall of jasmine and roses which the sisters had long since abandoned hope of discouraging. As always, he was overwhelmed by the sweetness: the *profumo* in the intensity of heat that shimmered with birdsong, with butterflies' and honeybees' wings. He sucked the air in greedily, taking in as much as he could, a fix to tide him over between visits to Santa Maggiore that had become more erratic, more infrequent; but barely enough breath escaped his lips to stir the wispy white feather that he found—that he would bring home to slip between the pages of the love poems he began to write when Lea died.

For a brief moment, the poetry had satisfied him, he found solace in sestinas, comfort in pentameter, iambs and anapestic feet—the flow from his pen like his very blood, the measure of his soul, the rhythms of his heart, it seemed to him, mysteriously transmuted into words into phrases into verses and stanzas into sonnets and laments shaped from air like breathing out; transpired.

Soon these outpourings were so prodigious that they defied the limitations of form, and finally of space. A terza rema, after Mrs. Browning, begun during this period was endless, its line numbers reaching literally infinity. In sheer quantity alone, his output was staggering; the body of his work enormous. But eventually, the poetry was no longer enough to contain his passion and so he began to write Italian romance novels instead. Published under the pen name, Georgiana, he had achieved notoriety and very nearly established something of a cult following. In the ponderously romantic world of his novels and his dreams, to Lea cast in the guises of multifarious heroines like Jean Simmons in *The Robe*, he Monsignore Valentino himself was Richard Burton, but mostly Victor Mature as in *The Egyptian* and *Androcles and the Lion*. He was Olivier's Hamlet to her Ophelia, John Mills' Pip to her Estella, Laughton's Henry to her young Bess, Charlton Heston and Gregory Peck in *The Big Country*, Burt Landcaster's preacherman in *Elmer Gantry*, especially *Spartacus* with Kirk Douglas, Olivier, Laughton. A Robert Mitchum to her *Angel Face*. She was an ingénue, dancing girl, castaway; he was a gladiator, centurion, prince—Brando as the emperor Napoleon and falling in love again to Frank Sinatra crooning a *Guys and Dolls* soundtrack—*Luck be a Lady Tonight!*

But through it all, there was that memory of her bare foot, her little pinkie toe clearing the convent wall, and he was clutching again at the ribbons that slipped through his fingers. And then there would never be words enough to fill the empty pages that were boundless; infinite: and there was not enough canoli cream in the universe to fill the gaping hole inside of him.

From the souvenir carts and vending stands of the small Sicilian town (which had become famous), together with key chains, wallets, and wind-up toys, they sold those little plastic viewers that looked like cameras. Images of Lea, clicking past in the miniature series of hand-tinted sepia postcards which had become browner and more brightly exposed over time, seemed startlingly strange and very, very old; while the colors of marzipan molds in the bakery windows looked like what angels would buy if they ate cake or sat at umbrella tables dunking any one of a variety of biscotti into sweet wine or espresso.

From café speakers strains of "Volare" floated above the crowds in the square filled with cages of birds, with birdsong and the beating of wings. "Oh! Oh!"

> I'm gonna live forever
> I'm gonna learn how to fly (High)
> I feel it coming together
> People will see me and die (Fame)
> I'm gonna make it to Heaven
> Light up the sky like a flame (Fame)
> I'm gonna live forever
> Baby, remember my name
> Remember, Remember, Remember, Remember
> —Irene Cara, "Fame"

Above the piazza, the progeny of Umberto Manna's pigeons still littered the sky, spilling over the rooftops with the music and ringing bells: the sound of Lea's soul pinned up in the windy sunlight like wedding sheets for all their watery eyes.

Annadora Perillo is a novelist and poet. She was born in the home of her grandparents, a palazzo in the ancient fortress-city of Bari, Italy. On her first birthday, she sailed for New York, beginning her childhood in the Bronx where, thanks to her father's travel business, Italy was never too far out of reach. The world lay at her feet. But life as an Italian-American princess in a large family was laced with blessings and sometimes curses. She found escape in books: transcendence in the power of words. At 17, she went to study in the ivory towers of Marymount College and Richmond College in London, receiving a BA in English and the Gold Medal in Creative Writing from Marymount. She has published and won several awards for her poetry and fiction. *Bella* was a finalist for the Heekin Foundation's James Fellowship for the Novel-in-Progress. She is retired from work in Rockland County, NY library youth services, and her home is now on the shores of coastal Carolina, where she lives happily ever after: a reader, a writer, and a dreamer. She has two grown sons (a broom and a cat).

Facebook: perilloannadora@gmail.com
Instagram: annadora159

Made in the USA
Middletown, DE
28 February 2025

71909380R00162